All the Dogs

All the Dogs

Daniel Bennett

**Tindal
Street
Press**

First published in March 2008
by Tindal Street Press Ltd
217 The Custard Factory, Gibb Street, Birmingham, B9 4AA
www.tindalstreet.co.uk

A CIP catalogue reference for this book is available
from the British Library

ISBN: 978 0 9551 384 3 0

Typeset by Country Setting, Kingsdown, Kent
Printed and bound in Great Britain by Clays Ltd, St Ives PLC

FSC
Mixed Sources
Product group from well-managed
forests and other controlled sources

Cert no. SGS - COC - 2061
www.fsc.org
© 1996 Forest Stewardship Council

For Catty

All the Dogs

I

They called the bar The Green Man: a bad joke like the black, sheet metal horses frozen mid-canter on the platform. The sign grinned down from the far end of the concourse: a man bearded with vines and leaves, eyes yellow as a snake's.

All the people in Birmingham station were somewhere else in their minds. Their eyes were X-rays, they moved through dreams. When Monkey's train pulled in, the platforms were packed four, five people deep, and as they stared through the windows all of them wanted to take his place. They could have had it – Monkey would have explained – but that was people for you: they yearn and they need and you can never tell them. The train stopped, and the tannoy coughed into life as he reached the door. The crowd chorused dismay like a brass band. The voice over the tannoy had brought bad news. It might have been the story of Monkey's life: to be a passenger on a terminated train.

He'd spent eight hours travelling west across the country only to be marooned in Birmingham: a tough journey, bad for his nerves, even if it hadn't been his first day of freedom in over six months. During the last hour, as the train crawled through a landscape that had long been obscured by the rain, he'd walked out to the corridor to light a cigarette. The conductor pounced on him straight away. In the old days, Monkey might have put up more of a fight, or at least skulked off to another corner of the train. Now he gave in meekly. After six months in the clinic, he'd been programmed to see life as a succession of rules and risks: he was an institutionalized Monkey, dribbling at a bell. That morning, he'd left a rehabilitation clinic based in the middle of the Norfolk fens. The landscape was bleak and lonely, without cover or comfort: you were an easy target and you couldn't hide. The oldest inmate was twenty-five, the youngest seventeen, and the six-month programme (women for half the year, men for the next half) would be their last chance. No substitute treatment was offered. The clinic practised residential therapy: removing addicts from the environmental triggers that maintained their needs. Alcohol, coke and crack: these needs were many. Monkey's was heroin.

When he reached the concourse Monkey discovered that his connection had been delayed, indefinitely. A scrambled tannoy message blamed the rain. All around, people staring at monitors or through the windows of the concourse café, longing for families and late-night meals, the favourite TV programme and central heating, the dogs who come to meet you and the dogs who don't. Because Monkey couldn't cope with the larger scale of his journey, he narrowed it down and headed for the bar. It was the only place in the station where they allowed you to smoke.

The Green Man hadn't been The Green Man the last time Monkey had passed through Birmingham. The distant past was only the latest conceit. The Flying Scotsman, The Nelson, The Shakespeare: the various names had plumbed heritage, descending further and further into what we have left behind. When Monkey pushed inside, the cigarette smoke hung like a bad dream over the heads of

4

the customers. People sat around the tables always with an eye on the timetable monitor in the corner, and the news brought only delays. A silent television flickered through the evening news. Monkey lit a cigarette, swapping glances with his reflection in the mirror behind the bar. All around him Christmas decorations leered: a cardiac Santa, an angel planted upon a dead star, a snowman stained yellow by nicotine. He sipped from his beer, trying to celebrate his freedom, ignoring the quiet voice of fear.

During his stretch in prison, a chaplain had once joined Monkey's table for the evening meal. Over gritty mashed potatoes and sausage meat stew, the chaplain had given a chat about Jesus and forgiveness, softening it with a joke about fishes and loaves. He managed to persuade a few people around, those like Monkey who were facing their first sentence, easily scared and looking for something to cling to. Monkey steeled himself for more of the same treatment inside the clinic. He spent the whole of the first week waiting for God to leap out and reveal himself. He looked for Him everywhere, in the daily lectures, in the posters in the games room, in what was said before meals. The head counsellor's first lecture had done little to remove his suspicions. The inmates were not to fall, he had warned. If they did, they would be punished. It would be hard work but worth it. The rewards would come in the life to come. Monkey smelled God throughout.

But instead, Monkey was judged by the league. From the first day, the inmates' behaviour was marked by a system of points, the resulting competition recorded on a whiteboard in the common room. On their final day, so they were told, the inmates' departure times would be staggered, and a better league standing meant an earlier release. The points system was never properly explained. In private meetings, the counsellors claimed to be applying a method used by behavioural scientists from a study originating from a university in the USA, but the methods were questionable, arbitrary. An inmate would trash the common room and see himself rise by two places in the rankings, while another could play copycat and end up at the bottom of the league. An inmate could go to bed in fourth place and wake in the morning having dropped three places. In this way, the head counsellor explained, no one could expect simply to flatter their way to a quick release. Those six months ticked by in boredom and pain, humiliation and anger, masturbation and table tennis. The league became only a minor feature of those days. While the leader could be blamed for anything from the weather to the quality of the Sunday meal, the inmates eventually gave up the competition. To be the first to leave the clinic, even by a matter of hours, felt more like a penance. The liberty which had so often betrayed them had been replaced by a benevolent routine. They couldn't imagine leaving it behind.

The night before the inmates' release, the counsellors threw a small party in the common room. A table offered sandwiches and crisps, bottles of cola and ice cream. A pathetic triad of balloons hung from the ceiling, dangling like the sexual organs of a traitor. Music played over the stereo, but none of the inmates felt like dancing. Most sat around on the plastic chairs, brooding upon their return to whatever life lay waiting for them outside. Then a fight broke out between two inmates who had waited six months for the chance. Lewis from Croydon spent the whole night telling anyone who would listen that there were girls coming. 'I swear to you, I saw them. They're in a van outside. It's our reward.'

Monkey sat on a plastic chair near the back of the room, making himself sick on ice cream and cola. As he retreated from the party, he retreated from his release. The idea of Herointown had started to spread inside his mind. Monkey cut himself another slab of Neapolitan while the head counsellor started upon his farewell speech. All that had passed had been easy, he said. The inmates had lived by the rules away from home, but the true test would come outside the clinic. He stood by the door, as though he was ready for a quick escape, the whiteboard facing the wall beside him. The suspicious, God-rhetoric returned. They were not to fail. If they did they would be punished. 'It will be difficult. For all of you, life will never be the same again.'

'All that remains is to sort out who will be leaving first.' He turned the whiteboard around. The league had been wiped away. Now, all the inmates' names were written in a jumble on one side of the board. On the other, there was an equals sign and the number one. The head counsellor waited as all the residents took it in, and cleared his throat.

'You are all at the same point.'

It was a bad night on the rails. Monkey waited over an hour until the tannoy announced his train. But he ignored it. The warmth of The Green Man called to him. He fed the fruit machine with coins, smoking another cigarette, ordering another drink. When this failed to distract him, he sat by the window, staring out over the concourse. The commuters wandered under the white lights, lost and despondent, waiting to be freed. Monkey thought about how Birmingham station had always been a gateway for him. He'd travel out here when he was skiving from school, riding on the train without a ticket, hiding from the conductor in the toilets. He'd shoplift CDs in the shopping precinct, he'd buy hash from the back room of a nearby minicab firm. When his needs became more immediate, he stopped leaving the town.

Somewhere along the line, maybe between his third and fourth beer, an old man joined him at the bar. He must have been in his late sixties, overweight and drink-shot, the veins bunched like greenflies under the skin of his nose. As soon as he took his place beside Monkey, the barman called over.

'I've warned you before. Buy a drink or you're out.'

The old man had already started moving back towards the door when Monkey took out his money.

'It's all right,' he said. 'I'll get one in.'

Monkey didn't know why. Perhaps he'd spent too much of the day alone; perhaps he was looking for someone worse off than himself. The barman glared at him as he served the beer. The old man took the glass without a word, gulping from it, his larynx grasping, pulsing.

'Think I've met you before,' he said to Monkey, wiping his mouth with the back of his hand.

'Don't think so.'

'Down in London.' He half-sang, which should have been a warning.

'Never been to London.'

'London in hot weather.' The old man lifted his pint glass and sipped from it, thoughtful now, restrained. 'The red chimes bring us messages.'

He grinned, revealing teeth like stubs of toffee. The barman caught Monkey's eye. Why does no one listen? he seemed to say with his level stare, his grim, disappointed scowl. When did people stop caring?

'The gale picked up when I played,' the old man said. 'It pulled up trees and there was nowhere to run.'

Most of the time, his voice was almost quiet. Only occasional words were barked out, rasping through rotten teeth and beer foam. Soon, most of the pub stared over, distracted from the silent TV set and a timetable with no times. Monkey started acting up to the attention. He'd had a few drinks now; he and the old man were a double act, there to entertain.

'It is lonely in the white,' the old man said. 'My wife was anxious in the corridors.'

'I know what you mean.'

'Our lives cancelled,' he said. 'They killed me in winter.'

'Isn't it your round?'

'Clocks and arithmetic,' he said. 'The heart wouldn't give up.'

'You're a poet.'

'I am carnival,' he said. 'I fear the rain on new stones.'

'You're a poet. You're a fucking poet.'

Monkey called him that after the poet who would visit the clinic. A man in his late forties, chewed by life and always with a cigarette in his hand, he first visited one Wednesday morning. Everyone sat on plastic chairs in the common room, the inmates gathered about him in a circle. No one really knew why they were there, the poet included. 'Someone's paying me for this, so I guess we'd better get started.' Forget what they might know about poetry, he said, a poem was a portrait of the mind. A person might only ever write one poem, but one poem might explain a whole life. He read out examples. Some were poems, some was only talk: the poet was a distracted man, prone to digressions. 'The woman you see from a train window. A drink with your father. Dawn in a white room. Brixton market. The light that stays on your retina when you close your eyes. Poems, lads. Poems, all of them.'

He sent each of the inmates away with a red notebook, the kind old people use for their savings. He told them to write down their thoughts, and to work on turning them into poems. 'If you're looking for a way to make the day pass, take up chess. But, who knows, this might help you reflect on a few things.' Monkey hadn't really known what was expected of him, but that night, lying on his bunk, he wrote something that eventually he called Herointown:

I was bored in Herointown
but then I wasn't bored.
I scored heroin in Herointown
and the streets weren't so bad
when it rained in Herointown
it was like sunshine
like Mali or Hollywood
places I haven't been

He'd read it out at the next session, feeling like an idiot, but apart from Lewis from Croydon, no one had laughed. When Monkey had finished, the poet had sat forward in his seat, gave a little clap. 'Yes, yes. Good, good.' But Monkey hadn't liked the look in his eyes, so that night, he burned the poem in the toilet. After that, Monkey started disrupting the poet's sessions and the other inmates soon joined in. They would whistle whenever the poet talked, coughing out swear words when anyone tried to read; Lewis from Croydon did something horrible to 'Dover Beach'. Soon everyone joined in and when the poet lost control, the clinic cancelled his contract. Monkey didn't escape punishment. He went up two places in the league.

Really, the old drinker didn't look anything like the poet from the clinic. Monkey only called him that as some kind of revenge. It gave him something to say, as they sat in front of the lights and silver of the bar, the other customers anxious and irritable around them, the clock ticking down above the television. 'You're a poet, you're a fucking poet,' Monkey said, because it helped him ignore the voice in his head, the one that hadn't stopped all day. 'Herointown,' it said, over and over. 'You're going back to Herointown.'

On the last train home, Monkey lit a cigarette by the open window, staring out at the umbilicus of wrack that linked Birmingham to Wolverhampton. Red is the colour of that area: the empty brick warehouses, junkyards and copper-coloured canals a reminder of how quickly innovation can collapse into decay. Herointown rolled closer with each turn of the wheels. Monkey tossed his cigarette out and went to find a seat. After Wolverhampton he stared out as the edges of the city receded, soon replaced by the tangled dark of woods and the bare, moon-soaked fields. Rain fell, intermittent, lazy rain. Monkey sat back in his seat, staring out at the landscape, at the ghost of his face reflected on the glass. Thirty miles reeled slowly. As the train pulled in, he realized he was approaching home.

2

When Monkey was born he had a thin strip of dark down running from the nape of his neck to the base of his spine. His mother Rose gave him the nickname in hospital. On her way to a New Year's party, she'd flipped her car on a patch of black ice. She spent two hours pinned inside, taking nips from a bottle of Tia Maria while chatting to one of the firemen. When he finally pulled her free, Rose gave him her number and they sang 'Auld Lang Syne' as the car was towed away. A car crash, an emergency worker, and, two weeks later, a slipped diaphragm. Rose would always call Monkey her precious accident. He grew up acting as though the haphazard nature of his conception had been embedded in his genes.

Not long after his twentieth birthday, Rose kicked Monkey out of the house. It was a high, diverting summer: Monkey had lost three jobs within a month and, by making him fend for himself, Rose wanted to teach him a lesson in continuity which she'd never really learned for herself. The fireman had fled when he found out Rose was pregnant; only eighteen, she'd moved from job to job, she and Monkey growing up together, more like siblings than mother and son. Monkey's days were a succession of chance connections and easy trust; he could usually find a floor for the night, so being homeless didn't worry him. When he couldn't, he slept out in public gardens or under bridges, waking to the dawn, a first cigarette mixing with morning air.

He'd known Teal for weeks without knowing he sold heroin. It made little difference. Monkey wasn't strong on morality and heroin was only one drug amongst many; the association had been an intriguing dimension of an excellent summer. The first night he stayed over at Teal's place, Monkey joined five other people scattered over beanbags and sofa cushions, while a *Faces of Death* video played. The scenes of fatalities in plane crashes, car wrecks, fairground rides, escalators and sports fields were awful, but once you started looking you couldn't look away. Everyone took their turn with the heroin. When it came to Monkey: why not? He put the pipe to his lips, coughing when the smoke hit his lungs. When Teal moved on, Monkey sat watching a bridge collapse in Ecuador, flat on his back, totally removed.

From then on, heroin followed Monkey like a dog. For a while, he managed to keep working, but gradually the gaps between jobs grew longer and longer, an emptiness that could be filled only by heroin. Soon, crime was the easiest way to keep himself supplied with the daily bag. He stole mobiles from crowded lunchtime pubs; he smashed car windows for briefcases and stereos. He'd shoplift from the supermarket off the bypass and tour the poorer areas of the town, selling from door to door. No one was ever surprised to find him on their doorstep, offering soap powder and air freshener, salmon steaks and blocks of Red Leicester. It was part of the sadness of those areas, the hungry economy.

He'd lived on last chances since his late teens, but when the police picked him up with ten mobile phones in a carrier bag, he discovered that everything had changed.

Without heroin, the cell closed in upon him: he couldn't sleep, he endured a long solitude of shit. He felt chilled to the soul and the coldest point was a sliver of ice inside his mind: the realization that he was addicted. When he stood up in front of the magistrate a few days later, she read his whole life on the sheets of paper in front of her, which included a report from the doctor who had administered the methadone.

'It doesn't make very good reading, does it?' Her eyes were cold behind the half-dark lenses of her glasses. She offered Monkey six months in the clinic. Fail there, and the sentence would be carried over to prison. It was the latest in a long line of last chances. The magistrate seemed to read his mind. 'I hope you realize how hard this is going to be,' she said, moving on to the papers for her next case. 'I hope you realize how difficult it is to change.'

When he left the train that night, he was treated to his first sight of Herointown over the low wall of the platform. Landmarks glowed under streetlights: the sandstone castle, the football stadium, the old newspaper offices, the market clock tower. In the clinic, one of the counsellors had pinned a map of the moon to the wall of the games room. Marsh of Sleep, Bay of Rainbows, Sea of Cold, Marsh of Decay: Monkey would read the names to himself, sitting around on a Sunday evening, with nothing else to do. He left the station car park and crossed the road; soon he was walking along the river. Whorls and eddies span upon the surface of the water: the currents waiting to drag someone under. The names in the games room came back to him. The river lay coiled around the whole town, high and fast and hungry: a stream of need.

Monkey headed over to see Lennox. He lived like a hermit in a flat on the west side of town. Over the years,

Monkey had spent days, sometimes weeks, sleeping on the badly fitting carpet tiles in his kitchen, eating Lennox's food, smoking his hash. Lennox had always been an easy victim. He could be easily persuaded: to offer a meal or a place to stay, to provide a loan that would never be repaid, to be always *there*. Once, when he'd been staying in Lennox's flat, Monkey had taken the TV and sold it in the junkshop downstairs. When they met again a few weeks later, Lennox had shaken his head wearily. 'You can't do that to friends. It's out of order. Really out of order.' Monkey hadn't been sure if he'd meant the TV.

This time, Lennox took him in readily, especially when Monkey offered to buy the beer. They spent their time in the main room of the flat, where a one-eyed alien offered a thick carrot spliff from a poster above the mattress. *Take Me To Your Dealer!* They played football on an out-of-date games console, smoked cigarettes and drank lager while the rain pecked at the window. It hadn't stopped since Monkey arrived. The banks of the river had burst, flooding a section of the town park. They could see it from the kitchen window. As the days passed, it became littered by jetsam from all these ruined homes: bikes and bar-becues, footballs and watering cans, children's toys and garden furniture. One afternoon, Monkey saw a garden shed, bobbing along like some failed Noah's Ark.

Monkey only left the flat to buy food from the shop around the corner: an errand bartered as rent. Mostly, the time passed quietly. Lennox didn't ask about Monkey's time in the clinic. He'd acquired a block of rich dark resin – from where he wouldn't say – which he smoked out of a small pipe sculpted out of pink quartz. Monkey declined his offer to share. Fuelled by the hash, Lennox chattered about a book on alien abduction, a plan for connecting to a neighbour's satellite TV, some of the recent misadventures of mutual friends. Only when he mentioned Lucas did Monkey start paying attention. Lucas had been arrested after smashing shop windows in the town centre. The police had discovered a small amount of cocaine in his jeans. He'd only escaped a charge because his father knew someone high up in the force. Afterwards, the Vegan had stepped in: setting up a room in a commune on the outskirts of the town, a place for Lucas to clear his head.

'Weren't you two close for a while?' Lennox's gaze seemed all-comprehending and huge, but it was only the effects of bad light and good hash.

'That's right.'

'Must make you kind of sick?'

'What do you mean?'

'That you don't have people to step in for you. You end up doing six months in a clinic. Lucas ends up pulling up spuds with a bunch of hippies. Not exactly going to make you believe in justice.' Lennox paused, his lips pursed in front of the quartz pipe. 'Still, the Vegan was never going to step in for you. Not after what you did with that rack of lamb.'

Soon, Christmas ruled on TV, bright and white and ersatz. Christmas in DIY shops and chemists, log cabins and submarines, on beaches, at dentists, estate agents, deep within the craters of the moon. After too many adverts showing a beaming mother doling out turkey and gifts to perfect children, of family films, family hampers and family assortments, Monkey finally got the message, and left the flat to see Rose. The sky was clear, blue as a vein, the wind catching at him in sharp thin currents. To avoid a few familiar landmarks of his heroin days, he took a long route through the park, where the belly of the river sagged over the town. The pile of jetsam had grown over the previous days. A few people waded from the banks to salvage anything worth keeping, and caught by the flexing currents, a man in a rowboat tried to retrieve a chest of drawers while a Jack Russell yapped in the bow.

Rose rented a small terraced house on the west side of the town, not far from the bypass. When she opened the front door, she placed her hand flat against her chest.

'Oh God, you've escaped.'

'It's OK. They let me out.'

'I thought it was in a couple of weeks? You went inside on the 17th . . .' She began to count out the months on her fingers.

'Honestly. I got back a couple of days ago.'

She let him inside. They walked through to the dining room.

'Do you want tea?' Monkey tried not to notice as Rose picked her purse from the table on the way to the kitchen. 'You go and sit down. I'll bring it through.'

While he waited, he checked out the pictures upon the wall: Monkey in his school uniform, Monkey feeding a donkey, Monkey and Rose on a beach. He saw each one of them as a sign that he hadn't been completely forgotten over the past months. When Rose returned with the tea, they faced each other over the table. Family relics lay between them: a cruet set in the shape of tomatoes, place mats illustrated with Victorian racehorses, an ashtray from Paris. Rose toyed with her bright auburn hair, recently dyed; she'd lost weight. They'd last seen each other in the interview room at the police station when Monkey had been charged. He'd been dosed up with methadone at the time, barely able to use a cigarette lighter; Rose had been called as a responsible witness. They had sat side by side, flicking cigarettes into the same ashtray. She hadn't looked at him once.

Now, sitting together in the dining room, she studied

him carefully. 'So.' She offered a Dunhill. 'What do you want?'

He couldn't ignore how loaded she made that last word sound. 'Just to see you.'

'You're sure they let you out?' She glanced at the orange crust of her cigarette. 'I mean, I'm not going to get a call from the police?'

'My six months is up.'

'So that's it? You're cured? God, if they could only do something like that for cigarettes, I'd be laughing.' She smiled. 'Well, if you're cured, you're cured. Well done.'

'It's not as simple as that.' Monkey blew the steam from his tea. 'This Christmas is all part of the test. I have to get through the holidays and sign up with some people in town.'

'What about money?'

'They paid for my ticket home. And I still get benefits. But I was sort of hoping to get a job.'

'A job?' Rose didn't quite sneer.

'But in the meantime, I thought you might need some work doing around here. Help brighten the place up.'

'I don't think that's . . .'

Monkey didn't let her finish. He began extemporizing plans for the house, offering colour schemes and suitable places for shelves. Rose sipped from her tea and smoked her cigarette down to the filter; she wouldn't look him in the eye. 'I just want to pay you back for a few things,' Monkey continued. 'I've done a lot of thinking while I've been away, and . . .'

Rose screwed out her cigarette on to a limb of the Eiffel Tower. 'We'll need to talk first.'

He asked if he could use the toilet. He was surprised when she let him walk upstairs alone. In the old days, he would use that request as an excuse to ransack the house.

Once she'd realized what was happening, Rose started following him to the bathroom, and, still later, she stopped allowing him upstairs altogether. As Monkey made his way on to the landing, he glanced inside Rose's bedroom. A suitcase lay on the bed, an open mouth disgorging folded clothes. In the bathroom, a toilet bag lay half-packed upon the basin.

'Have you been somewhere?' he asked as he came back to the living room.

'You see,' Rose said. 'That's exactly what I wanted to talk to you about.'

'I met a man,' she explained. 'He's from around here, but he lives in Dubai now. He trained as a landscape gardener, but these days he builds golf courses. It's a huge business. Depending on how things go, I might be out there for a while.'

'When was I going to find out?'

She waved away the question. 'I knew you were getting out soon, of course I did.'

'But what am I meant to do?'

Rose shook her head. She stared at the table as though she were trying to aim a dart. 'Have you any idea what these past years have been like for me? When you were causing trouble, I didn't mind too much. You were young. You took after me. I could see that. I wouldn't listen to anyone at your age. It would have been hypocritical to start lecturing you. I didn't think you'd turned out that badly, anyway. You can always catch up school. People try to panic you into planning your whole life early these days. It isn't like that. It does people good to make mistakes.'

'Like me?' He hated how pathetic he sounded.

'Oh, I never thought of you as a *mistake*.' Rose reached over and grasped his sleeve, rubbing the material between her thumb and forefinger. 'But heroin. I couldn't understand it. Every time the door went, I thought it was either you begging money, or it was someone coming to tell me that you'd died. Something happened inside me during all of that. I kept . . . preparing myself for the worst. And once that was done, I felt this distance . . .'

She stood up and walked through to the kitchen. She went into the fridge and came back with her purse. She glanced at him, embarrassed. He had often wondered where she kept it. 'I want you to take this,' she said, pulling out a few notes. 'It's all I've got, but it'll see you through.'

'I didn't come round here for that.' But there was no point. She pressed the money into his hand.

'I'm sorry. Very sorry. But like I said, I've got a chance . . .'

And after that Monkey walked back to Lennox's flat. Instead of taking the long route through the park, he headed through town. The Christmas lights burned against the grey late-afternoon sky. Teenagers gathered on the benches opposite the shopping arcade, the shop windows sprayed with fake snow. Monkey cut down from the high street, passing an alleyway which led to the back of a department store. He hardly dared to look at it. Once, he and Lucas had bought heroin from a dealer here, hiding out from the Saturday crowds. The alleyway called after him as he hurried along, cut down the next street, threaded through the traffic. *Herointown*, it said. *Herointown*.

On Christmas day – thanks to Rose – Monkey and Lennox ate a processed turkey joint and got drunk on cheap supermarket whisky. Boxing Day saw them regret it. They watched Christmas films, played cards and console games, until they got bored with one another and Lennox headed out to meet friends. Monkey stayed behind, smoking, watching TV, looking out of the window at the town which he was beginning to fear. That dingy flat might have been the extent of Lennox's world, but Monkey could not have believed that it was large enough to contain his escape. Just when he was starting to climb the walls, he made a discovery and everything changed.

Whenever Monkey stayed over, he'd sleep in the kitchen. He even had a regular spot, underneath the window by a stack of carpet tiles. That evening, he'd headed to bed early because he wanted to avoid Lennox's drunken return. Lennox had seemed strangely reluctant about the old sleeping arrangements, but Monkey had talked him around. He'd taken a can of beer to bed, because it was the kind of ordinary pleasure denied him for six months. Reaching for his cigarettes, he spilled the can, and while trying to mop up the beer, he pulled away a section of carpet that came away quite easily. Apparently, it had been pulled away many times before. Monkey put his hand inside the hole underneath, and it didn't take him long to find the secret. A bag of pills, hundreds of white pills.

In the dark, Monkey lit a cigarette and stared from the window, at the town under rain. He could see the market clock, with its spear of steel lit up by streetlights. He could see the red brick castle on the hill to the west. To the east, the horseshoe curve of the river surrounded the main body of the town. He saw two of the bridges: one of green wrought iron, the other of grey stone. He saw the church, with its spire the colour of soiled bone. It was a sanctuary for a hundred gargoyles. As small as they were from this distance, he could see their faces twisted in contortions of stone. Their mouths were open and hungry. They were ready to eat.

3

The lake dominated the field, still and silver as a lens as it magnified the weak light of the December morning. The Vegan paused at the gate, taking in the view. Before him a chain of people moved over a field, some walking by the edge of the lake, some heading up towards a rise in the land. The scene was charged with potency, like an army glimpsed before a battle that would bring forever the weight of history to a place. The Vegan vaulted the gate, his rubber boots splashing into mud. He was involved with things again; for too long, he'd been away from the fight. In only a few minutes it would track him down.

Earlier, the protestors had assembled a couple of miles outside the village. The Vegan had been assigned to the group trailing the hunt from the start. Seated on a metal gate, he shared a flask of coffee with Spike and Griff, two teenagers with identically straggly Mohicans. The hunt gathered in the grounds of a hotel across the road. The staff offered trays of port-and-brandy to the riders, while the dogs sniffed around the grounds. A few taunts had been aimed in their direction, but these had been easy to ignore. When, finally, the riders set the horses trotting into the fields, the protestors followed behind. In the old days, before the ban, they would work ahead of the hunt, laying false trails, using horns to distract the dogs. Now, they carried camcorders and mobile phones. The change in laws had necessitated a change in tactics: instead of sabotage, this was surveillance.

To cover as much ground as possible, the protestors were spaced at predetermined points within a five-mile radius; the exact position of the hunt's trail would be co-ordinated by phone. By the time they passed the lake, around twenty people had gathered. The Vegan was walking alone by the edge of the lake when the quad bike leaped over a rise in the land. He watched it drive full pelt at a group of four protestors. This was at least fifty metres away and the delay of the sound of the engine, the shouts and screams as the protestors spilled from its path, made it all seem vaguely unreal. The Vegan stood, frozen. Five horse riders appeared to the right, the heavy thunder of their hooves similarly delayed. They bore down on another group of protestors, the riders whipping at anyone who crossed their path. A quad bike knocked someone to the ground. A man began to scream in pain.

The protestors nearest the Vegan began to run towards the fallen. Shaken, he joined them, if only to stay in company. He was halfway across the field when a rider came at him, hunting slow prey in open ground. Hooves tumbled over him like rocks. He pitched forward in the wet earth, the thin shriek of the whip passing close to his face.

'You fucking cunt!' the rider screamed over his shoulder, his voice glacial with the accent of the landed class. 'Why don't you stand up and fight!'

The Vegan picked himself up. Two men kicked the life out of a protestor on the ground. A female rider strained to whip at a man with a camcorder. One quad bike circled two protestors, while the other rider pulled a wheelie along the edge of the lake. Some protestors had already scattered towards the far field, while others headed for the copse. The Vegan turned, and ran back the way he had come.

An hour later he reached the rendezvous point, a deep lay-by only a few miles outside the village. Vans guarded the edges like barricades, while the protesters milled around the centre. As the Vegan walked inside, he noticed Spike (or was it Griff?) holding a wet towel to Griff's (Spike's?) bleeding head. A small crowd had gathered near one of the Land Rovers; nearby a man looked up apologetically from a pool of vomit while a woman rubbed his back. Glass from a broken car window lay in cubes on the ground. As the Vegan joined the back of the crowd, a woman glanced over at him. Her pink headscarf and khaki coat were stained with mud; she had tears in her eyes.

'It was just lying there when I got back. Just lying there, like *that*.' As the Vegan moved to walk past her, she reached for his arm. 'We weren't following them: they were leading us. The fucking bastards. They had it planned all along.'

A fox lay stretched out across the front seat of the Land Rover, a savage gash running from throat to bowels. The entrails dripped like a necklace from the steering wheel. The air reeked of the fox stench of urine and flowers, mixed with the coppery tang of fresh blood. Only one eye was visible: staring from a space on the tan seat, a few inches away from the fox's head. It lay bold and sinister, balancing on the angle of the stitching; placed, it seemed, with great care.

Someone must have called the police. Two officers in a squad car pulled up not long after the Vegan arrived, parking on the road beside the lay-by. A few of the protest leaders gathered to report the attack and pass on evidence of what might have been an illegal hunt. The Vegan remained near the back of the crowd, relieved that he'd left the pills in the safe house. Only a couple of years ago, at a hunt in

South Wales, he'd thrown a can of red paint over a police van and taken a few truncheon cracks around the head in return. Now he was a responsible citizen, apparently with the law on his side.

But nothing could change the old allegiances. The police weren't interested in the fox or the damage to the car. They blamed the attack in the fields on the protestors trespassing on private land. They even ignored the videotapes of the hunt. Soon, the argument degenerated. Some of the protestors began drumming on the cars, while the chants of 'Filth, filth, filth, filth' grew louder and louder. The woman in the pink headscarf screamed into the face of one of the officers. All very heated. The old days regained.

The protestors eventually dispersed. While the injured and disillusioned headed back to the town, word spread of a party up in the hills. The Vegan tagged along, hitching a ride in one of the vans. The narrow road uncoiled through bracken-covered hills littered with purple rock. The winter's day had all but slipped away as they pulled up outside the farmhouse. Word about the battle had travelled ahead: the gang were cheered inside, and a woman even kissed the Vegan on the cheek. He helped himself to tacos and bean salad from the kitchen, plucking a can of beer from the fridge. The atmosphere was thick and intoxicating, a steam of food and woodsmoke, of cigarettes and hash, of alcohol, incense and sweat. The change in music acted like a shift in seasons: a cauldron of dub bubbled in the kitchen; elsewhere frosty electronica cheeped.

Although he recognized a number of people, the Vegan stayed on the outside. He *talked*, but as far as he saw it, sex and inebriation were the only outcomes of a party; he disliked both because they made him lose control. That this made him lonely in life, and lousy at parties, didn't really concern him. He was a remote man, who cultivated relationships only for what they might be worth to him, who always remained hidden behind the alias: email and chat-room moniker, nickname and, he liked to think, nom de guerre. He had no ties or responsibilities, his belief system ever-evolving and autodidactic: a mishmash of anarchism, chaos theory and eastern mysticism. His isolation was a sign of his strength. After a couple of hours, he ended up on the second floor in a rickety room, with wide black beams and a sewing table covered with a Brazilian national flag. At first, he'd been joined by a young couple who had stared at him with drug-bloated eyes and never said a word. The Vegan wondered if he'd missed an opportunity to sell some of the pills. But soon the couple walked arm in arm to one of the bedrooms. The pulse of the party thudded beneath him, an anxious, distant heart. The Vegan had almost finished his beer when the door opened, and a man came inside, carrying a plastic bag filled with beer cans. He was tall and burly, his blue parka several sizes too small for him. A rash of reddish brown stubble spread over his jaw.

'Peace.'

'Peace,' the Vegan replied.

'Peace and quiet, I meant. None of that hippie crap.' The man stumbled slightly and, closing the door behind him, he slid down with his back against the wall. He raised his can to the Vegan as he came to rest.

'Never, ever trust a hippie. Am I right?'

'You are.' The Vegan raised his drink in return. 'On the nail.'

Bass thud-thudded in the floor. The man shifted his position. 'So were you there?'

'Where?'

'Where? Where else? The hunt.'

'I was there.'

'I hear it really kicked off.'

'It got quite nasty.'

'Still, I'll bet you were prepared for it. Been to a few of those things, I'll bet.'

By now, the Vegan was a little drunk and the events of the day made him get a little carried away. He described himself as a hardened campaigner, and talked about the old days, leading trails through the woods of Sussex, about the pitched battles from being caught between the huntsmen and the police. He even had a few scars from those years, but he would never rest, he explained, until he'd done all he could to rid the country of a rancid tradition. 'Sacrifices,' he said – and his own words excited him – 'are a necessary part of the fight.' He was in the middle of boasting about that particularly bad hunt in South Wales, when the man interrupted him.

'Is that where you learned to be such a fast runner?'

Taken aback, at first the Vegan didn't answer.

'I said, "Is that where you learned to be such a fast runner?"'

'Most people ran,' the Vegan stammered. 'Were you there?'

'Better things to do.'

'Like what?'

The man didn't reply, instead slapping a vague beat on the floor with his hand.

'It's easy to criticize when things go wrong. Especially if you're making no effort yourself.'

The man shook his head. 'You don't know what real action is. You've no idea.'

'We made our point. They know we're on to them.'

'Made your point? Riling a few toffs on horseback? You provided entertainment.' With his forefinger, he tapped out every syllable of that last word on to the floor. 'They look forward to it. Nothing they like better than you people acting to type. You add a bit of colour to the day. It's people like you who make up for them losing all their dogs.'

'So what did you do?'

'Today? Nothing. What will I do? That's a different question.'

Vague paranoia made the Vegan wonder if this challenge had been sent to him by some of the other protestors. What conspiracy was brewing in that steamy kitchen, what plot? The man went on to boast about his involvement in an underground campaign against high-profile animal oppressors. The directors of a pharmaceutical company, a leading vivisectionist, a television chef, a farmer who bred white mice for science: 'The crème-de-la-shit,' the man spat. Hoax calls, credit card fraud, identity theft, suspect devices posted to the families, vandalism of property: the tactics were varied.

'The point is,' he went on, 'if I wanted to go traipsing through the country on a Sunday morning, I'd take up hill-walking. You've got to think about the larger picture. Do you want to save animals? Or do you want to get to the source of how the animals are harmed? Bringing down the culture which allows this cruelty to operate, that's direct action. That's war. Because this is, after all, the war against science that we're fighting here. And I mean *we*,' he finished. 'Not *you*.'

'I have plans.'

'Plans? What plans?'

'Plans I can't talk about.'

'Of course you have.' The man swilled the dregs around the beer can. 'Great ideas. Big plans. They're amazing, I'm sure.'

In the silence that followed, the Vegan burned on frustrated rhetoric and self-justification. A number of comebacks swarmed inside of his mind, but he would never get the chance to use them. The man struggled to his feet, retrieving his carrier bag of beer. 'Right then. Fuck this. I'm off.'

With that, he staggered from the room. The Vegan fell asleep where he sat, curled up under an old blanket he pulled from the sofa. A few hours later he awoke, the first trace of grey morning stinging his hangover. He made his way downstairs, where people lay strewn unconscious in corridors, on armchairs, curled up under piles of coats, entwined with dogs. A man lay naked in the bath, snoring with his head against the taps, his morning glory pulsing to a dream. While he probably could have waited for a ride, the Vegan let himself out of the farmhouse and walked out to catch a bus. Later, riding through the bleached-out landscape with only the driver for company, his thoughts inevitably turned to the man in the blue parka. The Vegan told himself that he was only one of those twisted roots a person was likely to trip over, the gnarled kind, whose dreams would never bloom. But the accusation that the Vegan was wasting his time still rankled with him, however, and as his breath fogged the glass, he satisfied himself by thinking about his scheme for the Mansion.

By staying in the town, not only had the Vegan avoided another excruciating family Christmas, but he'd planned to sell the most recent batch of pills. The idea had been to head out to a few clubs in Birmingham over the New Year, but because of the hunt, and the likelihood of a run-in with the police, he felt it best to keep them out of his possession. During his hash-dealing days, the Vegan had often used Lennox's flat for storage whenever he felt like being cautious. He didn't trust Lennox – he didn't trust anyone – but he could rely on Lennox not to deviate from a certain pattern of behaviour. So he headed over to the flat the next day, pushing through the unlocked door and shuffling upstairs. Apart from the ground floor, the site of a junk-shop which never seemed to open, the rest of the building had been cut up into flats. The place had a high turnover of residents: students from the technical college, hospital out-patients, temporary factory workers, and all manner of transient losers – life's passers-through. Only Lennox remained, a fixture as tatty and battered as the hallway carpet.

When the Vegan knocked, Lennox opened his front door very, very quickly, which should have acted as a warning.

'Oh. It's you.'

'It's me.'

There was an invitation to make, but Lennox seemed reluctant. He looked down at the floor, his arm propping the door open, blocking the Vegan's way. 'Haven't seen you for . . .'

'Can I come in?'

'What, oh yeah, yeah of course. Sit down, sit down.' Lennox flopped down on to the sofa and began, immediately, to roll himself a cigarette. The Vegan closed the door and sat down in the armchair facing the sofa. A litter of CDs lay scattered across the carpet in front of the stereo, artists and titles scrawled upon the white cardboard sleeves in marker pen. Something god-awful was playing on the stereo. His cigarette rolled, Lennox smoked it sitting hunched forward, an elbow on his knee. He was unaccountably drawn to the weave of his carpet.

'Good Christmas?' It might have been a question, a statement, or two words drawn out of a bag.

'It was OK. You?'

'Up and down, up and down.'

Lennox stood up from the sofa, walked towards the

stereo, stopped halfway, retreated and sat back down. 'No, I uh, I like this track. I suppose it's like that,' he carried on. 'Christmas, I mean. Up and down. Doesn't everyone kill themselves at Christmas? Isn't it, like, the worst time of year?'

'Depends where it is, doesn't it?' the Vegan replied. 'I mean, they're hardly going to get the Christmas blues in Yemen.'

'No. Fair point.' Lennox chewed on a fingernail, ashed his cigarette in a mug, then stared at the point of his cigarette, an indistinct mark on the wall . . . anything but the Vegan.

'Cup of tea?'

'Thanks, no. I've just come to pick up those pills . . .'

'Right.' Lennox didn't move. On the stereo, a woman's voice sang, 'Take, take, take, take.'

'Right,' Lennox said again.

The Vegan coughed. 'So, if I can just . . .?'

'You see, the thing is,' Lennox interrupted, and the Vegan sat forward in his seat. 'The thing is . . . I've had Monkey staying over.'

Over the years, the Vegan had cultivated himself as a man of connections. He peddled a little hash, and if a person wanted anything more he knew where to direct them. He liked to think of himself as a guide to any young people who came his way, and while he'd always be intrigued by anyone with potential, Monkey would never have been considered. He'd always been too grasping, too chaotic, his brains tuned only into selfish hunger. Proof, for the Vegan, that the instinct for revolution had disappeared from a working class hypnotized by reality TV and Sky Sports. Besides, the Vegan would never ever forgive what Monkey had done with that rack of lamb. When he'd heard that Monkey had turned to heroin and allowed himself to be institutionalized, he was hardly surprised. No vision, the Vegan liked to say, and it was vision that he had admired the most. It was his own personal vision that had led him to become involved with the Mansion; a vision which also included Lucas. But now, Monkey had reappeared and in one act threatened to ruin everything.

It took the Vegan over a week to track him down. When New Year came, all he could think about was Monkey touring clubs and pubs with the bag of pills, spreading the product too close to the source. He trawled through the likely haunts. When he latched upon mutual acquaintances, his conversation would begin with questions about general well-being, only to become, casually, more pertinent. 'That's nice to hear, that's nice to hear. By the way, have you seen Monkey around?' After a wasted night of fireworks and crowds, he thought of calling the Mansion and warning Taylor and Charley, but the idea was too humiliating. 'I need to sort this,' he repeated to himself, a mantra that anchored him to the situation. 'I. Need. To Sort. This.'

He spent the next few days searching the town. Down in the shopping centre while sheep fought for bargains in the sales. Outside the derelict football ground, in the corridors of the condemned multi-storey car park. On the riverbank by the floating Thai restaurant. In McDonald's, KFC, Burger King, those baleful temples of meat. Through alleys and gullies, gutters and avenues, back streets and pathways, short cuts and tracks. Through Mardol, Bear Steps, Wyle Cop, Dogpole. Pacing a ley line in the public park that linked the round church to the public school, a marker stone measuring the gap. In the playing fields, upon the redundant platform of the railway station, pacing the walkways around the castle. Around the market:

exploring the corridors of fruit and clothing, of DVDs and paperbacks, of meat, meat, meat. In churchyards, under bridges, the back of department stores: those hostels for the rootless. He drove along the bypass; he paced stagnant playing fields drowned by the floods. He moved through pubs: the tourist traps, the dark wood locals, those regenerated into pine, lights and wine; a bright red demon threw rocks from a sign. He risked the right-wing gatherings, the amateur dramatics, the Karaoke nights and chess clubs, the football fans without a team. He passed playgrounds and pool halls, the prison and public toilets, the depressing intimacy of public baths. He kept moving. He'd have erased a whole steak of shoe leather, if he'd ever worn it.

He'd been drinking in The Swan when he bumped into Jed. Jed ran a record shop over the facing alleyway, but spent most of his time playing on The Swan's quiz machine, listening out for the shop bell to ring. No money in the machine, no customers, Jed bought the Vegan a drink and they sat in the corner by the fire. The Vegan was distracted and not good for conversation, but through such meditative silence, he would later think, comes enlightenment.

'Hey,' Jed said. 'You'll never guess who I saw on my way over.'

He'd seen Monkey hanging out in the town park, on one of the benches near the English bridge. The Vegan left the pub immediately, leaving Jed with two pints and no conversation. He found Monkey standing by the war memorial, drinking from a can of beer. The Vegan felt so relieved he might have thrown his arms around Monkey's shoulders, and so angry he might have wrung his neck.

'I've been looking all over for you.'

'Ah.' Monkey took a swig from his beer. 'I thought they might be yours.'

'How many have you sold?'

Monkey shrugged. 'A few.'

'I need to know. How many?'

'About twenty. I can't exactly say.'

'Where?' he said. 'Where did you sell them?'

'Well, last night I went out to Wolverhampton. Sold most in a club out there.'

'So none around here?' The Vegan began to feel better. This was OK.

'Well . . . At least, I *hadn't*. But then I bumped into a couple of old friends, and you know, we got talking and they needed something for tonight. And they had some friends. It was a big party. So I've sold about ten around here, but the rest . . .'

Thoughts of violence occurred to the Vegan. They were fleeting, exotic, oddly calming. Monkey took a sip of beer. Close up, he smelled stale and damp. His jeans were filthy, and the cuffs of his tracksuit top were black. It was a rotten pervasive smell, the smell of stagnant water.

'So where are you staying now?' the Vegan asked.

Monkey gestured to where the river dog-legged around the park. 'There's a house down on the riverfront. The ground floor's flooded, but you can get into the first floor up over the wall. It's been empty for a while, before the floods. There's a mattress in there. It's pretty damp, but it's OK. Better than sleeping out.'

'You haven't got anywhere else to go?' A solution occurred to him.

'Doesn't look like it.' Monkey scowled down into his beer can.

'You know I can't let you run around with those pills.'

'What are you going to do? Slit my throat?'

'No. But the police might have to get involved.'

Monkey laughed. 'And what would happen to you?'

'It's a good point,' the Vegan said. 'And it proves that

we need to rely on each other. I'd be a happy man if I never saw you again. But if you don't come with me now, and I call in the police, which one of us is going to suffer more? You've had, what, a week of freedom?'

Instead of answering, Monkey walked towards the war memorial. Beyond him, a bronze angel, with heavy wings and a halo of blades, towered against the ceiling of a stone pagoda, guarding a ledger of the fallen. Monkey swapped a glance with the angel and took a sip from his can.

'I don't suppose I have much choice,' he said, half-smiling as though he'd been offered exactly what he'd wanted.

Expecting more of a fight, the Vegan tried to hide his relief. 'I want you to come and meet some friends of mine,' he said. 'You can help them out, and in return, you get a place to stay. It doesn't have to be for ever. Just a few weeks. Just until we finish our business.'

'What about money?'

'We can work something out.'

'I mean, I can earn a lot with the pills by myself. I'll lose out on benefit.'

'I said, we can work something out.'

The angel stared at the sky behind him, its mouth a rictus of heavenly despair. Monkey dropped the beer can on the floor, crushed it with his heel.

'OK.'

As they left the park, they passed the distended river. Still littered with junk and preyed upon by gulls, the flood would rise and ebb forever: carrying away the things we long for and need.

4

Taylor always liked to boast that if it hadn't been for his drinking, the commune would never have started in the Mansion. After leaving home at sixteen, he'd moved in with his grandfather, in a large caravan on a plot of land out towards the Welsh border. The old man had worked as a farm labourer on one of the estates, but gradually, strip by strip, the land had fallen out of use and the men had been laid off. He lived in a state of near poverty, too old for any other kind of life. After his grandfather died, Taylor stayed on in the caravan, because despite the foam furniture, the cold and isolation, it was a lot more comfortable than home. Every Thursday he'd hitch into town to sign on; in summer he earned cash-in-hand picking fruit. All the while, he was continuing some of the old man's traditions, brewing barley wine in vats inside the caravan. In more than one way, it was the beginning of things.

One night, the caravan burned down. Taylor would never really piece together what had happened. He remembered waking in flames, the heat blank against his face, fire running along the inside of the walls. He threw himself out of the door on to the damp grass. Still drunk, he watched the fire seep through the shell of the vehicle; soon everything that he owned had been turned into quivering, tantalizing flames. With nothing to keep him in the field, he started to walk, but instead of heading into town, he turned the wrong way. Traffic hounded him in the dark, headlights caught him and horns chastised him, but Taylor kept walking. Finally, reason penetrated the alcohol and he headed down a B road. Lit only by the moon, he vaulted a hedge and found a patch of woodland. He passed out almost immediately, too drunk to care about the cold.

The sudden reality of morning often took Taylor by surprise, but even by his standards that night took a while to piece together. While stretching the cramps out of his body, he realized that he had nothing left at all. A flash of white brick showed between the trees. He was near a house, the only house for miles. He'd walked up the driveway, hoping to ask whoever lived there for some directions, dreaming that he might even meet the last surviving kind stranger, and be offered some breakfast. But the house was abandoned. Pigeons scattered from the broken front windows. A green lichen stain spread over the front steps, while vines writhed over the west wall. The door creaked open at his touch, and Taylor walked into the empty hallway. Once upon a time, there may have been a warm welcome. Smiling servants to take your coat, offer port from a decanter on a sideboard: Taylor had seen it all in films. Paintings of plump women and angular livestock, an ornate chintz bell pull, the diamond fractals of a Turkish carpet. Statues of weird gods with wild eyes and wide projectile tongues, arms blazing with daggers. A trove of empire booty.

By the time Taylor staggered through the front door, the warm welcome had frozen over. The hallway stank of must and damp. The wallpaper had fallen away in strips, leaving bare plaster, the colour of skin from which a bandage has been peeled. Most of the carpet had rotted away and people were so likely to trip over the remains that when the commune moved in, they ripped it out. Taylor spent the whole day searching the corridors, peering through dim rooms that shrieked with the ghosts of better times. He left that day only because he was hungry. If I could make it happen, he thought as he walked the miles back to the town, that would be my home.

A few years later, he was living with Charley in a large squat, set up in a derelict pub. Someone mentioned getting out of the town, setting up a co-operative and working the land. It might have been idle, dreamy talk, one of a series of what-ifs, but Taylor remembered the white building and put it forward as a site. They drove out the next day in their asthmatic Volkswagen van, to find the Mansion still abandoned. They walked in the grounds and discussed the changes they could make: where to place the vegetable patch, how to make use of the outhouse. Back on the front stone steps, the commune was formed. Over the years that followed, Taylor would look up at the façade and remember that first time he'd stumbled on to the Mansion, when he thought that the world had shifted without him and that he had no place. The Mansion was the only thing he had come close to achieving, what he would often describe as his finest hour. It had ticked and ticked and ticked away.

It was past twelve by the time Taylor left his room. He'd been hiding out all morning, struggling with the effects of the night before. As he walked the corridor towards the stairs, he wondered if he'd missed any chores; probably someone had been forced to cover for him, someone whose anger he'd now provoked. He felt guilty: the furious indiscriminate guilt of a hangover, and coupled with his sense of humiliation (Charley glaring at him, Charley turning away in bed, Charley hissing over her shoulder, 'Looks like I'm finishing myself') it made him walk even more heavily towards the stairs. His body felt disgusting, almost inhuman, draped about him like so much meat; he couldn't stop scratching at his beard.

The other residents would have been awake for hours. He could hear music from a room on the second floor, shouting down a corridor, and as he stepped down on to the landing, through the window he saw the Vegan's car, which could mean only bad news. Still unsure on his feet from a weirdly vertiginous hangover, he kept to the wall. There was no banister on the stairs, only the split spike of a dark mahogany post left behind by some looter who had got his angles of leverage wrong. During one of his sober days, Taylor had been looking for something to take his mind off the dwindling alcohol in his veins, and he'd set about sawing off the point, telling anyone who asked that it had been a death trap waiting to happen. He broke a blade, took a break, headed to the kitchen for more tools. The search led him to the pantry, the pantry contained the fridge, and on autopilot, he'd reached for a beer and popped the cap. When he staggered to bed that night, he'd stared in confusion at the half-sawn post. Most people blamed alcohol for their recklessness, but sobriety always left Taylor confused.

Charley was sitting at the long kitchen table, hunched into a high-collared brown cardigan, tapping a cigarette into an ashtray. The Vegan was leaning against the sink. He nodded as Taylor let himself into the room; when Charley saw him, she gestured towards the bench opposite. Taylor hardly dared look her in the eye. Instead, he headed to the sideboard and poured himself a mug of coffee. The bitter steam mingled with the smells of woodsmoke from the Aga and the lingering odours of the breakfast eggs, tobacco and the greasy stink of dog hair. Most of the dogs were outside, either tagging along with some of the residents, or dreaming on the main steps at the front of the house. Only the greyhound had stayed behind, curled up in the cardboard box it used as a bed.

'You're not going to believe what mess he's gone and got us into.' As Taylor sipped his coffee, Charley described how a batch of pills had been stolen from the Vegan's safe house. While he'd reclaimed most of the pills, he'd panicked: bringing the thief over to the Mansion because he thought it was too dangerous to let him stay free.

'Marvellous, don't you think?' Charley raised her cigarette to her mouth. 'I mean, doesn't he know what kind of state we're in here?'

Pale and flat and wide, with an oddly stubby chin, the Vegan's face had always reminded Taylor of a split pear, the brown eyes bland as pips. While Charley took Taylor through what had happened, the Vegan had remained mostly indifferent, but finally, he decided to defend himself.

'None of this would have happened,' he said, in a bored, neutral voice, 'if you'd managed to keep your appointment.'

'Oh please,' Charley sneered. 'Don't even begin to try to blame me for this. Pete was out of town. The pills needed to be sold.'

Before Christmas, Charley had been unable to meet with the dealer, and rather than keep the pills, she'd given them to the Vegan, insisting that he sell them over the New Year. It represented a comedown for Charley, as the Vegan had originally planned to make and sell the pills himself, passing on the proceeds to the Mansion. She had vetoed this idea immediately, arguing that it gave him too much control. Instead, she had found her own dealer, who, apart from this one time, had been reliable.

'Anyway,' she continued, 'if this is what happens when

you start selling them, I'm only glad that I didn't listen to you before.'

Taylor could see the whole argument flaring up again. 'Excuse me. But where is this kid?'

'He's in the car,' the Vegan said. 'I told him to wait. I told him we needed to discuss things. Which we are doing.'

'I don't think we're discussing anything. You're just turning up and telling me I've got to take him in.'

'It makes sense.'

'It makes sense? Like this place is a fucking hotel. I can't believe that you didn't think this through.'

The argument started to prod at Taylor's headache. 'But if you think about it,' he said, wanting to put an end to things, 'it might not be a bad idea. We are short-handed at the moment.'

One of the residents had left the house a couple of weeks before Christmas. After too many run-ins with Charley over missed chores, incompetent work, and simple bad chemistry, she'd put his membership to the vote. The other residents had complied, probably out of boredom. Taylor had chosen the wrong tactic: Charley shot him a look of utter malevolence, and the Vegan found room to manoeuvre.

'You see? People come and go. I don't see what the problem is now. I don't remember this fuss, say, when I suggested taking Lucas in. I don't remember any of this then.'

The remark about Lucas seemed deliberately pointed. Taylor wondered if the Mansion had been talking and if the Vegan had listened. This was unlikely. The younger residents found the Vegan a boring anachronism; the rest, if anything, found him almost juvenile. But whether intended or accidental, the mention of Lucas was enough to knock Charley out of her stride.

'That is completely different.' She concentrated on crushing her cigarette out into the ashtray.

'But I don't see how.'

'Oh for God's sake!' She clawed at the air between them with a lash of her left hand. 'It's different because I say it is. We took Lucas in as a favour. He had nothing to do with the other arrangement. He posed no threat.'

Taylor marvelled at how effortlessly the Vegan was able to goad Charley. He had become a regular visitor to the Mansion, tagging along with one of the residents who had long since moved on. Self-absorbed, opinionated, humourless except for his own abstruse jokes, it would be tempting to think of him as a dreamer, except that he seemed incapable of so intimate a thing as a dream. He'd travelled, of course, seeing Europe and India, as well as living all over the UK. No one knew how he lived, but he owned a small terraced house on the fringe of one of the better areas in the town. While he appeared to enjoy the atmosphere of the Mansion, he'd always find fault with some aspect of the set-up, and his ideas for changes were always wildly impractical. One night, Charley had challenged him to join them. 'Shame to let all those big ideas go to waste.' He'd refused. Proof, Charley said later, that he was afraid of the work.

One night, he'd caught Taylor in a weak mood. This was when the Mansion was first beginning to fail, when the last of the other founder members had moved on. Takings from the stall were down, the garden was badly attended, repair work around the house was being postponed and forgotten. Taylor and the Vegan had got drunk together, and Taylor had let his mouth run away from him, blaming their failure on the fact that they had been left with nothing but kids to work the place, blaming anything but his own failure. The truth was that neither he nor Charley were suited to head the Mansion. It required a certain tolerance, a patience and authority, which neither of them possessed. Really, it required love, and Taylor had come to realize that both he and Charley were too needy to dole this out. Taylor would rather have been a rebellious child than any kind of father figure. 'I'm not suited to it,' he'd told the Vegan. 'It's not me.'

The Vegan had made a proposal. It would be risky but lucrative. Sacrifices would need to be made, a few principles postponed, but if things were really as bad as they sounded, then this would be acceptable. He talked about some time he'd spent in Holland. Friends he'd been staying with had known a group of people who had set up an MDMA laboratory out in the countryside. The Vegan had never visited – they didn't exactly offer tours – but from the way it had been described to him, the Vegan was sure that it could be made to work at the Mansion. Once all the chemicals and equipment had been bought, it was all self-financing, even lucrative. The process was sensitive, but the location of the Mansion was ideal. Over the next few weeks, the Vegan trawled the internet, coming up with formulae and methodologies. He reported back to Taylor and Charley; there were secretive meetings in the cramped office off the main hall. At first, Charley had been against the idea. It was too much of a risk, too dangerous, ludicrous. To persuade her, the Vegan had put up some of the money as an interest-free loan. He called it a gesture towards the spirit of the place. The pills would need to cover the overheads – the equipment, the chemicals – but that would be easy. When Charley had grudgingly agreed, the Vegan went to work. He acquired a stock of ex-pharmaceutical equipment from a warehouse sale and picked up the base chemicals over the internet: an investment the Vegan had forecast to recover. Taylor and Charley cleared out an outhouse and, to explain the lock and chain, they told the residents that the Vegan was using the place for storage. The Vegan had postponed his principles (for personal consumption he only approved of natural highs) and tested the pills. They worked. But it had taken nine months to start production and the delays had set them back a long way. Despite a healthy supply to the dealer, they were still clawing through their debts. Instead of salvation it had become contention: a bone to start a fight.

A new round was starting now.

'I take it you've told him that we've been making the pills here?' Charley asked.

The Vegan shrugged, looking suddenly uncomfortable. 'Well, yes. On the way over.'

'I thought you wouldn't be able to keep that to yourself.'

'He'd guessed anyway.'

If this kid had to join, Charley went on, he could help the Vegan in the laboratory. After all, he'd been complaining that there was too much work for one person, and that this was the main reason things had taken so long. Surely he'd solved his own problem?

The Vegan looked like he'd been slapped. 'That won't work at all.'

'You can make it work. You'll have to make it work.' She glanced over at Taylor.

'I agree,' he said, knowing it was expected of him.

'But what if I don't?'

'Then . . .' Charley shrugged. 'I guess we call a halt to things.'

The threat was clear: the Mansion might not survive, but then neither would the Vegan pay off his debts. He got up to leave soon after. He said he wanted to talk about things; Charley retorted that there was nothing to say. After the back door closed, Taylor nodded over at her.

'You did that well.'

She scowled at him. 'Don't ever contradict me in front of him again.'

'I didn't!'

'We *are* short-handed at the moment,' she repeated at him, her voice thick with parody. 'We might not be so fucking short-handed if you could drag yourself out of bed on time.'

She stormed out, leaving Taylor to welcome the new arrival by himself. He'd expected a recovering heroin addict to be a little more threatening, but, pale and stringy, Monkey was only another kid to add to the Mansion's brood. Taylor made him a cup of strong milky tea and a cheese sandwich, and sat down with him at the kitchen table. Furtive and nervy, even while eating Monkey couldn't stop playing with his cigarette pack, or the lighter, or the pile of straw coasters, moving each as though they were pieces of some cryptic game.

'If I run out of fags, where do I go?' he asked Taylor, with his mouth half-full, as though this practicality had been calculated by his game with the cigarettes and coasters. Taylor told him about a village shop about five miles west, otherwise he could place an order with anyone going into town.

After Monkey finished his sandwich, Taylor showed him upstairs. He'd decided to offer him one of the few habitable rooms on the third floor: a box room, with just enough space for the narrow camp bed.

'It's a bit damp,' Taylor said.

An ugly brown stain stretched across one wall, while on another the plaster bubbled like spit. Monkey walked to the window, peeling back the strip of paisley material that was used as a curtain, glancing at the grey light of the January day.

'Don't worry,' he said. 'I'm used to it.'

'Yeah, I meant to say . . .'

Monkey turned. 'What?'

'Your clothes.' Taylor pointed at the caked mud at the bottom of Monkey's jeans. 'If you want to put on a wash, help yourself. The machine is in the utility room, behind the kitchen.'

'Can someone show me how it works? I've only got this pair. . .'

The kid seemed genuinely flustered by the idea. 'Yes, I'll show you,' Taylor said. 'But you better start pulling your weight as soon as possible. You're not exactly welcome company.'

Taylor thought he'd struck the right note at the time, but when Monkey didn't come down for the evening meal, he regretted the way he'd spoken. I'm no disciplinarian, he told himself not for the first time. I shrink from inflicting pain.

After the meal, Charley worked on next week's rota. Taylor joined her at the table. The night before, they'd ended up in her room; unfortunately, not for the first time, Taylor had failed to perform. The memory of this humiliation had kept him hiding in bed all morning. Now, he needed to be close to her again, even though it made him feel almost frantic. While Charley worked on the rota, he played nervously with his beard: gathering it like rope between thumb and forefinger, his eyes downcast upon his gut. No such thing as cellulite for him: this was prime, solid fat, a swollen, rubbery corpulence. In company, he would joke about it, slap the gut and boast about the years it had taken to cultivate such a trophy. In private moments of clarity, he didn't really feel like boasting.

He'd opened his first beer, drinking it slowly to match Charley's sips of green tea. The other residents had drifted away after the evening meal. The three dogs – the collie, the retriever and a yellow greyhound – lay on their blankets, sedated by the smells of cooking and the heat from the Aga. The windows had blushed with mist.

'What do you think we should do about this new kid?' Charley scowled thoughtfully. As she looked down at the rota, her lips pursed over the rim of her mug.

'What do you mean?'

'There'll be hell to pay if he doesn't work.'

Taylor sipped from his beer. 'Put him down for washing up a couple of times a week. The rest of the time, have it look like he's working with me.'

Charley accepted this without comment, filling in a few boxes on the rota. 'I've been thinking.'

'What?'

She pushed the paper away, toying with the pen. 'Now that we've got this extra help, I think we should increase our production. The last time I met Pete, he asked me if we could supply more at a time.'

'Didn't we agree not to do that?' The Vegan had argued, and they had agreed, that it would be better to choose one contact and stick with a modest, steady supply over a long period of time.

'I know what we agreed. But things have changed.'

'Well, if it's possible . . .'

'I might talk it through with him. See what he's got in mind.'

Charley rolled another cigarette, folding the tobacco into a liquorice paper. Once, lying together in bed, she'd told Taylor about how, when she was fifteen, she'd spent practically every penny she earned watching *Cabaret* at the local cinema, hypnotized by Liza Minnelli as Sally Bowles. The film inspired Charley to dye her hair, to wear green silk scarves, and develop a hopeless lesbian crush on a girl in the fifth form who had Liza Minnelli's skinny figure and calf-like eyes. Now, past forty, when green silk had been replaced by battered jeans and cardigans, for Charley these liquorice paper cigarettes were the last remains of that trampy glamour, because they reminded her of cigars.

Taylor longed for her again. As he sipped from his beer, he pictured Charley naked: hazel-eyed and dirty blonde, her hips rolling disdainfully on top of him, back arched, breasts aloof, her armpits hairy and humid as a pair of groins. The first trace of alcohol in his blood made the image all the more powerful; he told himself that Charley would loathe him if she could read his mind. He was deluded: after last night, she would probably have laughed. In the depths of his drinking, Taylor thought that he should leave the Mansion, and give Charley the freedom that she claimed she needed. Unfortunately, he was devoted. Charley was the closest thing he had ever had to a life partner, and it drove him crazy when she didn't look upon him in the same way.

Charley gestured to the bottle. 'How many of those have you had?'

'First of the day.'

'But you still couldn't do without?' Charley shook her head. 'You've got *such* a problem.'

'I'm only sticking with what keeps me happy,' Taylor retorted.

'Taylor, Taylor,' Charley's hazel eyes were alive with cruelty. 'If you stick to that, it's the only thing that will.'

5

Monkey spent his first days like a ghost on that lonely third floor. He would sleep most of the day, and when hungry, head down to the kitchen, picking over leftovers for his evening meal. When his cigarettes ran out, he asked Taylor to pick some up on his next run into town; when the last of his money ran out, it meant helping to sort out the ruined rooms on the third floor.

Not long after Monkey's arrival, Taylor took him on a short tour of the grounds. They started out towards the forest from the back door, passing a small brick shed (now used for the brewery), a chicken run and a goat pen. It was early in the morning, but already a few residents were at work in the market garden: some on a set of empty beds, sowing the winter seed for broad beans; some harvesting kale and leeks. The garden stretched for over three acres at the back of the house. Taylor led Monkey amongst the rows of French beans planted under glass, behind the greenhouse. A wheelbarrow lay upturned over a litter of bamboo stalks and chicken wire, a margarine container black with rainwater, a grey tennis ball. At the corner at the top of the drive – an outcast from both the forest and the house – stood the cottage: orange brick roofed with purple slate, little more than two rooms placed on top of one another. It was the only building Taylor didn't mention during his tour.

At the edge of the garden, over two hundred metres away from the house, stood the outhouse. Taylor pointed it out as they walked back around to the front of the house. 'That's where we've set up the lab.'

He went on to tell Monkey about the conditions of his stay. Helping the Vegan make pills may have been exorbitant rent, but he couldn't really argue.

'When is that going to start?'

Taylor laughed. 'One of the things you'll get used to here is not to ask for work. It will come looking for you. As far as the Vegan's concerned, I can't say. He tends to keep his own hours, unfortunately. Drives Charley mad.'

A skill that the Vegan and Monkey shared. Charley had remained a distant figure during Monkey's first days in the house, but the only time they'd spoken she made it clear what she thought of him. 'I don't like the way you forced your way in here. Frankly, I hate everything you represent. But I suppose we'll just have to try and get along. We've got things to do.'

It started a week later, early in the morning. Monkey was woken by the sound of his bedroom door. As he blinked in the dark, he could make out Charley standing in the doorway. She kicked gently at the frame of the camp bed.

'Come on, wake up. I want you downstairs in the kitchen. It's a big day.'

'What time is it?'

'Just after five.'

By the time Monkey had walked downstairs Charley was sitting at the kitchen table, glancing over a crossword. She told him to help himself to breakfast. He made tea and managed to work out how to toast bread on the Aga, burning his fingertips on the hotplate.

'I got a call from the Vegan last night.' Charley sipped coffee while teasing a lock of her dirty-blond hair. 'He's coming over this morning to take you down to the lab.'

Monkey sat down opposite. Still half-asleep, he went for a sugar kick and smeared his toast with green lumpy jam from a jar on the table.

'What is this stuff?'

'Greengage. Robert makes it. By the way . . .' Without looking up, she gestured to a bin bag of clothes beside the table. 'I pulled these out for you.'

Monkey picked through the bag as he ate his toast, pulling out a couple of pairs of green combats, a black jumper, an assortment of faded T-shirts advertising, variously, Aberystwyth, Guinness, and the Territorial Army.

'People move on and leave things,' Charley said. 'Nothing special, I'm afraid, but you can't expect much.'

'No jeans?'

Charley burst out laughing. 'Wonderful. You arrive stinking like a ditch and you turn your nose up at some clean clothes.'

'I only asked for some jeans.'

'I just think it's funny, that's all. A skewed set of values.' She bowed her head, mockingly reverential, a bright look in her hazel eyes. 'Please excuse me.'

Despite the sarcasm, she was in a good mood; obviously, she was at her best early in the morning, which was probably why he hadn't seen her best before. She stole a cigarette from Monkey's pack and they talked about the early days of the Mansion.

'There were fifteen of us when we first came out here. Most came from the town, but there were a few from further away. We felt like we were escaping. You're too young to remember what that time was like, I guess. Thatcher, Major, they really did a job on this country, though you'd be stupid to think that anything has changed. You still get kicked in the face. New Labour only polished the boot.'

After years on the edge, the Mansion had offered those founder members a chance to create a society. At first, any ideological clashes had only galvanized the place. It didn't matter that the feminists distrusted the Marxists, that the anarchists picked fights with the Greens: the common purpose prevailed. People worked the same tasks, shared property, clothing; shared each other until the bed-hopping became more incestuous than liberating. But things drifted. People moved on, tired of the disputes, the claustrophobia; some worried they weren't doing *enough*. When a couple left to raise a child, Charley said, she'd realized that nothing would be the same. After a few more years, only she and Taylor remained from that original band. Now, the new arrivals had no real interest in the Mansion as an ideal. Most were kids, and if they wanted to escape the town, the reasons were usually more personal than political.

'It's the way things are, I'm afraid,' Charley went on. 'I mean, everyone *works* and they follow the rules, but there's something missing, some spark, some belief. I tell you, half of the kids that we get in here can last only so long without their consumerist crap. We even had to fight to ban mobiles.'

'How can you ban people from using a phone?'

'We've got *one*, of course, which we all use and contribute to. But it started getting ridiculous. Do you think we set this place up because we liked being surrounded by all of that? If they don't like the rules here, they can leave.'

The conversation stopped when the Vegan let himself in through the back door. He looked sleepy and irritable. He'd clipped his hair since Monkey had last seen him, which accentuated the impassiveness of his face. He and Charley swapped cursory greetings.

'There's coffee if you want it.'

'I won't. Thanks.'

'In that case, I won't keep you. I expect you'll both want to get started.'

'You still think this is a good idea?' The Vegan gestured to Monkey.

'I'm sure you'll both do very well,' Charley said, returning to her crossword. 'Close the door on your way out.'

Outside, the growing sunrise lay shattered over the front lawn, reflecting off the beads of moisture clinging to the grass. They headed around to the back of the house, stopping off at the Vegan's car along the way to pick up a whiteboard from the boot. The forest roared behind them in the morning wind, the green flames of the pine trees crackling in the grey sky. Early morning sparrows scattered over the garden, blithely ignoring the scarecrow which had been erected using an old orange jumper and a Tony Blair mask. The Vegan led Monkey down the path towards the outhouse, where one door was locked with a padlock and chain. He retrieved his keys and bent down to the lock, grinning at Monkey over his shoulder.

'Welcome to my world.'

As Monkey walked inside, the Vegan flicked the light switch, the bare strip bulb winking, once, twice, before staying lit. Most of the original features had been ripped out of the room, leaving behind only a huge white earthenware sink. An aluminium workbench had been set up in the middle, with a chest freezer against one wall and a fridge against the other. The lab equipment was lined up on the workbench: groups of flasks and stands and clamps, a hotplate connected to a car battery, a stir bar and a few metres of tubing, a pill machine and boss. The chemicals stood stacked on an aluminium shelving unit screwed to the wall opposite the door, stored in Tupperware containers, ice cream cartons, and spaghetti jars. The windows had been blocked out with black cardboard.

'So,' the Vegan said, 'what do you think?'

Monkey shrugged. 'It's about the best laboratory I've ever seen.'

'If you're going to keep up that attitude, things are going to get very boring, very quickly.'

First, they set up the whiteboard. This took longer than the Vegan had anticipated: when he tried to hammer in a nail, he succeeded only in chiselling a very loose hole into the damp sandstone. When he finally managed to get the whiteboard to stick, the Vegan produced a marker from his jacket and gestured for Monkey to sit down on a beer crate.

'Now, I want to give you a quick overview of what happens.'

The pen was uncapped, ink was applied. Monkey's worst fears were confirmed. After ten, fifteen minutes, during which the Vegan had picked the board from the floor three times, Monkey raised his hand.

'Listen . . .'

'What?'

'I learn faster when I'm doing things. Aren't we wasting time?'

The Vegan glanced between Monkey and the whiteboard, his face sour. 'OK. Then we'll start.'

Over the next months, the chemistry would structure Monkey's days. There were six stages, each of which took hours at a time, hours of work and again as many hours of waiting. The early work was almost pleasant. They'd cook up yellow safrole out of brown camphor, and the whole outhouse would fill with a sweet, wildflower smell. Later came ten hours with the fumes of formaldehyde and ammonium chloride, which made Monkey long for the smell of camphor. As the outhouse had no real ventilation apart from a split window that opened on a rusty hinge, often, the 45-degree gap wasn't enough, especially when the camphor overheated. A couple of times the fumes sent them running to the door for air. They spent all of this time inside the lab; the Vegan had agreed with Charley and Taylor not to draw attention to the place. So they ate sandwiches there and drank tea boiled over the Calor gas Bunsen burner. They pissed in the sink. But if this adventure over chemicals was meant to form a bond between Monkey and the Vegan, if they were meant to share moody cigarettes over the failures and high fives over successes, it failed. The Vegan was a cold master, fussy and meticulous. 'You really need to understand,' he'd repeat to Monkey. 'This isn't like cooking up a tin of beans. One slip and a whole couple of weeks' work will be up the spout.'

Once the Vegan had run the chemicals through the pill machine, they would mark each pill with a circle above a saltire. When Monkey asked him about the symbol, the Vegan smiled a knowing, sly smile. It was the pagan symbol for bane.

'It's my comment on things,' he explained. 'To be honest, I think this drug is a distraction. Supplying an emotion you can't create for yourself isn't my idea of what drugs should do. They should expand your mind, not entertain. You might as well watch TV.'

Apart from the smell of the chemicals, and headaches from too long under the strips lights, the Vegan's lectures were the worst feature of working in the lab. He'd always been this way: vocal, opinionated, self-righteous. For Monkey, the Vegan was always the last resort back in Heroin-town, and not only because he dealt mainly hash. Some drugs cost too much.

When Monkey made the mistake of asking him if he'd ever been worried about the residents discovering the lab, it set him off on a rant.

'As far as they know, I'm using the place for storage. That's what Charley and Taylor have told them, and you know what, it'll keep them happy. They live in their own little world.' He scowled at the thought of them. 'Everyone out there wants to escape from something. Ask them what they want, and I'm sure they could give you a big list of all the things that are wrong with the world, and how they would like them fixed. But really, do you know what they want personally?'

Monkey shrugged. 'No idea.'

'A quiet life.'

'And?'

'Seems a bit of a waste of this place, don't you think? I mean, I can take you on a tour of a hundred housing estates, and pretty much 99 per cent of people say the same thing. The great English dream. A quiet life, with no danger. To be uninvolved, on an island.'

'So why has no one found out about the lab?'

'Because no one asks any questions. Everyone here is so afraid that they'll lose what they've got, they take everything as it is, and they're happy.'

'If you've got such a low opinion of them, then why are you helping out?'

'Because the Mansion has potential, outside of the mess Charley and Taylor might, or might not, make out of it. Think about it: you've got this great house, probably built from empire money. It wasn't meant for the lower classes. Right away we're in interesting territory. It's a sign of revolution.

'In the right hands,' he went on, 'this place could become a seat of power. I see people, the right kind of people, coming from all over the world to be here.' He pointed at the floor. 'Something could happen, here. Something important.'

'And you really believe this?'

The Vegan sneered. 'You've never had any vision. That's always been your problem.'

The house and grounds, even his work with the Vegan, had been relatively straightforward compared to finding his place in the commune. By now, Monkey had started taking his meals with the other residents. Even if Charley hadn't used the rota to keep him isolated, he was no closer to being a part of the house. Names buzzed around him like wasps. Mealtime conversations saw him trying to tag along with old stories and private jokes. As Charley had made clear, there was a tension between the disparate older residents – Robert the cook, Magalene the acid casualty – and the various gangs of younger kids. These cliques were amorphous and apt to change. Members turning against old allies, sometimes on a whim. But Charley and Taylor tried to direct the energy of this tension into keeping the place functioning.

Monkey spent a lot of time brooding about one piece of Herointown which had fallen at his feet. From eavesdropping various conversations, he'd learned that Lucas had moved out to renovate the cottage in the Mansion's grounds. Though he remained an absent figure during Monkey's first couple of weeks, he finally appeared at one of the evening meals. Monkey had been sitting at the crowded kitchen table, fighting for elbow room over a meal of rice and fried cheese. When the back door opened, the conversation continued around the table; no one remarked upon the new arrival, and Lucas didn't volunteer himself. He kicked the mud off his boots, before piling a plate with leftovers from the sideboard. Monkey watched out of the corner of his eye as Lucas picked at his food, poured a glass of juice and bent down to feed the greyhound scraps from his plate. Suddenly, as he stood up, he locked his gaze with Monkey's without showing surprise, or even a hint at recognition. Monkey looked back down at his plate. Eventually, the back door creaked open, slammed closed.

After the meal, most of the residents gathered in the lounge, a large room warmed by a real fire. The room could have been a museum dedicated to the cast-offs of people who spent their whole lives passing through. A cracked electric globe, a computer monitor, a dragoon's sword, a fake skull, a set of bongos, an inflatable champagne bottle, an aluminium crutch: all had been discarded and now passed for decoration. The record player fed off LPs by Pentangle, Gloria Gaynor, Van Morrison, The Cramps, The Knack, George Formby, Elton John, The Fall and Belinda Carlisle. A huge burgundy chaise longue, like something from a nineteenth century brothel, stood next to a squashy foam sofa and three or four orange plastic stacking chairs. Someone had found the TV in a skip during market day in the town. Taylor had fixed it up during one of his sober days.

It was Friday night, so for the routine treat, Taylor pulled out a few bottles of home-made wine: damson, blackberry, and elderflower. The smell of green woodsmoke and fragrant incense fought the pervasive damp. Monkey only stayed long enough to drink a couple of glasses of the sour, chalky wine. While Robert acted as DJ, Taylor and Charley shouted over requests from their seats by the fire. An argument started between two of the younger residents. It soon became shrill and irritating. Monkey left while the others tried to restore the peace.

The air outside the living room made him shiver inside his tracksuit top. As he reached the first landing, Charley called after him from the hallway below.

'Going to bed?' She walked up the stairs, joining him on the landing.

'Yeah,' Monkey said. 'Only so much communal living I can stand.'

She responded to the sarcasm with a slight shake of her head. 'What was going on at dinner?'

'What do you mean?'

'When Lucas came in, I was looking at you. Your reaction was a little strange.'

Monkey shrugged. 'I knew him from before.'

A dark look flared inside Charley's eyes. 'I didn't know.'

'Why would you?'

'Would have been nice if I'd been told, that's all. Did the Vegan know?'

'Of course. Is it a problem?'

She shook her head, incredulous at the question. 'Well, *of course* it's a problem. It's bad enough that you're here. I don't need you to go cooking things up with Lucas.'

Monkey walked up to his room, tired of all the rules of this new freedom. He lay smoking on his bed with the lights off, lit only by the draw of his breath. A patch of sky showed through the blanket over the window. The country night was so very dark. It oozed in through the windows, it dripped down the walls. Eventually, Monkey crushed his cigarette out into a cracked mug and turned on to his side. On the second floor, a lone guitar played, the spare fragile chords hanging gently like smoke.

After she found out about his past association with Lucas, Charley's paranoia got the better of her. When Monkey wasn't working for the Vegan, or helping out with the Mansion's chores, he stayed in his room, lying on his camp bed, smoking cigarettes as he read an old yellow horror novel (bees: thousands of them) which he'd looted from the stack of books in the hallway downstairs. He thought very rarely about what he had left behind. Best to forget Herointown completely, as Herointown had forgotten him. Over a month since he'd last seen her, he decided to call Rose. When he couldn't find the phone in the office, he went through to the kitchen where Taylor sat drinking beer at the table and Robert was chopping onions by the sink.

'He's smelled the dinner,' Taylor laughed boozily when Monkey asked for the phone. 'And he wants to dial a pizza.'

Robert answered, without looking up from the stove. 'I think Jenn's got it. She's in the living room.'

Monkey found Jenn seated on the chaise longue, staring at the TV with the phone to her ear. She was a tall, skinny girl with hair the colour of flayed copper wire; she wore a pair of mustard-yellow dungarees. The TV had been turned to mute. An old seventies sitcom played, the silence giving a strange anxiety to the actors' movements. As Monkey turned to leave, Jenn gestured for him to stay.

'Yes of course. I will. Of course. No. I wouldn't do that. Yes. You too. Take care.'

'My mum,' she explained, as she hung up. 'She worries.'

'I was going to call home.'

'Well be my guest.' She handed over the phone. 'You're the new kid, aren't you?'

'That's right.'

'The mysterious new kid. Who everyone is talking about.'

'I didn't think anyone had noticed.'

'Don't let this place fool you. Just because they don't talk to you, doesn't mean they don't talk *about* you. It's what passes for etiquette.'

Monkey left the living room to avoid interruptions. Seated on the office chair underneath the files of accounts and farming manuals, he called Rose's number. Although he'd been rehearsing for a couple of days, he still wasn't sure what he would tell her. Whatever he said, she'd only think that he'd fallen back into Herointown. In the end, it didn't matter. The ringtone pulsed like sonar, describing the limits of an empty house. Eventually, he gave up and headed back to the kitchen with the phone. Jenn was out in the hallway, starting up the stairs. She called across to him, walking back down to the first step.

'Everything all right back home?'

'No answer.'

'Everyone out enjoying themselves?'

'You're probably right.'

He must have looked a woebegone, miserable Monkey, unloved and all alone. 'Listen,' she went on. 'There's a film on TV tonight. A few of us were going to stay up. You're welcome to join us. I'd have asked you before, but . . .'

'It's OK.'

'But next time, yeah?'

Back in his room, Monkey sat on his camp bed. Damp floors and peeling walls don't make much of a home, so he'd started decorating. Earlier that week, he'd magpied a trophy from the Vegan. During breaks in the laboratory, the Vegan would sit on an old plastic milk crate, drinking tea from a thermos, smoking a roll-up. Sometimes, he would read *The Tibetan Book of the Dead*, a small edition he kept in the button pocket of his khakis, but usually, he would leaf through one of his magazines. He liked to keep himself informed about everything from the conspiracy of cancer drugs, to the corporate hijacking of the Middle East; the magazines provided all of this along with generous doses of animal cruelty. An issue could not go by without some image of a seal being brained in Alaska or dogs being pumped with ketamine. A large pile of these publications had accumulated inside the lab. 'Help yourself,' the Vegan had told Monkey. 'They'll open your eyes, really they will.'

One of the photos showed a monkey restrained in a laboratory. The top of its skull had been removed and electrodes applied to its bare brain. But the monkey had shaken one paw free, and with a finger tried to root out the intrusive wire. Monkey pinned the picture opposite his bed, part decoration, part protest. It said everything.

6

One evening, it all became too much for Charley, and she walked out on Taylor after telling him that he'd never see her again. He took it the way he usually did, with his eyes on the ceiling and his right foot tapping the floor. Charley often wondered whether this little tic was his way of controlling his temper, but if Taylor had a fuse it burned down more slowly than a sun. Mostly this suited the balance of their relationship, but sometimes, when she longed for an argument, she wished that he would rise.

The whole mess had started like this. She'd spent the afternoon packing for the stall and even with all the help – she had four people on the rota – it was still a tiring, back-breaking job, not made easier by the fact that she had to supervise. No matter how often she begged people to be careful, something was always spoiled; on this occasion, Andrew dropped a beer crate, smashing most of the bottles.

'A little care next time!'

If anyone had to piss Charley off that morning, it might as well be Andrew. She'd known too many young men like him in her time: bed-sit geniuses who parroted big ideas to cover their lack of experience, they were irritants, mouthpieces for opinions, arguments for hire.

'It wouldn't hurt to use better boxes.' Andrew looked stung, not only because he knew that he was in the wrong, but because he realized that she was enjoying it. 'That one was bent out of shape.'

A boy who'd try to talk a tumour around. Charley sighed. 'Don't argue about this, please.' She kicked at the wet slush of broken glass. 'The box fell. Gravity took over, I'll grant you, but you dropped the box.'

'All I'm saying . . .'

'Just be more careful!'

Finally, with everything packed and stored in the van, she'd headed back into the house. There were other chores for the evening: she had to check the safe for the till float, as well as sort through some paperwork (the trading licence needed to be renewed) but she needed a break. After stopping in the kitchen to make a cup of tea, she walked through into the living room, allowing herself at least half an hour of TV, anything to occupy her mind. Instead, she was confronted by five or six kids in their late teens, a couple of them struggling with each other on the chaise longue. It might have been an ordinary evening in the Mansion's living room, except Charley didn't recognize a single one of them.

'Who are you?'

One of the boys started on introductions, but Charley cut him off. 'I'm not interested in your names. Who *are* you?'

'We're with Sadie. She's just gone upstairs.'

'And? What are you doing here?'

'It's kind of a party. At least, that's what Sadie said.'

When Charley walked out into the hallway, she found Sadie descending the stairs.

'I don't see what the problem is,' the girl said, when Charley demanded an explanation. 'They're just over for the evening.'

Sadie had lived in the Mansion for over two years; she

was hard-working, and had taken to the spirit of the commune as readily as anyone. Normally, Charley trusted her, but ever since they had started the pill-making, she had become anxious about having too many strangers in the house. If they wanted to stay and work, fine. They could be controlled, by the daily rota, by the rules. But casual visitors wandering around the house: she couldn't allow it.

'For a party?'

'It's not a party. It's a few friends.'

'And how long are they staying?'

'The evening. Well, maybe the night. I'm not sure.'

Charley took a deep breath. 'Sorry. It's not happening.'

A perfect expression of open-mouthed incredulity appeared on Sadie's face. 'Oh come on! New people come all the time. Look at that new kid . . .'

Charley didn't need to be reminded of Monkey. After telling Sadie bluntly that her guests would have to leave before the end of the evening, she went looking for Taylor, hoping for a little support, expecting him to understand. No sign of him in the kitchen, or the office, or outside in the brewery, she eventually tracked him down in one of the damp rooms on the third floor. With a stepladder set up and a toolbox lying open, he had, apparently, been working on the ceiling. But as Charley walked through the door, she saw him bend to hide a bottle behind a stack of boxes. When Taylor had only shrugged and said, 'I think you're overreacting,' an already infuriated Charley erupted. She talked Taylor through the situation with a sense of order and bitter purpose. How easy was it for Charley to cover for Monkey? Why was it that they had to protect someone who had stolen from them? Did Taylor think it was right that they didn't just leave him to the police, but that they took him in, housed and fed him? Did Taylor think that she should be forced into such positions without having anyone to back her up? Did Taylor think at all?

'I was fucking right!' She shouted this to nothing but air. It helped.

The evening was dull with the sullen threat of rain. As she walked up the gravel driveway her brain roared with the argument. Although she knew it was cold, she removed her cardigan, tied it around her waist and fanned her face with the back of her hand, a sign of her premenstrual state. It got worse each year: a hot flush – as though there was a spark somewhere inside her body and her blood was a fuel – and she'd lose herself to a few seconds of rage. This was certainly the main reason she'd blown up at Taylor, although if he'd dared mention it, she'd have clawed out his eyes. It didn't help that all the women in the Mansion had synchronized their periods, so that for a few days each month they traded blows on frayed nerves, the air a soup of bad hormonal feeling.

Half a mile down the road she managed to wind down. She jumped over a gate into a wheat field, sticking to the path beaten around the edges of the stubble, and headed for a large oak in the far corner. She leant against the tree trunk and rolled a caterpillar of Drum into a liquorice paper, staring at the fields beyond. Only recently, she'd read that a chemical company wanted permission to grow GM crops not far from here, a new round in a long running fight. She thought about the little men, the scientists, making a thousand and one calculations all designed to fuck things up. They were succeeding. Not for the first time, Charley thought about the kind of person scared by the unchecked morality of science, but who chose to make illegal pills to maintain a failing farm. She shook her head, threw the cigarette to the ground and screwed the paper beneath her heel: returning it to wood mulch and leaves.

Cold again, she pulled her cardigan over her shoulders and walked back up the field, out on to the road.

As she walked up the drive, she noticed a mellow orange light glowing in the downstairs window of the cottage: a signal of home, or a warning of rocks. Charley still couldn't decide. She walked quickly across the front lawn, around to the kitchen door. Inside, Taylor was sitting at the table, no longer hiding his bottle of beer. He looked over at her, trying to mask anxiety behind hurt, his need for her so great that he couldn't see that it was reciprocated. Because, obviously, she needed Taylor. Without him, and his unconditional need, Charley's disgust might easily become directed against herself. *Are you defeated yet?* she asked silently: not knowing if she meant by life or the games she played, unsure for a second which of them she queried.

Taylor wiped the beer foam from his beard with thumb and forefinger. 'Back then?' His voice contained a trace of sarcasm: his method of confrontation.

'Yes I am,' Charley replied. 'And if you don't piss me off, I might just stay.'

Call the Mansion a squat, and Charley would correct you. As a house – even as an idea – it was far more than that, and while the ideology might have drifted over the years, the commune had been founded upon principles beyond the happy chance of a rent-free roof. Still, commune or squat, Charley had lived in enough of these places to know that her surroundings would never really be her own. She liked to think she had relinquished the ordinary terror that craves property, but sometimes other people's influence on the house became too much. The Aga, installed like some donor's heart, had been rescued from a tip outside the town by other people. Other people had devised the calendar for the garden, other people had come up with a method of crop rotation to make best use of the soil. The piping in the first-floor bathroom, the installation of the electricity generator at the rear of the house: these were the successes of other people. It all served to remind Charley that since she and Taylor had taken charge, the Mansion had remained frozen. No time for new initiatives (perhaps no imagination for them), the residents lacking organization and purpose, advancing into nothing but increased stagnation: join it all together and it was her fault. She raged at this, spat fury at some imagined accuser who would dare to dump blame on her doorstep. Other forces too had influenced the Mansion's decline; she could, and did, blame supermarket culture, rampant social conformity, even the internal politics of the house. She was doing what she could.

Next morning was market day. Charley set her alarm for quarter to six. Not only did such an early start give her time to prepare, but in the silence, with only the dogs awake, it was her Mansion. After feeding the dogs, eating her breakfast and drinking a cup of strong, strong coffee, a Fairtrade blend bought cheaply from the market, she walked outside, taking her rucksack, and headed for the outhouse. It was a gloomy chilly morning, not quite dark and not quite light. The grey crystal of the sky revealed the fossilized crowns of stripped deciduous trees, precious as networks of coral against the horizon. In the outhouse, Charley retrieved the latest batch of pills from the freezer, which Monkey and the Vegan had produced over the previous week. As she stuffed the plastic bag into her rucksack, Charley felt a kind of groggy resentment at these twin threats upon her home, and she longed for the time when they would no longer be involved. After locking the outhouse, she headed for the van. It groaned reluctantly under the ignition, but she finally managed to bring it around. She pulled up outside the back of the house, shrugging out of the cardigan because she felt unusually hot. As she waited for everyone else, she rolled her first cigarette of the day. She looked out at the goats, sleepy in their pen, at the trees on the edge of the forest, stirring in the morning breeze, as though they too were coming alive. From the ribbon of smoke coming from the chimney of the cottage, she could tell that Lucas had started a fire.

When the radio newsreader announced eight o'clock, and no one had assembled outside, Charley headed around to the back door. By now, the kitchen was busy, some of the residents pulling on boots and gloves for their stints in the garden, while others were only just preparing breakfast. Charley rapped on the door to grab their attention. 'If you're working on the stall, can you hurry up. We're running late.'

Before returning outside, she talked briefly to Robert about the garden work over the coming months, and whether he needed any extra help with his plans for the kitchen. She had started looking to him more and more for help running the place, even though, at first, Robert hadn't really welcomed the responsibility. Dark and wiry, with a soft Scouse accent that he seemed ashamed of, he was a distant, solitary man, and when he wasn't working in the kitchen, he spent his time listening to football matches on the radio in his room. Since arriving a few years before, his work in the kitchen had been outstanding and it had been a relief when he'd recently agreed to take on more responsibility. As close as they were, Charley had begun to find Taylor too much of a liability.

Outside, the stall workers had gathered by the van. Charley realized that by a little trick of fate she would be working with Sadie, along with Jenn and a couple of the male residents to balance the gender mix. One look at

Sadie's face was enough to tell Charley that she hadn't been forgiven for cancelling her party, which would have been fine if they hadn't had to spend the whole day together.

They had to reach the market early to get a parking space, so Charley gunned the van along the bypass, goading herself on by feeding the tape player with a new punk compilation, courtesy of a friend in town. Jenn sat in the seat next to her, spending the whole journey chatting about the music, the day ahead (she was meeting her brother for lunch), about everything and nothing. Charley tuned out, too absorbed in her later meeting with Pete.

They reached the town centre as the attendant was opening up the makeshift car park behind the music hall. Charley flashed her trader's pass, drove on, and pulled up at a space near the entrance, by the crumbling sandstone wall. Once the stall had been set up, trade was good: they sold most of the fruit and apple juice, and shifted a fair amount of vegetables. But Charley also encountered the usual hassles: people complaining about the stock, that the vegetables weren't bleached the way you bought them in supermarkets, and people for whom the idea of 'organic' simply meant overpriced. One of Charley's gripes was the way that natural food had been so commercialized that people refused to trust it, but she tried to be patient. This was commerce, after all: smile and take people's money, hating them inside. It's what they *expected*.

Her appointment with Pete had been arranged for 3 p.m., this time in an amusement arcade around the back of the town square. Unfortunately, she was delayed. After Jenn had left for lunch, Charley let one of the boys pick up a prescription from the chemist. When three o'clock came and went, and there was still no sign of Jenn, she only had two people working the stall, when really it was too busy for three. So Charley spent twenty minutes waiting, with each customer she served picking at her patience. Finally, Jenn appeared on the other side of the square, distinctive with her bright copper hair and purple dungarees. When she saw Charley waiting, she hopped into a run. 'Don't bother *now*,' Charley shouted. 'Don't start hurrying *now*. I'm already late.'

'Sorry, sorry, sorry. I lost track of time.'

'What is wrong with you lot at the moment?' She glanced over at Sadie, making it clear that she hadn't forgiven her for the night before.

'It was my brother,' Jenn explained. 'He's back in town. I hadn't seen him for a while.'

Charley left Jenn babbling excuses and headed to the car park. She had left the rucksack stuffed behind the steering column to keep it out of sight; after retrieving it, she hurried towards the amusement arcade behind the shopping centre, anxious that Pete wouldn't have waited around. She found him feeding change into a fruit machine emblazoned with the logo of a Hollywood film. She'd met Pete through a friend of a friend of a friend; as far as he was concerned, the pills were made over the Welsh border by people who wanted to remain unknown. Pete was tall, good-looking, with light green eyes the colour of faded grass and skin the colour of milky coffee. He pushed at the buttons of the machine, his face vacant in the lights.

'Hit the jackpot?' she asked, standing at his shoulder.

Pete turned. ''Fraid we'll still be doing business for a while.'

'Make me feel wanted, why don't you.'

'Got everything?'

She tapped her rucksack. 'Sorry I'm late. I got caught up.'

'No problem, no problem. I live to wait.'

'Where shall we go?'

Pete pointed to the far corner. 'Over here. It's a blind spot for the one camera they've got in here.'

'Smart.'

'Oh, I cover all the bases,' Pete said. 'Not that they'll mind, I'm sure. They're more worried about someone ripping off the machines.'

They walked through to the back, past a woman in a change booth, counting pound coins into black plastic racks. Behind a partition wall by the solitary pool table, Pete unzipped his jacket and produced a roll of notes squeezed into a moneybag.

'Here's the money. Count it if you want.'

'It's OK, Pete. I trust you.'

She unzipped her rucksack and felt around for the pills. Wrapped tight in the bubble wrap they might have been a shattered antique, a collection of bones. Pete took the bag, thrust it into the pocket of his parka.

'Always a pleasure doing business with you.'

'Actually, I wanted a word.'

'I'm listening.' He looked suddenly tense, as though each extraneous word was an hour upon his time. This tension made Charley nervous. 'That is . . . What you were saying last time we met. About increasing supply of the pills. They've been thinking about it.'

'Right.'

'Are you still interested?'

'How much are we talking about? I'd need figures.'

'They're not really sure at the moment. They only asked me to sound you out.'

He scratched at the stubble on his cheek. 'Well, get them to put together a proposal.' There was a hardness to his voice, an icy precision. 'I can probably shift double what we're doing now, by branching out. But it would have to be soon.'

'Why's that.'

He shrugged. 'The way I see it, the whole thing is dying. Floods of cheap coke and heroin. Doesn't really mix with the old atmosphere. Those days are gone.'

'Are you sure it's not you?' Charley said. She smiled, although she suddenly felt alarmed. 'You never know, Pete. You might be getting old.'

He acknowledged it with a nod of his head. 'I'm not so sure. It's got this air about it now.'

'What do you mean?'

'Of the last days. There's too much fear about. Anxiety.' He patted his pocket. 'It takes a hell of a lot of these to fight it. It's the fading dream. Ecstasy turning to terror. It's the story of our days.'

They started packing up the stall around 5 p.m., and as the takings were reasonably healthy, Charley decided to take everyone for a drink rather than head straight home, sticking to halves because she was driving. She managed to repair things with Sadie, but Jenn was reluctant to patch things up, unable to keep that dreadful sarcasm out of her voice when Charley spoke to her. Anyway, Charley bumped into a couple of friends, and they caught up on news. For these rare opportunities to escape the Mansion, she enjoyed visiting the town, but the air of defeat always sent her running back. People in her circle tended to rebound here after their big adventures, whether they were making a homecoming or slipping into a slower pace of life. They'd returned from Mexico, or New Zealand, from teaching English in Japan or Poland; they were refugees from the old town houses in Hackney or Brixton, forced out by the stealth of regeneration. They came back chewed by life, their skin either leathery from too much sun, or pale and bloodless from city pollution, their minds porous from various kinds of abuse. They came here because the world had exhausted them, because in all the ways they'd been broken, they still longed for something which they felt they'd lost. They hated to think of failure and they hated to think of life, so they allowed themselves this last nostalgia, even though it was only an expression of frustrated rage.

When they reached home, the others headed off around to the back door, leaving Charley to bring up the rear after retrieving the takings from the van. When she opened the kitchen door, she was treated to the sight of Taylor drinking alone at the kitchen table. The others had walked right past, guessing it would be best to give them privacy. Instead of speaking, Charley filled a glass of water from the tap. She glanced over at the empties by the back door, the brown, clear and green bottles, which he would recycle, sterilize and reuse and this way turn a problem into a solution.

'Good day?' He scratched at the table with a grubby fingernail.

'Did well out of things, yes.'

'And the pills?'

'Pete's OK. There was no trouble.'

'Did you talk to him?' He paused to belch. 'About increasing his supply.'

'I think I'd rather talk about that when you're sober.'

Taylor scowled and reached for his glass. Drunk like this, he became caught in a pattern. The hand reached for the glass, the throat swallowed. It had nothing to do with the taste or feel of alcohol. It was a pattern repeated to supplant life, a monotonous function of depression. After living with him for so long, Charley had grown to understand what it really meant to drink.

'You're back late,' he said.

'I took everyone for a drink. Ran into a couple of people. Nothing wrong, is there?'

Taylor shrugged. His irises were tiny, receded to pinpricks. He stammered slightly as he went on. 'I just . . . I sometimes don't know with you, do I? Whether you're going to come back.'

She shook her head. 'I'm not really in the mood for this, Taylor. I'm tired.'

'I don't care if you're tired.' Taylor shook his head back and forth, a spastic, frantic gesture like a frustrated child on a slow fairground ride. 'I want to talk about this *now*.'

'What do you want to talk about?'

'I want to talk about you and me. I want to talk about you and Lucas. You said you were going to stop. It's getting ridiculous now. Everyone else knows. Everyone is laughing at us.'

'Taylor . . .'

'They think you're desperate because you're getting old. And me? What do they think of me?' He said this more to the table than to Charley. He talked to wood knots and splits in the pine.

'I'll tell you. They think I'm weak. They see me, putting up with all your crap. And they say . . .'

'You're not making sense Taylor.'

'. . . they say, he can't do *anything* but accept it.'

She headed for the kitchen door, went out into the hall. 'Taylor, I'm going to bed. That's all I want.'

'Ah fuck off,' he said, throwing out a hand. 'Don't take me for a moron. You can't stay away from him. You're hooked.'

That remark raged in her mind as Charley walked up to her room; it was infuriating to think that her motives were so visible. Even when she acted at her most obvious, she couldn't imagine that she was anything but concealed. It was another way by which she tried to maintain control. She undressed and pitched herself at the bed, but she couldn't sleep. Suddenly, it was two in the morning. The phosphorescent hands of the alarm clock taunted her. She pulled herself out of bed, and threw on clothes quickly to defeat the chill in the air: jeans, a T-shirt, a jumper. She left her room, letting the door close gently, treading lightly on the tired floorboards, angry with herself that she had to put up such a charade, but almost gleeful in the actual adventure of it. She moved down the stairs and into the kitchen. The dogs were her only audience. She retrieved a torch from underneath the sink, and pulled on her boots; the yellow greyhound trembled beside her in its bed. 'It's OK,' Charley whispered, patting the dog gently on the head. 'Really, it's fine.' Outside, she walked past the brewery and waded through the tall grass, the beam of the torch picking out shapes in the edge of the forest. A light was burning in the upstairs room of the cottage, the yellow glow of a candle. She walked quickly across the field, and entered through the dark ground-floor room, which was both lounge and rudimentary kitchen. Her hand reached out to navigate the furniture in the half light, and she lifted the latch of the thin planked door leading to the stairs.

In the bedroom, Lucas sat at the desk facing the narrow window, bent over an open notebook, a pen in his hand. His face was burned upon the black glass by the light of a candle: a ghost upon an old photographic plate. Charley stood at the doorway, waiting for him to indicate that he knew she was there. When he didn't look up, she spoke. 'Can we go to bed soon?'

'Are you tired?' His eyes moved to his shoulder to briefly acknowledge her presence, but quickly returned to the page.

'It's been a long day.'

She lay down upon the double bed, the springs of the ancient mattress squealing underneath her weight. For a while, she watched his reflection: the seriousness upon his long, slightly mean face as he looked down at his notebook. Before he'd moved out into the cottage, Charley couldn't remember finding him attractive, although she must have done. Only after he'd approached her about renovating the old cottage – asking her permission without the kind of weaselly flirtation that would have killed off any appeal – did she start to think about him. Not long after he moved in, she had visited him late one night, because she was bored and, although she hated to admit it, lonely. He hadn't been surprised; he'd hardly responded at all, although he had responded enough. A ready, energetic passivity: over the past months, this had kept her entertained. Or was it more than entertainment? Taylor's words came back to her. *You're hooked.* For a second, she saw Taylor suppliant at her feet, and she blinked, and suddenly Taylor wasn't there and she was looking at Lucas.

'I've been wondering.' She wanted him to respond, and this way offer slight proof that they reciprocated. He refused. 'We've got a new resident,' she went on. 'I think you know him.'

Only now did he glance up, his eyes searching for her reflection in the window pane.

'We spent some time together. It's not really important.' Finally, he turned to look at her. 'To me at least.'

'Meaning it is important to him?'

'Meaning I don't really care enough to think about it.' But he bit his lip and closed his notebook. 'We used to smoke heroin together.'

'Nasty.' It was the most that Lucas had ever given away about himself, but she tried not appear too intrigued.

He weighed the sentiment with a shake of his head. 'Whatever. We did.'

'Someone told me that he was an addict. He spent time in a clinic.'

'That's right.'

'And you?'

Lucas smiled. 'I came here.'

'You know what I mean.'

'With me, it didn't really stick.'

'You're lucky.'

By now Lucas had moved over to the bed, his shadow capsizing around the angles of the room. He began to undress, staring down at her with an absence in his blue eyes, an intelligent, emotionless vacancy which she chose to think of as detachment. *Like a scientist*, she told herself: *I have fallen in love with science.* She wriggled out of her clothes, and although the sheets were cold, they were almost a relief against her hot skin. Lucas lay down beside her, a hand sliding between her legs. His skin felt as cold as glass. 'Slowly,' she said, pushing against his shoulder and moving him back against the sheets. 'I want to kiss you first.' As she moved on top of him, she looked down through what little light penetrated the dark: the ever-fading candle, the discrete stars and the tarnished second-hand silver of the moon. As weak as it was, the light caught the absence in his eyes. And she found herself inside it.

7

The coming Spring was playing with Monkey. He felt restless and tense, the change of the season pressurizing the fluid of his kneecap, his frontal lobe, his sinuses, eyeballs and testicles. He felt overburdened and inflamed, a hungry gland, ready to burst. The need for sex drove you crazy once you came off heroin. In the clinic, the counsellors doled out porn to anyone who wanted it, and everyone eventually did. Monkey's room-mate Billy had spent six months thrashing himself raw, tiring out the springs on the top bunk. In Billy the lack of heroin had brought back an obsession long postponed: he was a dedicated, almost scholarly, wanker. After lights out, he'd discuss the various merits of The OK Sign over The Clasp, defend the application of Tabasco sauce and eucalyptus oil, make claims for the use of cookie dough ice cream ('Makes it last for hours'), a hole bored into a honeydew melon, a pint pot of chopped liver. No such luxuries in the clinic, but Billy improvised. One evening, Monkey returned to find him with a tourniquet around his wrist. He hadn't scored: he was cutting off the circulation to his hand. 'Feels like someone else is doing it,' he grinned. The bed springs started shrieking soon after. Billy would often long for Vaseline; Monkey would have settled for a little WD40.

During those early weeks in the Mansion, Monkey

spent a few nights in the camp bed alone with his hand. To take his mind off his needs, he raided the bookshelves between the kitchen and the living room. Amongst tattered Whole Earth catalogues, guidebooks to flora and fauna, outdoor manuals and local archaeology tracts, he found enough paperbacks to entertain him. Soon he lost himself in the various apocalypses of insects and pigs, rodents and crabs. When he wasn't working with the Vegan, he spent days living off books, strong cups of tea and cigarettes, only breaking off when he knew there were chores waiting for him in the house. After finishing the most recent consignment of pills, the Vegan had taken a couple of weeks off: replenishing the supplies, so he said. In an act of indirect revenge, Charley began setting Monkey to work. Feeding chickens, cleaning out the goat pen, digging trenches in the vegetable garden, cleaning floors and preparing meals: all the tasks came to him. The only thing he refused was to work on the market stall.

Partly because of the rota and partly through choice, Monkey spent as little time as possible with the other residents. Most of them had been barely interested in him, but after their first meeting in the living room, Jenn had remained friendly. Two or three evenings a week, they washed up together; Jenn spent most of her shifts working in the kitchen. 'You think I'm a little mother hen?' she asked, when he pointed this out. It turned out that she'd injured her back in a car crash and Charley had agreed to exclude her from the heavy lifting that came with garden work.

That evening, a full house sat down for a meal of vegetable bake followed by damson and apple crumble. Jenn and Monkey washed up the aftermath: pots, cutlery and dishes, the worst of them coated with burned fruit syrup. 'My god, this stuff is like road tar!' Jenn exclaimed, after scratching at one pan for nearly ten minutes. In the end, she threw Monkey the cloth. 'Come on, your turn . . .' Jenn took over wiping up, while Monkey scrubbed at the pan, dunking it repeatedly into the already greasy lukewarm water. The yellow greyhound padded towards them across the tiles. It began whining slightly, nuzzling against Jenn's side.

'Oh not *you*.' She pushed it away with her leg. 'I wish you'd stay away from me.'

'You don't like dogs?'

'My parents used to breed them. These nasty little spaniel things. Their skulls were very fragile, from years and years of inbreeding. A lot of the puppies didn't last a week. One slip and their skulls would shatter, just like that. We'd find them in the morning, lying perfect and still. I've seen enough dead puppies to last a lifetime.'

The yellow greyhound had moved close to the Aga, and sat eyeing them both as Jenn talked.

'Dog people have to be cold,' she went on. 'Training and discipline, runts of the litter: you can't let it affect you. My mum coped with it for a while but it finally sent her over the edge. She had a lot of problems. My brother was a bit wild. My dad was always away on business. And I mean, *business*.' She made a ring from one finger, and rubbed it over another. 'One day, Mum came down and found her favourite puppy, Samson. Somehow, the little thing had got trapped in the garage. I don't know what had gone through his head. He climbed up on the car, and when he was there, he climbed up some more. Pretty soon he was in the rafters of the house. Maybe the height got to him. He must have clawed at the roofing, got outside. At the time, we were having some work done. We lived on one of those estates on the new belt outside the town. Lots of mock Tudor and orange brick. There was scaffolding on the garage roof. Planks, and ladders. You know what builders leave around. Samson carried on. This was in the middle of winter. There were strong winds.'

'What happened?'

'What do you think? Samson got to the top of the house. He reached the very edge of his doggy world. What else could he do? He jumped.'

'Jesus.'

'Of course, I'm anthropomorphizing. Mum learned the word in her treatment. She invested too many human characteristics in her dogs. It's what caused the breakdown.'

'Did he die?'

'Cats land on their feet. Dogs go head first. Samson landed on his skull.'

'What did your mum do?'

'Had a breakdown. Right there by the side of the house. We found her clutching the headless dog. Very sad. We took her to the doctor. He pumped her full of pills.'

'And?'

'She got rid of the dogs. Spends her time dosed up to her eyeballs watching the TV. She likes golf. She likes golf *a lot*. It seems to make sense to her. Vijay and Tiger. Men in ridiculous clothes, tidying away little white balls. It has resonance.'

'Don't you feel sorry for her?'

Jenn shrugged. 'Everyone has a dead dog story. Everyone.'

They finished washing up and Monkey walked with her up the stairs. They stopped on the landing by the second floor. The moment had potential: he could have invited her up to the third floor, or found a way for Jenn to invite him back to her room.

'Well,' Jenn said, 'I'd better go.'

'I'll see you tomorrow.'

Somehow, the conversation slipped away. Back in his

room, he was a lonely frustrated Monkey on a single bed. He tried to sleep, and failing, he read. The night seeped in from the window; soon it swallowed the room. He smoked cigarettes but the glow made him feel insubstantial, a hallucination. A few of Billy's techniques came back to him, but he knew that if anything this made the frustration worse. In the end, he got up and dressed.

The house stirred around him as he walked down the stairs and let himself into the dark kitchen. One of the dogs – the collie, he saw in the triangle of light from the door – sat up from its bed and followed him as he searched for a torch under the sink and pulled on a coat. He pushed an intrusive snout away as he closed the door: the last thing Jenn needed was another headless dog. As he walked outside, the only sound was of the wind rushing through the heads of the trees. Within the goat pen, the brown one lay hunkered down on its hooves, eyeing him through the wire; the white one was nowhere to be seen. Something clack-clacked in the dark; something else replied. Monkey lit the torch, keeping the beam in front of him as he trudged towards the forest. Inside, he followed a long sunken ditch, a dried-up stream separating two parts of the forest. Soon, he lost track of how far he'd walked. The air was dank with the wet smells of leaves and earth. The forest trembled on the edges of the torchlight. He felt tired now, but he kept walking. In the same way he'd walked all over Herointown, describing a route filled by thefts and betrayals, a route which would usually lead to Teal.

When he heard the music, it seemed part of a dream. It was that indistinct, suffocated by the sounds of the forest, birds clattering amongst the branches, the wind in the leaves, the blood pulsing in his ears. It had the heavy thud-thud of a frightened heart, and if Monkey chose to scare himself with these midnight walks, it was because fear, at least, was a feeling. Looking to trace the source, he clambered up an incline where bright white electric light burst through the branches, the sound of a shrill voice and heavy bass straining the range of a set of car speakers. At the centre of a clearing, two vacant cars burned headlights towards a group of ten to fifteen people. Most were single men, but Monkey saw a few couples, the women dressed in short skirts and low tops, defying the cold spring night. Everyone watched another car, at the centre of the group. Monkey struggled down the verge, glimpsing movement on the inside. A naked couple lay together in the front seats. A woman with small breasts and dyed black hair sat astride a man, facing the crowd. The man rocked her back and forth over his hips.

'Yeah,' someone said in the crowd. 'Yeah.'

'Do it,' another voice said. 'Fucking do it.'

The air was thick with everyone's breath. Monkey had stopped inside the clearing, a few metres away from the edge of the crowd. One of the men noticed him: a tall, bony and stooped character, in tight white jeans. He kept checking his shoulder; when Monkey showed no signs of joining the crowd, he became agitated. Finally, he pulled his hands from his pockets.

'If you're going to join in, join in. If you only want to watch, you can fuck off.'

Monkey turned and walked back into the woods, wondering how far he needed to go to escape his needs.

Somehow, he lost the way back. A gully led deeper into the woods: he followed it for over half an hour, before he realized that he was heading deeper into the forest. He cut through the wood, but after a few paces he stumbled down a verge. It was a short drop, no more than a metre, but the fall knocked his breath away. He sat in the dark, imagining being lost forever: the grass covering his body, weaving through his hair, moss covering his bones. When he finally found the perimeter of the woods, he came out way down the front lawn, near the main road. He kept to the line of trees as he walked back towards the house. The cottage lay to his left, a light burning in the first-floor window. It was an incredible night, the sky so clear that the movement of the stars seemed almost visible, like handfuls of light caught in the action of being thrown. Monkey turned off the torch. Creatures rustled inside the forest, hidden late-night traffic. More approached him over the grass: Charley, walking quickly across the lawn, hunched inside her cardigan. She hadn't seen him. Monkey ducked back into the woods as she passed. She walked to the cottage and, checking her shoulder, let herself into the front door. Upstairs, the light burned for a few minutes longer; then it was gone.

At breakfast the next morning, fifteen people were squeezed on to benches around the kitchen table. Most meals, Monkey usually found himself crushed between Taylor and Charley – they were so close to him, he was surprised they didn't offer to taste his food – but that morning, he sat between Jenn and Andrew. Tall, with pale skin and mid-length curly brown hair, Andrew was always talking: debating, arguing, provoking. Now, he waited until everyone had started eating before he spoke.

'Did someone go out last night?'

Monkey didn't answer. He glanced over at Charley, but she continued leafing through paperwork.

'It's just, there were footprints all over the floor this morning,' Andrew went on. 'And the torch was left out on the side.'

Monkey raised his hand. 'That was me.'

'I'd just like to point out that I had to wash the floor

yesterday evening.' Andrew scowled, glancing around the table. 'When I came down it was a mess. It's actually quite disheartening to do a job and have it spoiled like that.'

'I went out for a walk.' Monkey continued with the story: how he hadn't been able to sleep and had gone out into the woods. When he described the group in the clearing, Taylor spoke up.

'I stumbled into one of those parties once. They arrange places to meet over the internet.' He sipped from his beer. 'They even have a name for it . . .'

'It's not that I mind you going out,' Andrew interrupted. 'But if it starts to impinge upon other people's work . . .'

Charley finally spoke. 'All right, Andrew. That's enough.'

'He's new. I just wanted to make it clear to him.'

'He's got the message.'

As everyone returned to their meal, Monkey tapped Andrew on the arm. 'I'm sorry. I'll make it up to you.'

He had to repay the debt later that night: Andrew asked him to take his shift washing up. The rota played a cruel, cruel lottery: Charley was drying. They cleared the table together in silence.

'What were you doing last night?' Although they were alone in the kitchen, she spoke in a low voice, barely audible above the chink and clatter of dishes and knives.

'The woods. I've already gone through this.'

'I'm not really happy with you wandering around the place like that.'

'What do you want to do, lock me in my room?'

She laughed. It was a hard, spiteful sound. 'I wish I could.'

'Wouldn't really work very well when I had to go out to the lab, though.'

'I suppose you're right.' She rubbed at the willow pattern plate: slowly erasing dead lovers transmigrated to birds. 'Did you really see that group of people?'

'Yeah. Of course.'

'I thought you might be making it up.'

'Didn't you hear Taylor? He's seen them too.'

'I thought he might be making it up as well.' Paranoia was the darkness in her eyes. 'Was it the only thing you saw?'

'I didn't *see* anything. I don't want to *know* anything.'

Before Charley could respond, the door sounded behind them. Jenn stood at the entrance, clearly realizing that she'd interrupted something.

'Sorry, I was . . . Have either of you two seen Robert?'

She left quickly. Charley followed soon after, leaving Monkey to finish the work alone. When he was done, he let himself outside. After the heat of the kitchen, the cool air welcomed him. He heard the door open behind him, the subtle leak of murmurs from inside, and turned to see Jenn pressing the door closed behind her. She walked across the paving slabs, her arms folded around her belly.

'Have you got a spare cigarette?'

He had three left in the pack. Anyone else, and he might have refused, but he offered her the pack. She lit the cigarette with her own lighter, rubbing a small, pearl-like flame over the tip until it caught. She smoked in silence, as though conscious that she'd intruded.

'Did you find Robert?' Monkey asked, even though he didn't really care.

'He's in his room. I'll leave it until morning. He fell out with Sadie over breakfast. I'm trying to keep the peace.' She inhaled from her cigarette. 'Were you enjoying the view?'

'It's beautiful.'

'You should go up on the roof. A few of us broke out there before you came. We did it for someone's birthday. Took a bottle of wine up there, had a bit to smoke. It was a clear night, like tonight, only summer, so it was warm. Beautiful.'

'I'll bet.'

'We can do it again. Maybe when it gets a bit lighter in the evening. Charley doesn't like people going up there. The place is rotten, falling apart. She says she doesn't want to have to cope with an accident.' She glanced at the orange eye of her cigarette. 'What was going on there between the two of you, anyway?'

'Who?'

'Charley.'

'Nothing, really.'

'Come on. She gave you a real grilling.'

Monkey hesitated. For a couple of months now, he'd been living in isolation. When anyone asked questions, he evaded them. He was a deep cover Monkey, fighting for survival, but he'd gone on like this for too long. So he told Jenn why he had come out here. It wasn't the whole truth: he left out the pills. That would have been an admission too far. Instead, he told her about heroin, how he'd become addicted, how he'd spent six months in the clinic rehabilitating. He apologized for telling her all of this. Jenn touched his arm, told him to carry on, it was fine, it was really all right. They smoked the last cigarettes. He told her about how he'd returned home, but that the whole town was like a trigger for him. He explained that he'd come out to the Mansion to escape, but that once Charley had found out, she became suspicious of him because he'd been an addict and a thief. The lies contained enough truth for Monkey to feel released.

'So what happens next?' Jenn had moved beside him on the step.

'I'll live here for a while.'

'But I guess . . .' Her voice trailed away.

'What?'

'Well, I mean . . . you'll have to go back there sooner or later.'

Only Magalene remained as they walked back inside. She must have been in her late forties, a distracted woman who, through her ability to botch the most basic of tasks, soaked up irritation from Charley like cotton wool over blood. They joined her at the kitchen table. Jenn retrieved tobacco and hash from a small antique tin, and rolled a spliff, her fingers moving with fluid ritual. Apart from cigarettes and the occasional drink, it was the first time Monkey had tried any kind of drug since his doses of methadone before the clinic. At some stage, Magalene decided upon a game. 'You'll like this. It'll scare you.' She ripped out a page of a notepad, and wrote a sentence at the very top; folding the paper to hide the sentence, she passed it over. 'Now you write something. But don't look,' she insisted, as Jenn went to lift the fold. 'That's the point.'

When Jenn had written her line, she folded the paper over and passed it on to Monkey.

'What do I write?'

'Anything,' Magalene said. 'The first thing that comes into your head.'

They took it in turns: writing a line, folding the paper and passing it around, until they reached the bottom of the page. Magalene unfurled the concertina of paper and read out the lines:

Autumn when we last met
A pan left on the stove
I don't know what I'm doing
I don't know what they said
Your last note on the yellow table
And why is the dog waiting by the door?

Or the black light in the glass
All of it useless we forget
The bright sky, a thousand stars
In the fire, the coals are white
And the bricks are white
And the fire was waiting as we walked inside

Magalene called it a poem. Jenn and Monkey called it a game. They played it again and again, the creased pieces of paper soon scattered around the table. *I saw the moonlight the idiots shouting in the corner*. At first, Monkey had only written down details from the room about them. He became more adventurous: writing fragments and half sentences, to clash with what came either side. *With summer passed none of us was clear the pain I felt when I left*. Jenn rolled another spliff, and the connections became more pronounced, the images more vibrant. *The angry traffic of my youth the boy who first loved me blue like the light the siren sounding the change*.

'It's amazing,' Magalene said, 'what kind of synchronicities occur.'

As she passed him a second spliff, Jenn's fingers lingered on Monkey's hand. *I'm no longer certain about home the trees why does it still seem so dirty?* When he looked over, her gaze was unflinching, inviting. She smiled at him. *That mellow biscuit taste unclear sky the kiss you offered the regular heartbeat of an animal*.

'Well, I'd better head up.' Jenn stubbed the remains of the spliff into the ashtray.

Magalene had spent over five minutes over her next line. 'But it's still early. We've got all night.'

'I've got a market trip tomorrow. I'd better get to bed.'

Monkey pushed his chair back from the table. 'I'll join you.'

The hallway amplified every step; each word echoed through the space above them. 'I haven't been up to the third floor,' Jenn said. 'I didn't think there were any rooms.'

'Mine's the only one. Taylor's cleaning up the rest of the floor.'

'You could show me. If you want.'

We are so obvious. Monkey's thoughts ran as seamless and diverse as one of the poems. *We are so obvious why is it wrong?* He let her inside. Jenn took in the camp bed on the floor, the scattered clothes, ashtrays and empty beer bottles pilfered from the brewery, the picture of the lab monkey on the wall.

'Nice place.' She turned to him, smiling. 'Do you get many visitors?'

They fell upon one another, struggling against clothes, moving down on to the camp bed, both so full of urgency that Monkey only lasted a few seconds. Afterwards, they breathed close together, musk as rich as pollen in the air. He lay with his head upon Jenn's thigh, his cool cheek close to her cool skin, the delicate lick of rust between her legs. He felt faint from his own blood: the endorphin rush, analgesic and tranquillizing, reminded him of heroin.

Jenn ran her fingers against his cheek.

'Are you OK?'

'I'm fine.' He played his fingers over her side, the cruel ragged imprint where her bra had bitten into the flesh. 'It's been a long time, that's all.'

It rained. The sky opened up over the Mansion, falling like rocks. It drummed against the window, beating furiously against the panes. Jenn and Monkey listened as they lay together on the camp bed, sharing cigarettes wet from each other's mouths, the blanket hardly big enough to cover them. Jenn tuned the radio into some pirate dance station, the beat and ecstasy of the music mixing with the sound of the rain. When the camp bed made too much noise, they lay down beneath the window, the rain fizzing on to their skin. It felt like the third floor was their whole world, that their breath echoed into nothing. For Monkey, it felt, more than anything, like recovery.

'I'd better go soon.'

They had lain together in silence, watching the morning grow brighter beyond the window until Jenn stirred under the covers.

'Why?'

'Market trip, remember? Besides, this place is terrible. Talk, talk, talk. It'd be better for you.'

'What do you mean?'

'I don't know. The way Charley was with you last night... She's run people out of here while I've been here. She's got a bit of a power trip going.'

Jenn settled the straps of her bra over her shoulders; after pulling on her jeans, she kissed his cheek. 'I'll see you later. Probably this evening.'

'OK.'

Monkey listened to the floorboards creak as she walked down the hall. For a while, he tried to sleep, but the daylight was already too heavy in the room, a cold nacreous grey. He wrapped the blanket around his shoulders, watching as morning leaked into the day. The rain fell like static over a TV screen, almost too fine to fall at all, licked by the slightest breeze. It lashed on to the cottage out on the front lawn, where, so he guessed, Lucas lay sleeping.

Two years before, Monkey and Lucas spent their days in the high attic room at the top of Lucas's parents' place, along the road from the English Bridge. The room was a litter of duvets and blankets and mattresses, books piled up on their sides in towers against the wall. Lucas had done a deal for a large quantity of heroin, which, for effect, he'd emptied into a cigar box. He and Monkey spent days in his room, what seemed like weeks, living only to smoke their way through it: a cool world, of transgressive heroism. The normal routine of life drifted through from the open window: sounds of traffic, street chatter, the distant sound of Lucas's parents in the floors below. It was easy to ignore it all, to lose themselves in the details which heroin brought alive: a scuff mark on the beige wall, the way the duvet was bunched up into the shape of a person, the light glorious through the wet window pane.

Sometimes, Lucas would pull up his chair to the window and spend hours looking down at the passers-by on the street, at the street itself. 'Out there,' he said once, 'in the hotel over the road, Thomas de Quincey stayed. Have you heard of him? He bummed around London, fell in love with a prostitute. He wrote about opium. He described staying in this town on his way to Wales, in a hotel with a ballroom. I didn't realize until recently that I went to that hotel when I was a kid. It was some old relative's birthday. A great-aunt or something. My family made a big deal about it. The whole family attended, coming from all over the country. She had lived to be a hundred, but she wasn't really with us any more, completely trapped in the past. My parents hired a band. I don't know where they found them. They played this song, most of us had never heard of it. It was the only time the old woman showed any sign of life. She kept asking for her brother, who'd been dead for about twenty years. She wanted to hear him sing that song again.'

One day the heroin ran out. They smoked the last of it in the morning, and once the effects had subsided, made plans to get some more. They had woken up into the middle of a drought. When Lucas got on his mobile, his contacts gave only bad news. Monkey made an abortive trip outside, but it was a random, peripatetic mission, taking him from pub to pub, dive to dive. No one was around, everyone was hungry. Those days were evil in Herointown, dogs growling over mean bones. They headed back to the attic with a bottle of tequila, hoping that a rapid fix of alcohol would take their minds off the overwhelming lack in their bodies. Lucas wanted music. He'd sold his stereo to help buy the bag of heroin, so he retrieved an old turntable, along with a stack of his parents' vinyl: Syd Barrett, *The White Album*, Roxy Music, and *Low* by David Bowie.

'I used to listen to this over and over when I was a kid,' Lucas said as Bowie started to sing. 'I thought it was the soundtrack to *The Man Who Fell to Earth,* which I hadn't seen. I had this whole film in my head which never existed.'

'What was it about?' Monkey would have listened to anything to ignore the itching inside his skin.

'It was the story of a man who works outside Berlin. He's a computer engineer in an industrial complex. He's called David. He's very thin, and pale, and he can't really connect with people. He lives in a house with a bunch of fucking freaks. His car is banged up, a wreck because he can't drive straight. But then one day, he goes to work at this industrial complex on the outskirts of Berlin. It's a huge place of blue glass and white walls. There's a new woman working there. Caroline. She's been transferred from another city.'

'Where?' Monkey asked.

Lucas shrugged, took a hit from the tequila bottle. 'I don't know. Düsseldorf. Anyway, David falls in love with her. She has this really savage magenta haircut. David invites her to a party at his freak house. The whole thing really kicks off, with people smashing windows, writing strange shit on the walls, and David and Caroline walk off down the street. David is drunk, so drunk that he asks Caroline to marry him. She tells him that she's attracted to him, but she has a secret. She's a spy from a rival corporation. She's infiltrated this plant where he works to find out about the company's secret project.

'It's a spaceship. They've been developing this spaceship, using technology they found embedded deep in the rock outside of Lascaux. The Nazis found it while they were looting caves during the Second World War. Wrecks of some weird alien machine. Ancient.'

Monkey laughed. 'Isn't that going a bit far?'

'Of course not!' Lucas had been looking at the floor, but at the interruption he glared over, incensed. 'I mean if you don't want to hear about it . . .'

'I do. Really.' The change in mood unsettled Monkey. 'Carry on.'

Lucas picked at the label of the tequila bottle. 'Caroline and David break into the industrial complex,' he went on. 'They steal the spaceship, fly it up out of its hangar before security can get to them. They leave the earth behind. They have sex drifting through space, spending years there, decades. They don't grow old, though. They fly through constellations, watch black holes and white dwarf stars. It's amazing.' He paused, frowned. He sipped from the bottle. 'And then, the spaceship lurches out of their control. It's set on a different course. A beacon on a remote planet has activated it. The spaceship lands on a planet. David and Caroline put on spacesuits and head outside. There's music playing. Even through the space suits, they can hear it. Strange music, words that don't make sense. They follow it to where it gets louder. It's a rock, a stone obelisk.'

'And?'

'It ends there. With them standing in front of this monolith, the music echoing out from the stone. It's all there is. It's the end.'

That night it rained: hard driving rain, lancing down against the windows, smashing itself into the roads, sending great torrents down the street. Monkey wrapped himself up in a duvet on one of the mattresses. His stomach was cramping badly and he was sweating, a nasty feverish sweat. He drifted in and out of sleep, conscious of Lucas moving around the room, hunting for cigarettes and Rizlas, the TV strobes lighting his shadow.

At some stage, Monkey woke to find Lucas lying next to him. 'It's cold,' he shivered, putting his arms around Monkey's waist. Monkey stared at a corner of the blue and white duvet. Inaction felt like the best action. Stasis and void. Silence.

Lucas broke it. 'Are you cold?'

His voice was gentle, tender in a way Monkey hadn't heard before. He placed his hand on to Monkey's front and, with halting fingers, he unbuttoned the fly of his jeans. Monkey closed his eyes. Traces of light burst upon his retina, oozing, dissipating into a blur. The rain hissed against the window. Opening his eyes, he stared into the pattern of white and blue upon the duvet cover: clouds against sky, surf on the edge of a wave. Lucas placed a hand on his hip, and rolled him on to his side.

The next morning, he left early, picking his way out of the room. On his way downstairs, he passed the lounge on the first floor. Dressed in a floral peignoir, Lucas's mother lay sprawled in front of the TV, cackling over Jeremy Kyle. Monkey headed out. Soon, he'd entered Herointown, its traffic and hunger. After stealing money from Rose's purse, after broken deals, bad contacts and two days of walking, he scared up some heroin. The numb void cut out a lot of confusion. Teal provided for him. Teal always would.

As Monkey looked out of the Mansion window, he searched for a feature in the geography that would divert him, but there was only the rain, illustrating the patterns of the wind as it swept across the country. It was like the Vegan had said once, as they'd walked over to the laboratory, 'Landscape is where we look when we're missing something. And what we're missing is it.'

8

In the late nineties, the Vegan had lost a rich uncle who, despite a lifetime of bad feeling, had preferred that his money be shared by his family than be dispersed into the state. The Vegan had travelled – a couple of years around France, Holland and Belgium – but this lump sum allowed him to be a little more ambitious. So he headed to India, to Himachal Pradesh. Squeezed by the pressure of Kashmir and Nepal, the territory is the tenuous nape from which the body of India hangs. Once the playground of the Raj, people lost themselves there for years, whole villages invaded by the dropout descendants of the colonials. Beautiful and ruthless, the area was notorious. The Vegan heard stories of people thrown from cliffs, of arrests without trial, of people turned off like so many lights.

The Vegan had headed out there looking forward to good drugs and great scenery. He rode trains and took buses, heading north through the Kullu valley. In Manali he'd hooked up with a pack of Brits, but after a few days, he was keen to move on. Sooner or later, someone was bound to talk wistfully about Marmite or to long for (strangely) cigarettes that come in packs of ten. To travel so far and meet only nostalgia didn't appeal to the Vegan. He worked his way along the Chandra river towards the border with Kashmir, inside an asthmatic bus that reeked of chicken shit and exhaust fumes. Beyond the window, men bathed in the Chandra, their skin the same colour as the water. Sedate cows grazed on the banks. On the high narrow roads, the white mist pooled among the green valleys, the high peaks sugared with snow. The Vegan lost himself in the scenery. An old woman slept perfectly upright in the seat next to him, gnarled and stiff, as dark as wood.

After a day of sightseeing in Udaipur, the Vegan wandered into the hills, entering a landscape which, for too long, had been trapped beyond glass. Apart from a group of men, trekking far along the pass ahead of him – he assumed they were shepherds or travellers – he saw no one. It was a relief to enter the forest. Here he walked under the lush canopy of pine, deodar, oak and rhododendron, blue magpies clattering through the branches. He came across marijuana plants that stood three metres high, knotted buds that reminded him of the matted dreadlocks of the holy men back in Manikaran. He spent the night in front of a small campfire, drinking tea and smoking weed, his mind flickering between exquisite clarity and fear.

Dawn barely threatened beyond the trees when the Vegan opened his eyes. A man stood at the edge of his camp. Short and wiry, his hair frayed from underneath a sweat-stained pagdi. He stood like a sentry, the Vegan thought, even before he saw the AK47. Without a word, the man raised the gun to his shoulder. When he heard the click the Vegan didn't really understand; the man frowned and pulled at the trigger again. When the gun still didn't fire, the man shook his head, smiling as though he expected the Vegan to share his dismay at malfunctioning equipment. He pulled the curved black clip from its socket, blew on the top, and gestured, lazily, with the rifle barrel, along the forest path. The Vegan sprang up and ran.

He returned to Shimla, and paid for a room in a Parsi hotel. After the night on the hillside, he needed comfort and security, the first of which, unfortunately, this establishment dealt out sparingly. Sheets went unchanged, bells unanswered; meals, when they arrived in the shabby dining room, were cold and congealed. Since the death of his wife, the owner had all but lost interest in his trade. 'It is a burden,' he told the Vegan, 'a terrible burden.' When the man wasn't distracted by his guests, he spent hours in the parlour next to the reception desk, sipping tea on a chintz-covered armchair while muttering at the picture of Zoroaster upon the wall. Five times a day, he'd pray before the flame from a small oil burner, the aroma of the smoke filling the whole foyer. After keeping the Vegan waiting at the front desk one time, the owner emerged from his prayers in a state of near ecstasy. The Vegan had been waiting for fresh bedding, but instead he got subjected to a lengthy monologue about the sacred fires of Zoroaster: how they moved from temple to temple, never extinguished, epic conflagrations older than communities and the stories they told. The owner explained that any building could be regarded as a temple, as long as it provided sanctuary for the flames. 'Agiary,' he called such a site. 'House of fire.'

The Vegan stayed on. Symptoms of nervous exhaustion had begun to display themselves: a numbness of the two smallest fingers on his right hand, a deep, seemingly drugged sleep, and restless days where the dull click of the AK47 sounded in his head. He managed to pull himself together, and walked outside into the streets of Shimla, hoping to lose himself among the bazaars. With its villas and toy train, there was something quaint and terrifying about Shimla, like a badly judged theme park. The Vegan found himself loathing it. This beautiful place, clinging to an almost mythical tradition amidst the kind of violence he'd experienced in the forest, was all too familiar. He had struck out for the world and ended up in a high outpost of Middle England. He imagined a great cataclysm of the surrounding mountains, the Himalayas turned topsy-turvy, their peaks crushing blameless, cosy Shimla and its superficial order. Something began to tick inside of him, some machine of change.

A few weeks later the events of that day made the international news. It was the curiosity story, filling two inches at the bottom of a tabloid page, later to be recycled in endless 'On This Day' magazine articles. The Vegan had made his way to the Sabzi Mandi, where sellers of silks, incense, candles and ornate wooden boxes offered their wares on low tables. After buying a pastry from a small shop on the Mall, he squatted down against a building of terracotta brick, looking back at the steep gradient leading back to the town. The morning was overcast and dull, the bright turmeric-yellow awnings of the stall stark against the terracotta-coloured buildings. The Vegan heard the screams, but didn't really pay attention.

No one could agree what drove the monkeys mad. Later theories blamed mating patterns, metal poisoning and mass hysteria. The Vegan had seen these scavengers everywhere on the fringes of Shimla. Tame enough to seek out food, they were still nervous around people, probably learning quickly to avoid tourists only out for a cute photo. As the screams began to sound closer and closer, the Vegan realized something was happening. In front of him, a man dropped a basket of silk to the ground and started running, a woman in Western clothing followed. The Vegan jumped to his feet. Hundreds of monkeys suddenly poured into the street, teeming over the pavements, jumping over tables, hissing, biting, shrieking. A woman in sari and leggings ran past him, screaming, a monkey riding her back like a jockey. The Vegan almost cried with laughter. It was beautiful, beautiful chaos, shaking the worn-down theme park of Shimla: a pack of monkey Jesuses scattering the moneylenders. The Vegan applauded them, his hands over his head, spraying crumbs from his pastry as he cheered.

One of the monkeys suddenly jagged in its path and leaped up at the Vegan's face. He didn't have time to protect himself. The monkey grabbed hold of the Vegan's hair, its grey face pushed against his nose. It began to eat the pastry crumbs from his mouth, nibbling, furtive, malignant. Finally, it scampered away, leaving the Vegan upon the ground. The pitted road bit into his cheek, but the coolness of the ground calmed him. He lost track of time. When someone bent down to him, rousing him with a word which he didn't understand, only then did he pick himself up. He walked home listlessly, feeling lost, persecuted, alien, blaming the streets around him, blaming the world. Back in the hotel, two rucksacks had been abandoned by the front desk. From a distant room came the sound of violent hammering; a South African woman was haranguing a member of staff about the quality of the food. The owner sat in his parlour. He gestured to a chair as the Vegan walked inside. They sat for the whole evening staring up at the picture of Zoroaster, never sharing a word.

The next time the Vegan drove over to the Mansion, Charley was waiting for him on the large stone steps by the front door. She wore her hair piled in a bun, an alarming feature which gave her the appearance of something simultaneously apocalyptic and staid, like a librarian in Hiroshima. A bright, wet morning glistened all around them, latent heat beginning to burn. Not even halfway through February and you could feel summer, waiting like a predator. The Vegan let himself out of his car. She watched him come, smoking thoughtfully; only when he'd reached the foot of the steps did she hail him.

'Morning.'

'Morning. You're up early.'

'I wanted to see you.'

It was a dispiriting way to begin the morning, but after his two-week break – which he had spent recharging himself, reading and thinking – the Vegan had anticipated a confrontation.

'Do you want to talk out here?'

'Not really. Let's walk across to the lab.'

She jumped, her boots splashing into gravel, crushing shells and stones, and began to walk to the outhouse. The Vegan didn't hurry to match her pace.

'Is Monkey down there, already?'

'He's in the kitchen. I asked him to wait behind.'

'What's this about?'

'I've been talking to my dealer in town.' She paused, waiting for him to catch up and they walked side by side, the long wet grass whipping against their clothes.

'And?'

'He's asked us if we can up the supply.'

The Vegan bristled immediately. 'I don't think that's a very good idea.'

'Why not?'

'It's just not what we agreed. Remember? You said you wanted to keep everything low key. You thought it would be safer.'

'Yes, well. Now I've changed my mind.'

'Look, I realize that this business with Monkey has got to you. But you need to relax, to calm down.'

Her eyes were dark, hollow, as brown as medicine bottles held up to the light. 'You mean I'm overreacting? Little woman getting the vapours.'

'No. I didn't mean that.'

'It's taking too long to show any sign of a profit.'

'So what do you suggest?'

She cleared her throat. 'I want to double production.'

'You're kidding.'

'I'm serious. You've got help now. That's double the workforce. The only problem I can see is if Pete can't sell them. But he thinks that he can.'

'What have you said to him?'

'I haven't mentioned that *we*'re making the pills. That's what we agreed. I've only asked him if there's a demand for a greater supply. He thinks there's no problem. But we have to move soon.'

The Vegan scratched his jaw. 'It's a lot of work. If you leave it with me, I'll think about it and –'

She didn't let him finish. 'I'm tired of letting you think. Defending your small corner of power. It's got to stop. The fact is that your big idea for getting us out of a hole has contributed nothing to the upkeep of this place.'

The Vegan could have argued all day. But he also knew that Charley was frustrated enough to dump the whole enterprise, and that if she did, he would lose his hold upon the Mansion. Better to concede, and find time to manoeuvre.

'OK,' he said. 'You're right. I'll get working on things.'

'Right.' She looked surprised at how quickly he'd surrendered. 'That's OK then. I'll tell Taylor.'

'I'll talk to Monkey today. We won't be able to start right away, of course. I'll have to order some more supplies in. That'll take a couple of weeks.'

Charley walked back to the house; Monkey came around to the lab not long after. The Vegan passed on Charley's plans, about which Monkey was wholly ambivalent.

'Yeah, well, you can kind of see her point, can't you?'

Monkeys make poor allies. They went to work: spending two hours mixing up the MDMA oil with Xylen and IPA, and then distilling the solution. Afterwards, the crystals were filtered, the solution poured through a coffee funnel into a jar. The crystals collected on the rim, a mottled yellowy-brown; when washed in acetone, they would appear white. By this time, they had over 15 grams of crystals, which they ran through the pill machine of 100 milligrams per pill. The final act was to mark the pills with the saltire-circle symbol, something that the Vegan usually left for Monkey. He sat back on the pile of plastic milk crates and pulled his tobacco from the pocket of his khakis. As he rolled a cigarette, he watched Monkey mark the pills with a punch, working swiftly, like a croupier apportioning chips.

'I've been surprised by you.'

'In what way?'

'Just the way you've taken to all of this. It makes me wonder whether I've been wrong about you all these years.' He picked a flake of tobacco from his lip. 'By the way, have you seen much of Lucas?'

Monkey shrugged, not looking up from the pills. 'He keeps to himself in that cottage. Besides, Charley wouldn't exactly be happy.'

'Why's that?'

'Well, for one thing, she hit the roof when she found out that I knew him. Thought that I'd tell him about the lab.' He stamped a pill and sent it sliding into the pile. 'I don't know why she thought he'd be interested. After all, she knows better than anyone that he's got other things on his mind.'

Monkey told the Vegan about a time when he'd been out walking late at night and seen Charley creeping into the cottage. Later, he'd discovered that most people in the Mansion knew they were seeing one another, Taylor included. 'If you want my opinion,' Monkey said, finally, 'pills or no pills, this whole place is going to fall apart.'

The Vegan felt almost triumphant. When he had first started his plans for the Mansion, he had been presented with a choice. He could have stood to one side and watched the whole place collapse, an inevitable trajectory given Taylor's confession. Even before, the Vegan had noticed a lack of purpose about the place: it was ailing, failing, dead upon its feet. It might have been easier to let the commune break up and allow everyone involved to drift away. He'd been tempted but then he realized that allowing the house to become abandoned again entailed too much risk; the site could easily be jeopardized. Better, he thought, to make himself a necessary part of a surviving Mansion. The pills gave him this opportunity.

He had first visited the house after returning from India, tagging along with one of the residents. His encounter in the forest still haunted the Vegan; but for a malfunction of a gun, he told himself, he would have been a dead man. His time in Shimla also remained with him: that mannered, superficial world, so much like home. His mind turned to revolution; he began reading in earnest, gleaning excerpts of Marx, Bakunin, Malatesta, and moving into the twentieth century by way of Adorno, Benjamin and Artaud. When he discovered Guy Debord and Situationism, the vision of Paris in 1968 became an ideal for him. In the Mansion, he saw a site where these ideals could find practice. The place was unique, almost a singular event. It deserved more than the current inhabitants, who, as the Vegan saw it, restricted their imaginations to the limits of their temporary escape. A new future for the house began to obsess him. In his vision, the place would be filled, not with people wanting to escape to the land, but with those dedicating themselves to revolution in art and politics. The

Vegan himself would be at the centre of this, more teacher than activist: Aristotle not Alexander.

When he began to look out for suitable pupils, Lucas had immediately impressed him. A Cambridge dropout with a voracious appetite for drugs, Lucas was already taking risks and experimenting. The Vegan shared some of his experiences; they took acid together, on long drives out into the countryside. He told Lucas about Himachal Pradesh and the morning of the gun; he mythologized this episode as the moment when his mind had truly come alive. Later, Lucas drifted out of his influence. The drugs got harder. A little opium now and then, that was fine, but the Vegan didn't approve of heroin, or the frenzied idiocy of cocaine. When Lucas had cracked up and come close to prison, the Vegan had stepped in. He'd been impressed by Lucas's crack-up: a *Kristallnacht* of middle England, fascist tactics turned against the capitalist machine. He talked to Charley and Taylor, and arranged for a place in the Mansion. It was the environment that would inspire Lucas.

It was a little before eight o'clock. A few lights showed in the windows of the Mansion, but only a few, and the first workers had yet to appear in the garden. Stopping off to retrieve a bottle of Jameson's from his car, the Vegan walked over to the cottage. When he had first visited the Mansion, the cottage had been little more than a wreck. Now there was a door where there had been no door, a clear windowpane where before there had only been glass tarnished to mercury. The Vegan knocked, but with no answer he pushed inside. The room was empty. A rug lay over the floorboards in front of the hearth; a fire burned in the grate, a kettle steamed on top of a stand. Behind an almost threadbare sofa, there was a door to the staircase; to the left the alcove kitchen looked out through a window mostly covered by ivy. Footsteps shook the steps behind the wall, and Lucas appeared. Irritation moved to surprise at the sight of the Vegan.

'It's you.'

'Just thought I'd come over.'

'Bit early to be passing, isn't it?' His voice was suspicious, unwelcoming.

'Doing a bit of work for Taylor,' the Vegan replied, deeming it insignificant with a slight wave of his hand. He tried to close the door behind him, but it remained stuck on the floorboards.

'Leave that. There's a knack to it.' Lucas had crossed the room, and bent down to the fire, where the kettle had begun to whistle softly. The Vegan sat down upon the settee.

'Anyway, I wondered what you were doing,' Lucas said. 'I've seen you coming and going for quite a while. Always early. But you've never come around before.'

'Thought I'd give you a bit of space,' the Vegan replied. 'Moving out here, I guessed you wanted it. Oh, by the way, I brought you this . . .' He withdrew the bottle of Jameson's from the deep pocket of his coat. 'Thought you could use something to keep the cold out.'

'Do you want some now?'

'No, I'm fine.'

Lucas produced another mug from a cupboard in the kitchen for tea. 'Two cups?' the Vegan said, smiling as Lucas handed the mug over. 'You live out here, by yourself, and you have two cups?'

'They were in the house.'

'Extravagant.' He wagged a mocking, pedagogic finger. 'When you could have stripped things down, you went for an extravagance.'

Although he had been half-joking, it occurred to him

that this was actually an almost Zen-like piece of wisdom. He smiled to himself, savouring it. Lucas, however, was distant, distracted; probably, the Vegan realized, he had only recently woken up. They sat in silence, the tea steaming in the cool air from the doorway. Upon a short shelf by the window, books lay stacked in piles. Some of them, he had recommended to Lucas; some of them Lucas had obviously found for himself.

'Are you reading?'

'No. I'm not reading.'

'Living out here and you're not reading? I can't believe it.'

Lucas sipped the tea, his mouth pursed and small, as he stared off at a point somewhere in the centre of the room.

'I've been writing,' he said eventually.

'Writing?'

'A bit.'

'Well that . . . That's even better.'

'Only a bit. Not really sure. Trying to piece things together. Want to get hold of things, you know. Work them out.'

'That's good. That's even better than reading.' He paused. 'Can I read it?'

'No. Not yet. Maybe when I've finished.'

The Vegan nodded approvingly. 'Make sure it has an agenda. That's all I'll say to you. Make sure it's controversial.' He flattened this last word into four syllables, drawing each of them out. 'Vision. Make sure it has vision. And don't let writing replace life. That's another important point. Don't let it replace action. Here and now, a time of reflection,' he went on. 'Writing is good. But it's not life. Don't forget that.' He sipped from his tea. 'But you won't. You know what you're doing.' He placed the mug down on the floor, and rested his chin on his folded hands, supporting his arms upon his knees: a posture, he felt, of single-minded seriousness. 'I *know*, you know what you're doing.'

'What do you mean?'

The Vegan held his gaze. 'You know what I mean. We both have our secrets, but in our way, we're both working towards the same thing.'

He had been preparing a lecture, of sorts. He wanted, in a veiled way, to promise Lucas that he had plans for him, and that those plans were in motion. He had barely started, however, when the door screeched on the floorboards, and a dog wriggled in through the crack. It was one of the Mansion's dogs, the skinny yellow greyhound. The Vegan had only ever seen it in the house, looking meek and terrified. Now, it darted around the room, sniffing at corners, hunting for whatever it is that all dogs want.

Lucas sat up immediately. 'That damn thing.'

'Relax.'

'I don't want to relax. It came in the other night and ate my food.'

'A little territorial aren't we? It's only a dog.'

'A dog I don't like.'

Lucas grabbed the greyhound by the collar, and dragged it towards the door, claws scraping on the boards. We define ourselves, the Vegan thought, by our attitude to dogs. Feed them, breed them, eat them, starve them, set them to fight or set them to run, inject them with hormones and radical cancer drugs, send them out to desiccate in the cockpit of a spaceship: we are them. And Lucas wouldn't allow one in his home. The Vegan couldn't help but feel disappointed. After the dog had been shut out, they talked in front of the fire. The Vegan asked how Lucas had been spending his time, making a number of vague references to the situation with Charley. Lucas refused to be led, however; in fact, he barely acknowledged these statements at all. They sat in silence, with only the sound of the flames popping around the logs in the fire, black tea bitter on the tongue. With the tea drunk, the morning brighter against the window pane, the Vegan decided to leave.

'I'll see you soon, anyway. Maybe the next time I'm here early, I'll come over.'

Outside, the dog was waiting. When the Vegan held out his hand, it sniffed at him tentatively before following him across the grass. The Vegan walked slowly, appreciating the morning, even though the conversation with Lucas had confused him. The boy had always been able to put him on edge. He remembered a time when they had taken acid together and Lucas had kissed him fully on the mouth. 'I thought you'd want it,' he'd said when the Vegan recoiled, and subtly, Lucas had accused him of being unprogressive and afraid. And now, through his relationship with Charley, Lucas was sowing discord within the Mansion. Even though the Vegan couldn't have planned things any better, something about their conversation had perturbed him.

As he walked towards the front of the house, he noticed that one of the residents sat on the front steps, not far from where he had parked his car. Tall, with pale skin and mid-length curly brown hair, he sipped from a mug while reading from a book. He had been leaning against the wall, but when he noticed the Vegan he sat forward, and placed both book and mug down on the steps beside him.

'Morning.' His voice echoed amongst the stone of the doorway. When the Vegan showed no sign of recognition, he continued. 'We met at a party here. It's a while ago now. I'm Andrew.'

The Vegan remembered. In the middle of a crowded

room, Andrew had made a great display of trying to buy hash from him. It had been an unwelcome intrusion, not only because the Vegan was a little sensitive about the people he sold to, but also because it was the same party where he had first approached Taylor with his plan for the Mansion.

'Were you visiting Lucas?' Andrew had retrieved his book and tucked it inside his suede coat.

'Just popping in on an old friend.'

'I didn't realize that you knew each other.'

The longer Andrew continued talking, the more the Vegan felt both flattered and irritated. He didn't reply. The dog had sat down on the gravel between them; he bent down to stroke its head as a way of distancing himself from the conversation without retreating. The dog moved closer and, as he crouched down, it sat back on its haunches, lifting its snout into the air.

'It's trying to get above you,' Andrew said. 'Competing with you for a place.'

The Vegan didn't look over. 'Is that right?'

'If it lifts its head, it thinks that it's above you in rank.' His laugh was piercing, almost adolescent. 'Dogs are always looking to move up the pack.'

'Then the dog should sit up on the steps, shouldn't it?' the Vegan replied. 'That way, it would be able to look down on everyone.'

He was still savouring the retort as he walked back to the car. Andrew had headed back inside the house, but the yellow greyhound remained on the steps. The Vegan waved at it as he walked to the car. As he pulled away, he looked forward to a day away from the Mansion, which he would spend catching up with some reading, cooking a meal, maybe driving out to a favourite spot on the outskirts of the town to do a bit of walking as the sun went down.

Something still troubled him, however. As he passed the cottage, he thought of Lucas again. A thin wisp of grey smoke drifted from the chimney. He wondered if anything was burning.

9

'So where would you go?'
'What do you mean?'
'If you could go anywhere, where would it be?'
'I'm not sure. I haven't thought.'
'You haven't thought about travelling? Everyone thinks about travel.'

Three a.m., a time which over the last weeks belonged to them, Monkey and Jenn would lie on the camp bed in his room, sharing cigarettes and talking.

'My mum's gone to Dubai.'
'So you'd like to go to Dubai?'
'I suppose. Actually, no. Probably not.'
'So nowhere else?'
'Not really. I've spent the last few years thinking about other things.'
'About heroin?'

In his dreams, Monkey would find himself smoking heroin in an unknown room at the Mansion. When the fumes hit his lungs the taint of the drug was so real that he felt like he had fallen. Beyond the Mansion, Herointown was always waiting for him: a geography of triggers and reminders, trajectories of an old life. He refused every offer to return, taking on extra shifts around the Mansion to compensate for not working on the stall. While Jenn found something worldly and impressive about his heroin days, she didn't talk to him about his rehabilitation. Even if she had, Monkey would have struggled to explain it. He had only recently found out for himself. It was like Normandy.

One night they'd watched a documentary on TV. It was a rare evening, when everyone else had deserted the living room. On the screen, an old soldier had been taken back to the battlefields of northern France. The camera followed him around fields and hills and beaches, the medals in rows upon his blazer, his neat white moustache perfect above his thin, proper mouth. He talked to the camera, pointing out seemingly innocuous patches of land, a rock he'd taken shelter behind, a path where a friend had been blown to pieces by a grenade, a patch of grass where he'd killed a man with a bayonet. Here he bent down, letting a hand trail through the grass. The tears were bright and full in his eyes. 'You won't understand,' he began, but his voice faltered.

That a landscape could do that to you . . . Monkey understood everything.

Mornings, he worked early in the lab until eight, after which Charley liked him to keep a low profile. After the evening meal, he'd meet Jenn in one of the corridors on the second floor. They had tried to be discreet: in Monkey's case because he wanted to hide things from Charley; in Jenn's because she hated the gossip. It was impossible to avoid this kind of talk in the Mansion, however. Monkey had encountered silences whenever he had walked into a room, he'd spotted knowing glances whenever there was innocent contact between him and Jenn in public. After spending most of the night together, Jenn would head back to her room.

One Saturday, Jenn left for the market. They'd said

goodbye in the dark, Jenn struggling into her clothes and kissing him before she left. Monkey spent the day by himself. After work – cleaning out the goat pen and helping Robert in the kitchen – he spent the afternoon reading H.P. Lovecraft, a book Jenn had bought for him from a market stall, as he'd finished everything in the Mansion's library. After that, he headed down for the evening meal. As the stall workers ate later than the other residents, that night only a small group sat down together. It was a low-key meal. Charley and Robert spent most of the time talking about some new plans for the stall. Taylor tagged at the heels of the conversation, interrupting, elaborating and irritating both of them. He was jealous, Monkey guessed. The van pulled up about half an hour after they'd finished their meal. Monkey was still sitting at the table. Taylor was halfway through a story about the time he had driven drunk the wrong way down a motorway. Cool, detached Monkey, uninvolved and calm, listened to Taylor as the market workers trooped into the kitchen; only when the back door closed did he glance over casually to look for Jenn. Only Jenn wasn't there.

He guessed that she'd been delayed in coming around to the kitchen, so he stayed where he was sitting. Andrew, Magalene and the other workers sat down at the table, and Robert served up the meal. The talk turned to the day at work, the takings and the customers. Eventually, Monkey grew tired of waiting and asked Andrew what had happened to Jenn.

'I think she might be staying over in town.'

'Why do you say that?'

'She went off at the end with a friend.'

'A friend?'

'Some guy. He met her from the stall.'

Monkey left the kitchen soon after. The look on his face

had been so transparent with disappointment and hurt that he'd been unable to stay. He went outside, needing the air. He wanted to get away, feign the escape he couldn't allow himself to make. He walked across the vegetable gardens, to a rusted gate in the middle of a long, angled hedge. He sat, shivering in the evening air, feeling sick and lost, and a little mad from the thoughts that crammed into his mind. He smoked cigarette after cigarette, until the nicotine ached in his veins.

On his way back to the house, a black Mini had pulled up in the drive. Jenn stood by the front steps, talking to a man: tall, lank and pale, with short hair gelled like fangs over his forehead. He laughed at something Jenn said and Monkey suddenly saw the resemblance. 'This is a friend of mine,' Jenn said as Monkey approached. 'This is my brother, Mark.'

Mark stared at Monkey, slicing away at him with slow blinks of his green eyes. 'So you live here?'

'That's right.'

'Enjoy it?'

'It's OK.'

'It's OK,' Mark repeated. He turned once more to Jenn. 'So you'll think about it. About coming home?'

Jenn pushed him gently towards the car. 'I don't want to talk about this now,' she continued. 'I've told you.' Monkey left them to the last scraps of their argument. Eventually, Mark started off, spinning wheels against the gravel.

'He met me at the stall,' Jenn explained, as they watched his headlights ride up the drive.

'I didn't know what had happened to you.' Monkey tried to keep the edge out of his voice. 'When you didn't come back.'

Jenn scanned his face. 'Wait a minute. Were you jealous? You were, weren't you?'

'You didn't come back, so I thought . . .'

She stopped in her tracks. 'No wait. You didn't . . . You saw me with Mark and you thought . . .'

'I didn't know what to think. Andrew said someone met you from the stall.'

'Are you angry with me?' Jenn bit her lip, a look of hostility in her eyes. 'Because if I want to meet my brother . . .'

He was angry, but he couldn't admit it. 'No, I'm not angry. I was worried.'

It was too late. Jenn didn't talk to him as they walked back. Her hand stayed limp when he reached out to take it. Inside the hallway, she muttered some excuse and headed through to the living room. He spent a few minutes *almost* heading upstairs, *almost* going back outside, before he followed. She sat talking to Sadie and Magalene and wouldn't look him in the eye. Monkey stayed for a while, trying to tune into the TV, flicking through the records, toying with the dragoon's sword which stood upright in the corner by the window. Each time he looked over, Jenn blanked him completely.

Although the room had been cold, Monkey burned as he walked out into the hallway. His pulse was furious, his breathing shallow: he wanted to run but had no idea where to go. At times like this he remembered his first few months in the clinic, when he'd still suffered symptoms of withdrawal. An irregularity to his heart, an adrenal heat in the pit of his stomach; he'd lived in a permanent state of panic, always being hunted without being chased. The view out of the windows had obsessed him – the bland fens, sliced by trenches, pooled with water – because he'd thought that it offered escape. But at heart, he'd known that the world and its freedom would have been too much for him, that whatever route he took would return him to one place. *Herointown*: it was during this time that the phrase had started up in his head. *Herointown*: he'd never realized that it was large enough to cover the whole world.

In the end, he walked upstairs and spent an hour exploring the vacant rooms of the third floor. Taylor had torn out the interiors of most, but in some it was still possible to find traces of the building's past. An old rag doll with a woollen smile. A hat with blue feathers. A clump of handwritten letters, the sentiments illegible from damp. A sepia photograph of a young woman sitting in a garden, the image tarnished with age. Sometimes, Monkey and Jenn would pick around these rooms and it could seem almost inspiring to find these trinkets of history: a privilege to be appreciated. Now, he felt like the intruder he was, as though there were lives that claimed the house legitimately, as though by staying here, somehow all of them were being judged. There were ghosts trapped in the glass of old mirrors, memories rubbing fingerprints into the walls.

He was on his way back downstairs, when he encountered Jenn.

'I was just coming to see you. Can we talk?'

They walked outside, on to the steps. The night had closed in, drowning with a white mist. The forest appeared as a mass of vague fluctuating, a distant encirclement of monsters. Jenn settled down on the steps, hugging her knees to her chest.

'About earlier. I want to explain.'

Monkey shrugged. 'You don't have to explain anything.'

'We're not going to get very far if you keep sulking.' Her eyes were serious, and she bit nervously at the sleeve of her jumper. 'Mark's been putting a bit of pressure on me to go back home. He met me from work to go through it all again.'

'Why does he care about you being out here?'

'Mum wasn't very well last year. I told you about my dad? He had a couple of affairs. Well, one day while I was at college, she had to be taken to hospital. It was an overdose of pills. When she came around, she insisted that she'd got the dosage wrong. It was all a big mistake, ha ha ha. Forget her own head if it wasn't screwed on. The thing is, Mark was the first one to find her. He told me later that she'd left a note for Dad. A suicide note. It was really nasty, really detailed. All about their marriage.'

'Did you read it?'

'Mark wouldn't let me see it. Said he burned it. At first, he went a bit crazy because of it all. Punched my dad. Moved out of the house, to Manchester. I was working in one of the shops near the market stall, a health food shop. I met some of the Mansion's residents. They offered me a place here, and I thought, why not?

'Mark found out and suddenly he changed. He came back to town. Now, rather than getting angry with Dad for putting Mum in this state, he thinks that the family needs to get together and everything will be all right. Of course, ideally, I should be back at home looking after Mum. It's his crusade. It makes me laugh really, considering the way he's behaved in the past. It's just stupid hypocrisy.'

'I'm sorry.'

'I'm sorry too. Believe me. About all of it.' She paused. 'But yes, I'm sorry about the way I reacted. I guess I should have known you'd be worried. But the way you were acting, I lost my temper. I've got too many controlling young men in my life as it is . . .'

It was a guarded apology, but he understood. He'd irritated her; in fact, he'd irritated himself. She shifted closer to him, and rested her head on his shoulder. 'Can we go inside. I'm freezing out here.'

They spent the night together, and, as it was a Sunday,

Jenn stayed right through until the morning. They parted at the top of the stairs. 'I'm going to spend some time with Sadie today,' she said, before heading back to her room. 'Is that OK?'

Monkey spent the day alone. He helped Robert out in the kitchen and, later, as part of the afternoon's rota, he gathered logs. They were stacked up in a pile at the back of the house, covered under tarpaulin. He'd brought the wicker basket from the kitchen, a huge thing the size of a tin bath; overloading it, he struggled to carry it back. He was taking a break when he saw Charley walking back from the garden. She cut across to meet him.

'Do you need a hand?'

'Thanks, yeah.'

They walked back to gather a few logs before carrying on.

'By the way,' Charley said. 'I've been meaning to ask. What was all that about, yesterday?'

'What do you mean?'

'You were a little anxious. About Jenn.'

'No. Not really. She was bringing back some cigarettes for me.'

Charley burst out laughing. 'Oh please.'

'It's true.'

'If you think I don't know what goes on under my own roof, then you're wrong.' Her eyes scanned across his face as though she were reading from a book. 'Don't get too close. That's all. Don't make any mistakes.' Her voice was calm, almost soothing. 'I don't expect you to live like a monk. But I want you to be careful. Even by accident, if any of them find out about what we're doing . . . I can't let that happen. The house, what we're doing here: it's much bigger than you. And Jenn.'

They picked up the log basket together and walked back to the house. Charley didn't mention it again. It was a warning, and he took it as such. Monkey didn't argue. After all, there were worse things that she could have discovered.

After complaining that the work was taking up too much of his time, the Vegan had started to leave Monkey alone in the laboratory. He'd arrive in the morning, set up the apparatus for the session and take Monkey through what needed to be done that morning. The whiteboard had now been fixed to the wall, scrawled with formulae and temperatures and timings in green marker pen. Over the weeks, Monkey had been made to read through the instructions once a day, so that he knew the entire formula off by heart, Ammonium Chloride right through to Zubrick. Once he was satisfied that Monkey had things in hand, the Vegan would walk back to his car and drive home. Monkey was left to himself, free from the Vegan's moods, his music, his magazines. The Vegan had even cut him a key for the outhouse door.

Always ready to abuse a trust, Monkey had started a little hideaway in his room. Underneath the window, the floorboards had given way in the damp. Here, wrapped in a sock, tied with a piece of twine, and pushed deep underneath the floor, was Monkey's personal collection: a bag of pills he would add to a few at a time, skimming off every new batch. This bag represented the future, no longer restricted to that stultifying mantra of recovery, *one day at a time*. Done with the Mansion, Monkey planned to head off to a new town, to sell pills and save money. There was a symmetry which Monkey enjoyed: Plan A became Plan B, but Plan B quickly became Plan A. Only the landscape had changed.

'I still can't believe you've never thought of travel.'

'I might have changed my mind. We should get away. Together.'

'Where should we go?'

'Wherever you want. Wherever you feel like running to catch yourself up. What was it you said?'

'I say a lot of things. I do a great deal of talking.'

'"I want to run so fast I catch myself up."'

'Yes. That sounds like one of mine.'

'We could head to a beach somewhere at the end of the world. Live in a beach hut. Fish for food.'

'And how would we do this?'

'What do you mean?'

'I'm talking finances. Money is my concern. Beach huts require backing. We'd need investors.'

'If I could . . .'

'Are you going to move some money around? Are you going to sell some shares?'

'If I could sort things out. You'd want to come, wouldn't you?'

'Of course. But how will you sort things?'

'I'm in the middle of something,' Monkey said. 'I'm making plans.'

10

The dream had been to retreat to the woods like a sage. During his first few weeks at the Mansion, Lucas had read a thin paperback of Zen stories, and although those parables of wisdom had seemed crazy, wilfully cryptic and obscure, the ideal had stayed with him. Brewing tea over the flames of an open fire. Learning the calls of birds. Spending days reading, reflecting, working. Staying clean and lucid and sober, except for late-night whisky drunk from a tin mug. Evenings would be spent watching the fire: the thick white smoke pooling in the crevices of green bark, the smell possessing a deeper, ancient significance. A time of eloquent simplicity: this had been the dream.

He woke at 5 a.m. in the chilly bedroom and threw himself out of bed, pulling on his jeans and parka to guard against the cold. Mist was hanging low over the landscape, woven into the space between the trees, drifting slowly over the grass. The Mansion almost appeared diffused, as though the white stone was slowly bleeding into the mist. Lucas cupped his hands under the tap and splashed the water on to his face. The cold was lethal, but there was nothing like it for waking him in the morning, and as he dried his face, he almost screamed with relief at the warmth of the towel.

Glancing across the fields, he saw two figures walking

quickly from behind the house, two figures he recognized. It wasn't the first time that he'd seen Monkey and the Vegan walking together at this time in the morning. Even before the Vegan's last visit – which Lucas had found utterly baffling – he'd guessed that some secret was being played out not far away from him. He pushed his face deep into the towel, the material abrasive on his skin. *Something is happening*, he told himself. *Something is happening but I am not involved.* Inside, he spent half an hour raising a fire in the grate, and when it filled the hearth, he made tea and toast over the flames. He liked the smell of the woodsmoke in the morning, the way it permeated the bread. He liked to eat his breakfast and sit back in the armchair, watching the fire. It was a good thing, simple, and Lucas had grown to appreciate the value of the good, simple things.

It had been his birthday at the beginning of March; his mother had driven over from the town with a birthday cake and a parcel wrapped in glitzy silver paper. 'I hope you like the colour,' she said as he unwrapped the green cashmere jumper, which a few hours later he would donate to the communal clothes chest. Better was the box of dried food – pasta, rice, as well as a few tins; and a little upper-income decadence, porcini mushrooms. 'I thought you could probably do with a few things.'

She liked the cottage, telling him that it reminded her of a place she had stayed once in Cornwall with an old boyfriend. She was fond of passing on such spurious details of what had, apparently, been a youth filled with talent and promise. When she asked to be shown around the main house ('To meet some of your friends') Lucas had refused. 'It's not really that kind of place.' Instead, he made her a cup of tea, and they picked at slices of cake. She smoked six cigarettes during the hour that she stayed, her conversation switching between a manic, uncomfortable chatter and morose silence. She was probably drinking again.

Eventually, Lucas made it clear that she had to leave. 'I've got to work over at the house, so . . .' He walked her out to the car, which she had driven over the grass to the door of the cottage. As she paused by the driver's door, her eyes levelled upon him with a look that was piercing but laden with concern. She brushed her palm over his hair, and kissed his cheek.

'Just look after yourself. OK?'

Tracing things back, his breakdown had probably started when he headed to Cambridge, where he'd intended to study political science, and had lasted not even a term. There were a number of reasons for this failure, and the day might well come when Lucas would answer to them: that he was spoiled, middle class; that during his time in that city of ritual and intelligence, he'd withdrawn in the face of the competition involved in his studies; that the antipathy between his parents had marked him more than he would admit; that really he had always looked to the outer world – drugs and people and ideas which were not his own – to supply something which was lacking inside. Perhaps it was none of these things, or rather, they had all affected him because he had been cracked from the start.

After dropping out, he stayed on in Cambridge for a while, moving in with a girlfriend. This had ended nastily. Lucas had fled to London, living on an endless stream of bad credit. He returned home after a plea from his mother, who'd paid off a few of his debts. He navigated the various excesses of his home town, until those excesses broke him: casual friends, lots of drugs, flirting with crime because it felt like the last thing expected of him. Credit card fraud, drug dealing; finally, he'd plunged into an act of vandalism which took even him by surprise. He no longer remembered much about that day in the high street. He was hardly sleeping, spending days on end in his high attic room without seeing another person, living to a different clock, with different needs. One afternoon, he had walked out along the tangle of streets, the daylight almost silver on his retina. Passing a parade of shops (CDs and shoes, mobiles and fast food) he saw a face through a window, a face that he'd disliked. Rage had overtaken him. Loose tarmac from roadworks had done the job. With one window smashed, why not break another? Lucas was laughing when some public-spirited passer-by wrestled him to the ground. Later, when reason leaked back into his mind, the act lost its comedy. He was left with the dreadful feeling that the face he'd hoped to smash had been his own.

But now it was time for work, so, after eating, Lucas walked out of the back door, and waded through the grass towards the Mansion. When he reached the gravel path, he headed around to the kitchen, letting his fingers trail against the rough wall. Some mornings, waking with the dawn, which, no matter how many blankets he had strung up over the window, always roused him, the house would gleam back at him, as white as an eye. But nothing, Lucas often told himself, is really that pure. Up close, the brick was mottled with soot from the chimney and the remains of rotten leaves flushed from the gutter. Approaching the kitchen, his fingers found an airbrick furred by a spider's web, the tiny architect withered by the side.

In the kitchen, a few residents were milling around, finishing off breakfast before the day's chores. Conversation bubbled amid the steam. Taylor and Charley sat over at the kitchen table; Taylor with his back to the door. Charley had glanced over as Lucas pushed inside, but only at the sound of the door. Since then, she'd ignored him, as did everyone else in the kitchen. He checked the rota and found that first of all he was down for the goats. Rather than head back outside straight away, he spent a while warming himself in front of the Aga, although he wasn't especially cold. He stood with his back pressed to the oven, feeling the metal heat through the material of his parka. Eventually, Taylor stood up and walked over to the sink, carrying his and Charley's coffee mugs. He blanked Lucas completely.

'I wanted to ask you something.' Lucas was surprised both that he'd spoken and how loud his voice sounded.

The hot water steamed between them. Taylor didn't speak. Two of the residents were whispering to each other by the chest freezer.

'It's about the cottage,' Lucas continued. 'I'm having trouble with one of the walls.'

'And?'

'And I wondered if you'd help me. Come over and have a look.'

Taylor seemed unwilling to understand. 'You expect me to help you fix up the cottage?'

'It's in the bedroom,' Lucas explained, as though that made things easier. 'The north wall of the bedroom.'

Taylor would have liked to be angry, Lucas guessed, except he couldn't really achieve anger. A long time ago, the impulse had been redirected to feed his self-disgust. Instead, he looked destroyed. His eye retracted as though from shock. He sucked in a little hair from his beard, and he let his coffee cup drop on to the draining board. As he walked away, a loud, meaningless conversation started at the kitchen table. Charley didn't look over once.

Lucas left by the back door and walked around to the goat pen. The pines at the edge of the forest stood like rigid, bristled plumes. Inside the pen, the white was chewing grass, while the brown sat on a patch of raised ground, hooves folded beneath its body. It stared as Lucas walked over, the thin pupils like slits in the grey irises. Lucas started sweeping out the A-shaped corrugated shelter and checked the shit for signs of illness. The brown goat was prone to attacks of diarrhoea. 'That's my luck all over,' Taylor had once said to him. 'Most goats can eat their way out of a cage but I buy a goat with a bad stomach.' This had been a few weeks into his stay at the Mansion, when he and Taylor still talked.

Everything looked healthy today; Lucas scooped feed from the sturdy plastic container, scattering it over the ground. Afterwards, he sat down on a stone by the side of the pen as the goats grazed. He imagined a vast herd of goats let loose on the world, chewing their way through buildings and forests and bomb shelters and office blocks, ravenous and unstoppable. Apart from the brown goat, he reminded himself, the one with bad guts. He looked up into the cold blue of the sky, appreciating the tranquillity of spring.

He was closing up the goat pen when he saw Monkey again, this time walking over towards the edge of the forest with one of the residents, the girl with bright red hair whose name he could never remember. They walked apart from one another, but occasionally one would reach for the other in gestures of habitual, almost unconscious intimacy. Lucas watched them until they disappeared into the woods. When he'd realized that Monkey was staying in the Mansion, it had been something of an irritation. Suddenly, there was a familiar face in this cast of strangers. It confused him, and when he thought of Monkey's morning assignations with the Vegan, something gnawed at him, an insistent dog of unease.

As he was free for an hour, rather than taking lunch, he went for a walk. At first, he started out in the opposite direction to the outhouse, following the path that Monkey and his girlfriend had taken, almost as though he were fooling himself, leading himself along with his eyes covered. Instead of heading into the woods, however, he cut across gardens, vaulting the gate at the back. He described a long circuit of the Mansion's grounds, hidden by the tall hedges from any possible observer. When he came to the back of the outhouse, he zipped up his parka and, hood up and hands withdrawn, he pushed himself through a hole in the bushes. The usual detritus had gathered here: shreds of black bin liner, dog shit desiccated to white powder, a crisp packet, the brand name erased by years of exposure. The windows of the building were covered from the inside, but in one, the cardboard had curled away from a corner. Through this gap, he could see a metal table and the dull reflection of glassware, a wide, perfect stretch of white metal, like the top of a fridge.

Back in the cottage, when evening came, he cooked up a tin of beans and sausages over the fire, taken from the box of supplies in his cupboard. Loneliness crept upon him in these hours. He'd brought a lot of books with him when he'd first arrived, some of which the Vegan had recommended. Bataille, Debord, Thomas Mann, Frazer, Kierkegaard: as a bibliography it might have been impressive, but warped by the damp, still unread, these books were now no more than trinkets of pretentious intent. He simply didn't have the mind for them any more. Instead, he spent a lot of time staring at the cottage walls, but when this became too much, he walked over to the Mansion. If asked why he was there, he excused himself by saying that he was hungry, or he needed the bathroom, or that he was searching for tools. The truth was that he was very rarely asked. After a few moments of human contact, he would return to the cottage. Although sometimes it scared him, the world made sense to him out here.

After his meal, he broke up the embers of the fire and poured a shot of Jameson's into the tin mug. He headed upstairs. In the bedroom, he lit a candle on the desk, sipping his whisky, as he stared out of the window. He liked to see the woods at this time of the evening, as the colour slowly seeped out of the world. He stood for a while, wondering what that darkness hid, and when he felt ready, he sat down at the desk and retrieved a battered diary from one of the drawers. He flicked through the pages before writing, but when he did, his pace was furious, the pen describing minute jags and generous curlicues, a cartography of scrawl. The next morning, he would leaf through the pages again and try to decipher what he'd written, perhaps in bed before he dressed. To be surprised by the details of your life: this, for Lucas, was the essential outcome of writing. A breeze stirred the conifers in front of him, stealing his attention. He reached for his mug of whisky as he looked through the window. Chips of white gloss peeled on the frame. Bored some evenings, Lucas would pick at the paint flakes, creating profiles and caricatures against the dark wood. Some were benevolent, some threatening: familiars and demons lurking on the periphery. Sometimes, even as he looked at them, these shapes would disappear.

When he heard the front door scrape against the boards, he put down his pen and replaced his journal in his desk drawer. Feet worried the floorboards of the stairs and the bedroom door opened. In the mirror of the dark window, he saw Charley entering the room and turned to face her.

'I wasn't sure it was you.'

She stood in the doorway with her arms folded inside the baggy sleeves of a green jumper. 'What on earth was going on earlier?'

'What do you mean?'

'In the kitchen with Taylor?'

'I was asking him a question.'

'You asked him to fix a wall in the bedroom.'

'So?'

'In the *bedroom*.'

Lucas shrugged. 'I don't know, I don't like the way he ignores me. I just wanted to see how he'd react.'

'He only has one way to react and he started not long after you left. And now he's flat on his back in his room, snoring.'

She lowered herself on to a corner of the mattress. 'I'm really fucking furious with you, Lucas. I don't really need any of this right now.'

Lucas knew that Charley had secrets because she told him. She didn't describe them, of course, but with her air of undefined mystery, her constant fatigue about unnamed events, it was obvious that she was involved with events that couldn't be shared.

'You mean Monkey?' he said, risking a little involvement to put her in her place.

Charley had been scowling, but at this remark, her face relaxed, attentive, suspicious.

'What do you mean?'

'You've complained about him before,' he replied. 'That's all.'

'Have you been speaking to him?'

Lucas laughed. 'No. He runs away whenever he sees me coming.'

'You're sure?'

'Have you ever seen us together?'

'Well no. No, I haven't.' She paused. 'What happened between you two anyway?' The suspicion had dimmed slightly, but she stared at him with a cool, level gaze.

'I think I've already told you.'

'Just because you took heroin together? He can't stand the sight of you.'

'Well, there's more than that.'

Lucas had stood up from the desk, and, bringing his tin mug with him, he sat down on the edge of the bed. Charley gestured silently and he passed the mug over to her. 'Well . . .' She sipped at the whisky. 'You were saying?'

He told her about the night he and Monkey had spent together in his room, while they were coming off heroin. He elaborated what had been a very ordinary sexual experience into something worldly, intense, intrinsic to his character, long suppressed. It was only when he was half-way through the story that he realized that, in throwing this part of himself at her to watch her feed, he was testing Charley. At one detail, she had let out a high-pitched cry, only to cover her mouth with her hand. 'Well, well, well.' Her voice brimmed with sarcastic glee. 'Did you both enjoy yourself?'

'Why do you find it so funny?' He kept his voice neutral, calming.

She shrugged. 'I don't know. You should see him some times when you walk into the room.' She was gloating, horribly. 'Oh, that's wonderful.'

'You seem so surprised by it.'

'Well, I am.'

'But it shouldn't really be so surprising, should it? After all, it's only sex.'

A look of seriousness tugged at her face. 'Yes, yes of course. Don't get me wrong . . . I don't think there's anything wrong with it. Believe me, with my past. Well . . .'

'So you've had similar experiences?'

'Well no. Nothing happened. But when I was a teenager, you know, I had crushes.'

'But you never acted on them?'

Charley could tell from his face that something was wrong. 'What is this?' she asked, reaching out to touch his leg. He realized how much Charley needed him: whether to make up for her relationship with Taylor, to escape her responsibilities in the house, or to reward herself with a secret, selfish vice. This insight surprised him, and, coming so soon after her glee, he found it very easy to hate her.

They went to bed. Charley moved over him, charged with an urgency, a purpose. 'Tell me what to do,' she said to him at one stage. 'Tell me what you want.' But he didn't answer. He lost himself all over her, and even when she asked him again, reaching out and holding his face with her hand, he ignored the question, which seemed to him entirely meaningless.

11

'The failure of punk was that it conceded defeat before the battle had even been fought. Political oppression, corporate evil, the random violence of an ignorant mainstream: everything was brought on to the individual. The wearing of heavy boots was for defence not aggression. The music was only the screams of the beaten. It's self-immolation. Sid and Nancy died for you. They took the aesthetic to its very limit. It's Jesus Christ with nappy pin earrings instead of thorns.'

'I disagree completely,' Charley said. 'I think you're wrong.'

Andrew's face was a picture of smug authority. Watching him, Charley revelled in the feeling of warm, comfortable loathing for a contrary opinion. It was late afternoon, and she had been reading in her chair in the living room. Andrew had been talking to one of the other residents about punk. Raised from her book by the conversation, Charley had joined in, thinking she could share some of her memories of Stoke Newington in the seventies; she'd lived on Amhurst Road, haunt of the Angry Brigade. Andrew had dismissed everything with a casual, patronizing wave of his hand. She wouldn't accept this from anyone, but that it was Andrew made it all the worse. Philosophy courses and testosterone made for a dangerous combination.

'How am I wrong?' He smiled, the way he always did when he knew an argument was brewing. 'Enlighten me.'

'People actually wanted to kill the Sex Pistols,' Charley continued. 'You don't know what that means. After the Bill Grundy interview, people wanted to have them hanged.'

'The first feeding frenzy of tabloid television. Just because the media provokes a reaction doesn't make that action genuine.'

'But *killing* them? Don't you understand?'

'In America, people wanted to kill Muddy Waters, Bo Diddley and Little Richard. People *did* kill Robert Johnson. Why ignore that?'

'That was racism. It wasn't a cultural debate.'

'How can you say that? I really can't understand why, in the face of punk, we tend to ignore the blues? It's the precursor of punk, but something wholly potent. It was the defining moment of the last century. A cultural event born from the meeting of continents.'

'You're ridiculous.'

'The history of the blues is the secret history of the first half of the twentieth century. Every major act in the larger scheme has a corresponding trope in the music. Charlie Patton was the First World War. Muddy Waters went electric and invented Vietnam. It's occult, literal black magic.'

'You don't know what you're talking about.'

'No, *your* thinking is limited. You're spoon-fed by Sunday supplements. You believe DJs. It's like *Fox News*. It's dogma. Punk was the purest form of white blues, I'll concede that. But that potency was limited to fashion and a two-three-year *zeitgeist*. Its continual appraisal as something worthy and defiant, as something momentous, is simply racism.'

'I don't have to listen to this. I don't have to be lectured by a kid.'

'Who's lecturing? I'm only trying to put forward a debate. I'm interested in the possibilities.'

'You're offending me. You're hectoring.'

'I expected too much. I was interested in your perspective. But you're too close to the subject.'

'I'm bored now. I'm tired of the insults.'

'You're stuck. You can't escape how it felt to understand what it meant. It's very sad. It really is awful to see an intelligent person stagnate.'

'You need to live a little,' Charley said. 'You're too young to appreciate these things. How can you understand events if you don't live through them.'

'Right. The esoterics of being involved. The cult of what happened. If you have to ask the question, you'll never know the answer. It's disturbing. It's the beginnings of fascism.'

'You're absurd.'

'I mean it. Don't question the established truths. Conform. Punk was good. World is flat. Earth is the centre of things. So long Copernicus. Columbus went down the waterfall. He's down there gasping for air with the turtles that support the world on their backs.'

'You're overreaching now. Really, you're embarrassing yourself.'

'The fight might be lost, but we're still young as long as we can remember punk. The world was a safer place. We could leave our back doors open for gentle homeless punks to come and eat in our kitchens. And they would polish their safety pins on the cloths we provided. It was a beautiful time.'

'You're talking to yourself. No one is listening. Thank you for a stimulating conversation. Now, goodbye.'

Life in the Mansion could be infuriating, but Charley always walked away from an argument feeling satisfied. She was bright enough to provoke people, sharp enough to point them into blind alleys, solid enough to stop them escaping. She'd cultivated her intelligence in isolation. Universities were factories of dogma, newspapers and magazines were only adverts, other people – increasingly – were *wrong*. She read for herself: books lining the floor and surfaces of her room. Her intelligence was a secret weapon, but as she grew older, she used it less as a secret and more as a weapon. Taylor told her that he found this embarrassing: she was points-scoring with people more than twenty years her junior; there was bound to be an inequality. As far as Charley was concerned, this was only another example of how Taylor had been defeated. She knew he'd never appreciate the power of the game.

After his encounter with Lucas, Taylor had refused even to speak to Charley. He'd taken himself off rota and spent the day getting drunk. Because she felt guilty about the way he'd been humiliated, she'd stopped by his room to look in on him. He lay on his bed, flat on his back, wearing only a stretched Metallica T-shirt. Disgust chased away guilt. She headed over to see Lucas, thinking – if anything – that Taylor deserved it. The evening didn't work out as she'd hoped. Lucas had been more distant than usual, even when he'd told her about his relationship with Monkey. When they went to bed, he went about the business of fucking her with the automatic fury of a machine. The next morning, she had dressed while he slept, and although everything between them had become un-settled and charged with hidden meaning, she had bent down to kiss him as a gesture for herself. Even before her lips touched his skin, he had awoken, an empty look of confused hatred in his pale eyes. Sleepily, he'd pushed her away and turned on his side. She'd left feeling rejected, loathed; naturally, she'd headed to see Taylor.

He was teasing the dogs when Charley came through the

kitchen door. They stood around him in chorus – the collie, the retriever, the Alsatian and the meek yellow greyhound – as Taylor dangled an old leather lead in front of them.

'What are you up to?'

He didn't look at her. 'I'm just taking them out.'

'Can I come along?'

He shrugged. 'I can't stop you.'

She had things to keep her occupied. Late March, she organized the seeding of carrots, turnips and parsnip beds; this year she wanted to try the strawberry plants early. But she wanted to be close to Taylor. He led her through the back door, turning left to keep the cottage behind him. She'd thought they might head out into the forest, but instead Taylor led them down past the outhouse, out towards the fields beyond. 'Don't you feel better,' she said – thinking of the laboratory locked up beyond that door – 'knowing that we'll be getting a bit more money coming in?'

'I haven't really thought about it.' His voice was sulky, dismissive.

'Well you *should*.' She was trying to be playful, but succeeded only in sounding caustic. 'If things work out we can stop the whole thing.'

Taylor glanced over. 'What do you mean?'

'Just an idea, really. But as soon as we've paid off the initial outlay and the Vegan's loan, I think we should call a stop to production. I've had enough of dealing with the hassle.'

'But then we're back to square one.'

Charley shrugged. 'Yes, well, I'm starting to feel a bit more positive. Let's see what the May festival is like. That's always a good time of year. If we have a good festival, then we can make some more plans. Look into expanding the business. Doing deliveries, mail order, get a website.'

She wanted to finish their deal with the Vegan. That much was fully thought out. Right now, the idea that she'd be able to find time to organize the rest of it by herself seemed insane. That she'd be able to find support among this gang of bored malcontents – in some of them, she was sure, inertia developed into clinical depression – was laughable. Breakfast and dinner were successes. To finish each market day with money in the till. A roof when it rained. *Jesus, but where did my energy go?* she asked herself. *What happened to the belief?*

They walked in silence behind the Mansion, down into the adjoining fields. A lone cypress stood like a peacock feather amongst a group of stripped sycamores, their bare crowns running like rivulets into the sky. Three of the dogs ran wild in front of Charley and Taylor: the collie and the bitch retriever and the Alsatian. Only the yellow greyhound stayed beside them, quivering, timid, its huge eyes turned to them whenever they looked down. Charley and Taylor didn't speak until they reached a gate into the next field. While the dogs struggled through a gap in the hedge, Taylor climbed the gate and held out his hand to Charley.

'I can manage, thanks.'

'I was only trying to help.'

'I know. I can see. But there's no need. I can climb over myself.'

Taylor walked away into the field. Charley jumped down into the mud, and, hurrying in her stride, she caught up. When she reached for his arm, however, he shrugged her away.

'Don't be like that.'

'I'm not being like anything. It's just . . . You're always trying to fight me. No matter what I do.'

Charley looked out across the fields. 'I am . . .' she began, but 'sorry' really wouldn't come. '. . . in a bad mood.

I had an argument with Andrew. You know what he's like. He was goading me about punk. He said that the time, not just the music, but the whole attitude . . . it was an illusion. He says that people like me only hold on to those days because we can't let go.'

'He's probably right.'

'I think the day I have to admit that Andrew is right about anything is the day I hang myself.' Before she could stop, the remark gave way to a more important truth. 'He makes me feel like I've failed. I hate it.'

She surprised herself by her vulnerability. Taylor saw it too. When he spoke, his voice was soft, almost calming.

'But you haven't failed.'

'Try telling Andrew that.'

'Where would Andrew sit around all day if it wasn't for you? The house wouldn't keep going. You know that.'

By now the dogs had wandered far ahead. The hills in the distance rose in savage blue and purple peaks against the background of the sky, the clouds above a spit of quartz inside a stone. Charley wanted to believe Taylor. Why else had she come for him, if not for his assurance? This need she had for him: still he couldn't see it.

'I feel close to something out here,' she said, wanting to change the subject. 'Something more permanent.'

'The old ways.' Taylor had a voice from a horror film.

'You can laugh, but I'm being serious now. Ever since we've lived out here, I've felt this way.'

'Folk knowledge,' he grinned. 'Country senses.'

'Something genuine. Away from all the trash that people in the town have become mired in. An authenticity, I guess.'

'The laws of the land. They're controlling us, Charley.' The way Taylor winked, she almost felt he was warning her of something.

'There's just a connection,' she continued, trying to explain something which had suddenly run away from her. 'It's why we can't lose the house. It's why we're doing what we have to. This is our place. We belong here.'

The three dogs roamed ahead, sniffing out trails in the fields, hunting through the undulations of the land: old tracks and mounds, long covered and forgotten. There were structures and settlements hidden in these fields, whole civilizations. She reached out and took Taylor's hand, grateful that despite everything – all their misunderstandings, weaknesses and betrayals – that he was near her at this moment. He pointed out patches of chickweed and groundsel, and Charley listened, giving him encouragement when he needed it. He was trying to impress her, and she allowed herself to be impressed. As they reached the brow of the hill, they looked down into a shallow valley where a herd of deer grazed at the edge of a stretch of woodland.

'Look at that,' Taylor said, alive to the miracle.

'Beautiful.'

Before either of them could react, the greyhound sprinted away down the hill. The deer scattered as it approached but, kicked by a flailing leg, one fell behind. The dog leaped upon it. 'Oh my god!' Charley heard herself say: the sight was that shocking to her. The dog hung at the deer's flank, as though caught in the act of mounting; only when the deer bucked did it fall. Now Charley saw the prize: the tail in the dog's mouth, ripped out to the root, fleecy and white, insubstantial as cloud. The deer bounded for the woods, hindquarters streaked with blood. Taylor walked down. The greyhound trotted to meet him, shaing the tail in its jaws: snapping an imaginary neck. Charley realized two things as she watched this, confluent and yet still distinct. You trust a dog for its nature, but its nature is only ever trained; eventually, a dog will behave like a dog.

She felt disappointed and foolish, shocked and, yes, disgusted. While Taylor pulled at its collar, the greyhound grinned around the sodden tail. It looked up at Charley, eyes timid, huge, expectant.

'He wants you to praise him,' Taylor said.

It was early afternoon as they crossed back into the garden, where a scattered group of ten residents was still working at the beds. The back of the house rose behind them, white plaster veined with ivy. The scene had a timelessness and dislocation; something distant and pure. Think of poetry and the land, Charley told herself. Forget yellow dogs. She heard the car engine as they crossed the gate and, although it was louder than she would have expected, she hardly paid attention. Only as they crossed the path through the garden – Charley counting the workers to make sure that no one had skipped their stint – did Taylor mention it.

'Where's that coming from?' he said. 'It doesn't sound like the driveway.'

They had reached the greenhouse, when the sound of the engine grew louder, and a black Mini appeared from beyond the house. It had mounted the grass on the other side of the garden and, rolling dangerously with the slope of the land, the driver sent it speeding towards the outhouse. For some reason, Charley thought it was a police raid and she began to run *towards* the car. Later this would seem significant: rather than run away, her instinct had been to protect the pills, and by extension the house. Just as she passed the greenhouse, the car skidded, bleeding two dark tracks behind its rear wheels as it cut up the grass. Someone was screaming from the open window, someone young. First her heart had pumped panic, now it fuelled anger. What was going on?

The residents had put down their tools. Charley walked among them until she reached Magalene, who stood with a hunk of broccoli in her red-gloved fist.

'Kids,' she explained. 'From the town.'

'Who are they?'

Magalene shrugged. 'Kids from the town. I've never seen them before.'

The car had stalled about a hundred metres away from the outhouse. Charley walked over as the driver tried to restart the engine. There were three young men in the car and, as she got closer, she saw the two passengers pass a bottle of vodka between them. 'You mad bastard, Marky,' the passenger in the back seat shouted at the driver. 'You mad fucking bastard.'

'I'm calling the police,' Charley said, as she approached. 'You can't do that around here.'

'I thought anyone could come here,' the driver said. 'I thought that was the point.' He was too tall for the Mini, cramped in the front seat. He was pale, with short hair gelled over his forehead, his face as hard as a knuckle. Apparently, it was Charley's day for coping with cocksure young men.

'Well, you're wrong.'

'But didn't you just move into the place, anyway?' He grinned. 'Isn't that what happened?'

'We need people who are prepared to work . . .'

'Jesus Christ,' the back seat passenger sneered. 'What the fuck is your problem?'

'My problem is you driving over my garden.'

By now, Taylor had reached her side, breathing heavily, brandishing a rake. 'What's going on?'

'Nothing. These boys were about to leave.'

'I don't think so,' the driver laughed, nastily.

Taylor gestured with the rake. 'How'd you like another paint job, mate?'

Jenn appeared beside them. Ignoring Charley and Taylor, she began shrieking at the driver.

'What the hell are you doing?'

'Oh here we go,' he said. 'Here she is.'

'Mark, you total fucking shit, what are you playing at?'

'You know him?'

'He's my brother.' Jenn turned back to the driver. 'What are you playing at?'

'Just came over to say hello.'

'Driving over the garden? What's going through your head?'

Charley let the family drama play itself out. She walked back towards the residents in the garden. 'OK.' She clapped her hands. 'Let's get back to work.' To lead the way, she started helping Magalene pull out the broccoli from the ground and toss it into the wheelbarrow. Taylor, realizing that he wouldn't be needed, returned the rake to the shed and whistled for the dogs. As the workers returned to the beds, Charley glanced up to see Monkey, standing on the far side of the garden. When he noticed that she'd seen him, he began picking weeds from the new seedlings.

The car drove away, departing with an aggressive blast of its horn as it vanished behind the house. Jenn walked over towards Charley, embarrassed and contrite. 'I'm really sorry. What can I say? He's a moron. He's decided that he doesn't like me living here.'

'I can't have that happen, Jenn.'

'I know, but . . .'

'It's not fair on the others. A lot of people live out here to escape behaviour like that.'

'I can't control him.'

'But you just said yourself, he doesn't like you living here.'

'He could come back, anyway. It might not just be about me.'

'Oh for fuck's sake Jenn, do you think people would actually want you to stay here now?'

When Jenn left, she had tears in her eyes, and predictably, neither she nor Monkey came down to the meal that evening. Charley would have liked to put it all behind her, but the earlier events dominated that night's conversation. It was a full house: almost twenty people gathered around the table, and those who had been at the scene elaborated to those who had not.

'I really don't want to go back to those days.' Magalene had started talking about it as soon as she sat down.

'We shouldn't blame Jenn, but still, if she's going to attract that kind of thing . . .'

'Pond life. Football tops and trainers. What more can you say?'

'They're the reason I don't go out on a Friday night.'

'They're the reason *I* want to go to New Zealand.'

'Trust me, they'll be there waiting for you on the beach. It's the budget airlines. Carrying them out there like rats.'

Sadie called over to Magalene. 'What do you mean about going back to those days?'

So eager was Taylor to join in, that he didn't bother to finish swallowing a mouthful of olive bread. 'It happened all of the time when we first moved in.'

'A couple of times,' Charley interrupted. 'Don't exaggerate.'

'It happened more than twice.' Taylor scowled, irritated at having his drama ruined. 'Anyway, mostly it was just like today. We'd get a few village boys back from a night on the town. Nothing else to do, so they thought they'd come around here. I think they used to come out here anyway, when the place was abandoned. A place to drink, to smash things up. I grew up with people like that. I know them. Once they found out there were people living here, or worse, people they didn't understand, then they came back. We had a few battles.' He glanced over at Charley. 'Remember that time we had to fight a bunch of them on the front step. It was like a Western or something.'

'You lost a tooth.' Despite herself, Charley was laughing.

'I did, yeah.' He pulled back his lip to show the gap between molars. 'And there was that guy, he only lived here for about six months. What was his name?'

'Keith? No. Kevin.'

'It was Kelvin.'

Taylor nodded. 'Kelvin. He beat one of them up with his mandolin. I'll never forget it. He broke the bastard's nose. But not the mandolin. There's a lesson there.'

Magalene shuddered. 'Like I said, I don't want to go back to those times.'

'I don't care what anyone says.' Andrew grinned. 'I loved it. When the car came around the side of the house . . . It was like the coming of the barbarians.'

Later, Charley would feel angry that she'd been so intimidated by the events of that afternoon. Too often in the Mansion, the town and its people became the only justification for a certain way of life, and in that they were so integral, that any real sense of purpose was impossible. *As long as we're not them*, a lot of the residents seemed to say, *as long as we're not there, then we're OK*. But define yourself in opposition and you end up relying upon what you profess to spurn; you have nothing else. Charley often found herself gnawed by the idea that this, ultimately, represented the real reason for the Mansion's failure. As she worked until late in the office, she started now and then at what she thought was the sound of the car returning. It was horrible to be reminded how fragile her life's foundations were: that she lived in an abandoned house discovered by accident, shared with a collection of interchangeable strangers. Nothing, nothing, she said to herself. Nothing is mine.

After finishing in the office, she moved through to the living room, and watched the late-night news with a few other residents, even vegging halfway through a film until she realized it was utterly appalling. Up in her room, she tried reading – *Jane Eyre*, for about the hundredth time – but her mind wandered. She lay fully clothed on her bed, wondering if it was only her loneliness that kept her awake.

Out in the corridor, coming back from the bathroom, she bumped into Taylor.

'Bit late for you, isn't it?' he asked. Even though he carried a half full bottle of wine with him, he appeared fairly lucid, almost relaxed. 'Haven't you got the market tomorrow?'

'I can't sleep.'

'Not worried are you?'

'A bit. Just tense about it all. I keep expecting to hear that car coming up the drive.'

Their voices echoed in the still corridor. In a room far inside the house, someone began to laugh, the young voice verging on hysteria. Charley gestured to the bottle of wine. 'Got enough to share?'

Taylor let her into his bedroom. A reef of dirty combats, T-shirts and underwear lay on the floor, which he pushed under the bed with his foot. A torn poster advertising a sixties horror film glared down from the wall. In the background, the silhouette of a gang of torch-wielding villagers advanced on an old dark house; on the steps, a wolfman snarled over a screaming blonde, a crease in the paper spoiling her generous décolletage. Charley and Taylor sat down together on the bed, taking it in turns to drink from the bottle, while music whined through the speakers of an old tape player.

'It's when they headed for the outhouse,' Charley explained. 'That's when I really panicked.'

'You didn't let it stop you, though. You went right after them.'

'Like an idiot,' she agreed. The wine was bitter and sharp, though not unpleasant. She laughed, shaking her head. 'You turning up with that rake. My hero.'

Taylor flinched, thinking that she was being sarcastic. She was reminded of the yellow greyhound, the way that even when she went to stroke it, it prepared itself for a blow. Only when she touched her palm to his cheek did Taylor smile.

'It's nice to have you around here. Seems like it's been a while.'

'It's been far too long.'

She stripped quickly. Taylor moved to turn off the light, while she slid under the cold covers. The moon was very bright through the window, an almost perfect silver glinted on the glass. Away from it, Taylor was a dark form in darkness as he undressed. 'Let's take it slowly,' he said, as he appeared into the light. At first she didn't realize what he meant, thinking it was said as a promise. She reached out for him, but he pushed her back, the pressure of his fingers definite against her shoulder. 'It's OK. I'll start.' She lay back and closed her eyes as he moved over her. The bedsprings shivered, regular and automatic; she squirmed against the feel of his beard. She opened her eyes to see the outline of the film poster on the wall; turning her head, she shifted slightly under the pressure of his hand. Again she reached out, but he pushed her away. 'It's OK.' His voice was thick. 'I'm OK.' She closed her eyes. A breeze picked up and rattled the window latch. The mattress shivered beneath her. When she opened her eyes again, she saw the wolfman leaning over the creased, cartoon blonde.

'This isn't working.' She had her hands on his head.

'What?' His voice was still thick. 'What's wrong?'

She lay her fingers against his side and began to slip away out of the side of the bed. 'I'm sorry. It's not working.'

He shifted. 'Wait a minute . . .'

'It's me,' she said, as she struggled into her jeans. 'Really. It's just not right. I can't relax. It was earlier. It's put me on edge.' She pulled her jumper over her head. 'I'll just get back to my room.'

She left him, already turning away from the door. Back in her room, she climbed into bed. She lay with her face against the pillow, staring at a bare white patch of wall, against which the light of the moon illuminated the shadows of the window pane. Every chip or crack on the glass, the damage and dirt of an age, the rugged blistered paint of the frame and even a long thin flaw which she'd never noticed before: a cinema upon her wall. And Charley waited for something to happen.

12

Secrets run like rats: pushed away and marginalized, they head towards the dark to thrive. Taylor had an ugly chore waiting for him that morning, so to postpone it for as long as possible, he disappeared into the forest. He made sure to take a couple of guidebooks with him, one for wild flowers, one for birds: something to concentrate on rather than the drink. Last time he was in town, he'd bought a set of these books (mushrooms and butterflies, grasses and freshwater fish): all filled with identification templates, colour-coded keys and Latin taxonomy. To understand the land, that had been the grand idea: he'd stash them in his room, and become an after hours scholar. He saw himself dazzling the residents: advising on safe mushrooms to pick from the forest floor, songs of stonechats and goldfinches, proper times for baiting pike, perfect herbs for natural highs; the old sage. Not a big secret, but he had precious few of his own, and the novelty was exciting. To be a drunk leaves your life laid open: you betray yourself and rarely remember the betrayal. But through the code of a kept secret, honour and character could be rebuilt, even dignity. And Taylor needed dignity. Over a week since Charley had come back to his room, and they'd hardly spoken. The dogs were his company now.

They set the pathways for these walks, their tails the slinky rudders negotiating wilful turns, their noses tuned into invisible intelligence. Taylor trudged behind for an hour or so, sometimes shouting out an order to indulge that comforting lie of all dog walkers, that somehow they are in control. Led, finally, into a small clearing, he took a break. While the dogs moved about in ever-widening circles, he sat upon a fallen sycamore and flicked through his guidebooks (was that a patch of ragwort off the path? 'Gentlemen, let us marvel at the song of a thrush'), taking occasional hits of rum from a hip flask. The rum was harsh, cheap white Jamaican rum from an off-licence in the town. He winced at the burn. As soon as the Vegan was finished with the outhouse, Taylor wanted to build a still and make some border moonshine, English poteen. It couldn't be any worse than the rum.

Only when he stood up did he realize that he'd been left behind by the dogs. He found them off one of the pathways that ran from the clearing: gathered around an old shed set back in the woods, they sniffed at the earth, sniffed at the door. Probably it was a groundsman's shed, derelict for years, the wood split and rotten, joints lined with moss as green as the felt roof. Even if the padlock could have been closed, the doorhinges had separated from the wood; Taylor didn't so much open the door as cause it finally to fall. Burned out matches and fag butts mixed with dead leaves on the floor. A berry of orange mould oozed in a nearby corner. But no tools, no traps, no twine, no machinery. They weren't the purpose.

The first clue was a red satin bra hanging from a rusted hook by the only window, black lace embroidered with grey webs. Matching panties yawned on the floor nearby. There was even a hint of romance: a bottle of Cutty Sark, lying on its side, had a pink candle shoved into the neck.

Maybe the shed had been a nest for doggers, but doggers had clean cars, they hooked up on the internet, GPS guided them, they bathed their dirty knees in suburban bathrooms; doggers don't need sheds. Taylor wondered if there was something in the air, a stimulant in the water, an energy in the land, the whole geography rife with fertility and lust. Someone should advertise it: carve a priapic man in chalk upon a hillside. He thought of Charley, and for too many reasons wondered what she'd say about *that*. In the corner gloom, he found a magazine: a woman with blond hair (obviously dyed) stared up from the creased pages. Black damp had engulfed most of the picture, but her vagina bloomed between a pair of green nylons. Hairstyle, make-up, the blue-and-white graph paper duvet cover, all belonged to the 1980s. Taylor picked up the magazine, flicked through the pages, compelled by the sense of morbid desperation, the reek of a secret kept hidden so long it had turned to rot. Christ, he told himself, the place really must have an energy if it can turn *me* on.

In the end, he dropped the magazine to the floor, took a hit from the rum bottle and walked back outside. The collie was pawing at a patch of ground: underneath leaves and dried bark, Taylor revealed a skull, what looked like a sheep's skull, almost perfectly intact. While the collie moved off to sniff out more treasures, he brushed the skull down, screwing out the caked dirt from the sockets with his little finger, placing it carefully inside his jacket pocket. His grandfather had collected skulls from his walks, boiling them clean in a pot on the gas stove, and mounting them around the confines of his caravan. Skulls of birds, squirrels, sheep and calves had decorated the fake panelling of the furniture, while the clammy smell of steam from the pot had often clung to the air. The portable TV had displayed the old man's favourite: a lacquer-painted skull of a grass snake, which had slid across his path while walking. He'd killed it with his stick.

Thinking about the old man only reminded Taylor of the job waiting back at the house. He took a nip of rum and began walking back towards the house, heavy legged, despondent, whistling for the dogs. Still easily diverted – if Taylor was accomplished at anything, it was avoiding responsibility – he killed time by stopping at the red brick building at the back of the kitchen, the brewery. Unlocking the padlock – this one clean and silver, without a blob of corrosion – he paused inside the door, breathing deeply. He could bottle that smell: the damp brick and wood, the sharp, sour tang of spilled fermenting fruit, of hops and malt, of *everything*. Elderberry, elderflower, gooseberry, rhubarb, carrot and blackberry: the wine breathed inside demijohns, plop-plopping the water airlocks. In the beer vats, yeast cells fed and died, swarming with silent fury under clouds of foam. Taylor checked the thermometer, tapped on a few of the jars, poured himself a small tin cup of beer; he indulged the rituals. The morning sun through the translucent corrugated panes, simultaneously tinted and more accurate: if Taylor ever filmed happy childhood memories, he'd use this light. Winter in the old days had seen the cannier residents congregating here, after Taylor rigged a heater up to the generator. He'd soon put a lock on the door. The fruits of the labour were available to everyone, but the site was sacrosanct: Taylor's private temple. As he stood there now, the taste of hops in green beer fizzing upon his tongue, he felt almost complete. He shook his head and sighed. He couldn't postpone his chore any longer. It was time to head to the chicken coop.

Originally, the residents had wanted to let the chickens run free, one of many rustic dreams that had been annihilated by foxes and the frankly tiresome search for eggs.

Caged inside a long stretch of wire, the wooden coop stood over three metres tall, one wall decorated by the giant red head of a graffiti cockerel (drawn by a resident; Taylor forgot her name) the run littered with shreds of bark, logs and rocks: the freedom of free-range birds. As he opened the door, the air throbbed with chicken conversation, a sound that had always seemed warm to him, like water bubbling. Most of the birds were resting on the deep shelves fixed into the walls, while a couple pecked at the large plastic bowls of feed and water. Already the planks were littered with feathers and the air stank of the sour, slightly chalky smell of bird shit. The day before, when Andrew had returned from his shift cleaning out the coop – and after a lot of griping about what was, everyone knew, one of the worst jobs – he'd mentioned one of the chickens. Misshapen and mostly bald, its comb was the colour of strawberry milkshake, its neck drooping and flaccid. Whenever this chicken moved for feed or water, the others would attack it. Taylor spotted the outcast bird immediately, sitting apart from the others on the highest shelf. Birds scattered as he stepped forward, some making abortive attempts at flight, others scrambling against the wall; a couple made it out into the run. Taylor reached up like he was taking the last meagre toy from the most meagre toyshop: the bird came to him more placidly than any chicken should. Probably it knew. As he brought it down, another chicken launched itself from the floor, pecking at the outcast bird before Taylor knocked it away. He kicked the door open and walked outside. Screams followed.

Any hermaphrodite chicken is soon excluded from the brood. Taylor's grandfather had always called these birds Will-Jills, because you couldn't tell if they were Will or Jill. Outside the coop, Taylor walked towards the house, adjusting the Will-Jill in his hands. A single orange eye regarded him from the small leathery face. There was very little choice. If the bird didn't starve, the other chickens would slowly peck it to death. This was Taylor's chore within the house: no one else could stomach it. He could hardly stomach it himself. 'But you've got to,' Charley had insisted. 'You know what to do.' Worst of all, this time there would be no rewards. Taylor wasn't a vegetarian by choice – he ate according to Charley's conscience – and every so often he and Robert would meet for a meal late at night, after conspiring to make one of the healthier chickens disappear. These were usually extravagant, almost decadent affairs – Robert's chicken-in-cider was a hymn to finer times – but there would be no such treats with the Will-Jill. Its flesh was limp and pallid, like something congealed; the best thing would be to boil up the carcass for the dogs.

Outside the run, Taylor adjusted the chicken in his hands. The claws he clasped in his left fist, and keeping the head facing downwards, with his right he took a firm grip on the neck. 'Like you're an archer pulling on a bow,' the old man had always said. He'd kept chickens on his land, locked up from night predators in the remains of a wrecked Hillman Imp. You'd see the chickens fluttering inside the windscreen: pea-brained, furious creatures getting nowhere inside a car. No, Taylor hadn't missed the town at all. He'd fetch eggs in the morning, picking them from the dashboard and glove compartments, or from holes gouged into the sponge of the seats. And afterwards, a fry-up with the old man: bacon, traded for casual mucking-out at a pig farm up the road; mushrooms picked from the fields. Tea so strong it supported the spoon. Sometimes, the old man laced it with a jigger of whisky: a generous celebration of transient days.

A sudden peck at his hand reminded Taylor to hurry along: this was a chicken sick of its mortal coil. He tightened his grip and pulled. There was a soft, barely audible click, and the weight of the body swung away heavily in his arm, but as the wetness spread over his fingers and dripped on to the grass, he realized that he'd pulled too hard. The old man would either have laughed himself stupid or kicked Taylor up the backside. Blood pulsed from the neck, squirting over his fingers, the chicken's head sharp and, suddenly, definite in his right hand. The orange eye still glared at him as he tossed it into the plastic bag.

As Taylor washed his hands at the outdoor tap, he remembered the sheep skull in his coat pocket. After hosing off the remaining mud from the bone, he decided to use it to decorate the goat pen, a little bit of Wild West exotica added to this drunk man's gulch. The brown goat sat with its legs folded under its body as Taylor let himself in through the gate; it regarded him steadily as it chewed on the grass. The white one was nuzzling against one of the fence posts. Taylor walked over to the shelter and set about finding the best place to position the skull, hanging it from one of the nails that had, at some time, been hammered into the wood. He didn't notice Lucas until he was impossible to avoid: hitching the wire of the gate and letting himself into the pen. Taylor scowled and stared back at the skull. This was an unfair development. Lucas was a secret which had strayed. The cottage was supposed to house him, secluded from everyone.

'What do you want?'

'Obeying the rota.' Lucas said. He glanced over at the carrier bag by the fence. 'How's the black magic?'

'What?'

Lucas gestured to the carrier bag. 'Killing chickens, putting up skulls. Black magic.'

Taylor grunted in reply. He wanted to leave, but he didn't want to be chased away. Lucas moved to Taylor's side, leaning back to perch upon the yellow plastic feed barrel.

'So,' he said. 'Roast or soup?'

'What?'

'It's chicken tonight I take it?'

'Have it if you want.' Taylor gestured to the carrier bag. 'I was going to feed it to the dogs.'

'Just an ordinary day in the country. Wake up, take some air, rip a head of a chicken. Is that anger management?' A person playing games had never looked so joyless. Lucas bit his lip, shifting on the edge of the feed barrel.

Taylor ignored the last part. 'It was sick.'

'Sick how?'

'There was something wrong with it.' He felt unable to justify himself, unsure of why he should. 'It would have been cruel to let it live.'

'That's a lot of responsibility. Deciding what's wrong with something.'

'It's a fucking chicken! These things need to be done.'

'Not sure I could cope with it, though.'

Taylor shook his head. 'I really don't want to have this conversation.'

'About chickens or responsibilities?'

'Any conversation. I just don't want to talk to you.'

Lucas looked suddenly stung. 'I'm sorry. I'm just interested. You know what I thought.' As he stood up and walked behind Taylor, his voice became more intimate, as though they really had something to share. 'It's stupid, I know, but . . . I thought you were telling me something.'

'What?'

'I thought it was a curse. Skulls and dead chickens. Because of me and Charley.' Lucas nodded to himself. 'But now I know. These things need to be done.'

*

Robert stood over the stove, stirring the contents of a huge cast-iron pot with a long metal spoon. Taylor paused at the back door to kick off his boots, and leaving the carrier bag on the kitchen table, he walked through to the pantry. He pulled one of his beers from the shelf behind the fridge and cracked open the top. Robert glanced over.

'Hair of the dog, yeah?'

'Yeah.' Taylor actually growled. 'Something like that.'

The first beer went down like black molasses. He couldn't stop it, couldn't tear it off the stream. He might have given himself over to it entirely, except that Robert wanted to talk.

'Killed that chicken, then?'

'Yeah.' Taylor sipped from his beer. 'Cracked its neck.' He broke the consonants against the back of his teeth.

'I'll boil it up,' Robert said. 'Soon as I'm done with this.'

'What are you cooking?'

'Just some jam. For the May festival. Had the fruit in the freezer all winter. Thought I might as well use it.'

'Jam.' Taylor said the word as Bob Marley might, dragging it out nice and slow. 'Jam.' Ten minutes passed. He drank two more beers. 'Jam,' he said once more, because he was in love with the way it sounded. 'Jam.'

He was occupied like this when Charley came into the room. Probably, she had things to discuss with Robert: plans for the stall, for the future of the Mansion. It could all burn, as far as Taylor cared: it could collapse into the ground.

'You've started early.' She didn't disguise her irritation.

Taylor grinned, sweetly. 'I've just been talking to your boyfriend.'

The words almost tripped Charley over: her secret let

loose into the kitchen. Gone was the sarcastic assurance; when she called over to Robert, her voice caught in her throat. 'Listen, do you mind if we have a bit of time alone?'

Robert had shrunk over the stove, but he shrugged, almost helplessly. 'I've got to stir the jam.'

'You can take it off the heat.'

'Yeah, but if I do that it'll be spoiled.'

'Robert . . .'

'The pan is red hot. Even if I take it off the heat it'll still burn.'

'Then let it burn.'

'I don't want to. I've spent the whole morning on this.'

Charley seethed for a second. 'Fine.' She walked over to the cooker. 'Robert. Please. I'll stir the jam. Can you give us a couple of minutes?'

He held the spoon up in the pot until Charley took it from him.

'Just keep a nice steady motion. Keep the bowl of the spoon moving along the bottom. Don't let the mixture stick.'

'I think I can manage.'

'If it burns even slightly, all of it will be ruined. The taste will affect the whole thing. One mistake and it's gone. Pay attention.'

As Robert walked through to the hallway, Taylor hunched low over the kitchen table, staring at his bottle of beer. Charley faced away from him, stirring the jam. He reached out and placed his hand on the carrier bag. Through the thin skin of plastic, he could feel the feathers of the bird. He took a sip of beer, and then placed the bottle on the table, exactly at the point he'd picked it up, matching the bottom with the wet ring on the wood. He placed his chin on the lip of the bottle. 'Jam,' he whispered to himself in his Bob Marley voice. 'We're jamming.'

'I take it you're talking about Lucas.'

She hadn't turned around, but stood facing the blank wall behind the stove. Taylor coughed. 'That's right.' As he took another hit of beer, it occurred to him to say, 'Well how many boyfriends have you got?' but he decided, this time, to stay quiet. Keep it simple, he thought. I don't want to know.

'So what's brought this on?' Finally, when she turned to face him, one hand still stirring the jam, she had none of the defiance that he might have expected. She chewed her lip, shifting her weight, nervously, from foot to foot. Taylor saw these actions very clearly, as though they had been laid out on a table and itemized. He told her about his conversation with Lucas out in the goat pen.

'But that's crazy.'

'Of *course*, it's crazy,' Taylor snapped back. '*He* is crazy. I don't care what happens behind my back. You know that. But when it gets rubbed in my face, I can't take it.'

'Taylor . . .'

'I mean, for god's sake, I need all the dignity I can get.'

'So what do you want me to do?'

'He goes. That's what I'm saying. We kick him out.'

'Taylor, we can't . . .'

'I want him out of here!'

The beer bottle had moved from the print of the ring on the table. He reset it, and stared down the neck of the bottle, at the amber light trapped by the brown glass.

'Can you come here, please?'

Charley was looking at him, he could tell. He scowled and stared down at the table, at the patterns sealed under varnish, at the seam and knots of the wood.

'Taylor. Robert will kill me if I leave this. Please come here.'

He stood up, the bench squealing underneath him on

the tiles. He walked to Charley's side, and stood with his hand in his pockets, staring at the wall over the stove. When Charley reached out and touched his shoulder, Taylor looked at her. His eyes were suddenly wet. He wiped them with his thumb and forefinger, pinching his tear ducts with the pressure, his throat dry and trembling.

'Think about the festival,' Charley said. 'We need everyone we can get. There's going to be so much work.' She worked the silver spoon around and around the pan, metal singing against metal. 'You know that, don't you?'

'I know,' he said. He was crying freely now, and his voice caught in his throat. Charley put her arm on his shoulder, began to stroke his arm with strong circular motions.

'Ssssh. We only have to wait a few more weeks. Then we can make all the changes we want. Ssssh.'

'I know.' Taylor wiped the tears from his cheek.

'But until then, nothing can change. We can't risk it. I'm sorry.' Charley left the stove and put her arms around him. 'I'm really sorry that he hurt you. And I'll do everything to stop that happening again.'

'Thank you.' He was crying freely now. He gave himself over to her arms, whispering softly into her ear. 'Thank you so much.'

When Robert returned, Charley stepped back from the cooker and let him return to the jam. 'Here. I think everything should be fine.'

But Robert scowled as he tasted the jam. 'It's ruined. The whole thing is ruined. It only needed one burn and it spoils. A whole morning's work, a whole batch of fruit, because you can't pay attention.'

To Taylor and Charley the jam tasted fine: sweet and rich, with the subdued bitterness of fruit skins. After Robert left, slamming the door as he went out into the hallway, they sat together at the kitchen table. The dogs moved underneath the table, whining for attention, scratching claws at the tiles. But they ignored them. They dipped the spoon into the pot, and smeared the jam on bread, ate it like honey from the spoon. The carcass of the chicken lay between them, forgotten on the table. Their lips and fingers were sticky with the sugary fruit. They couldn't taste the burn at all. Neither of them could tell that anything was wrong.

13

The prisoner of Monkey Island had been in the house for nearly three months, and not once had he left the grounds. All the other residents made runs into the town to help out on the stall, or to escape for a long weekend. Monkey always stayed behind. It had become something of a joke around the place. People told him he'd be a ghost Monkey, haunting the halls for years to come, rattling his chains, white-bearded and grey-faced, longing for the light of the sun.

A few days after Mark had driven over to the house, Jenn went back to town. She had to argue with Charley for the time off. 'I don't know what she expects. How does she expect me to stop him coming over if I don't meet him?' She was gone for nearly a week. Without her, Monkey worked long hours in the laboratory, piecing together his own batch of pills whenever the Vegan turned his back. The Mansion crackled with the usual histrionics. Magalene fell out with Sadie. Andrew and Charley couldn't stand the sight of one another. People whispered about Charley and Lucas behind Taylor's back. A couple of residents complained about Jenn, probably realizing that Monkey was listening. 'First we get her nasty family driving all over the place. Now we have to cover her shifts.'

On the day Jenn returned, he'd spent the morning in the outhouse with the Vegan, and a couple of hours in the afternoon helping in the garden. Finally released, he'd headed to the bathroom on the second floor, and stewed in a bath for half an hour, smoking cigarettes and drinking tea, reading *The Fall of the House of Usher*. He'd only been back in his room for ten minutes when Jenn appeared at the door.

'When did you get back?'

'A couple of minutes ago. Come on, I want to show you something.'

'What?'

'Charley's still in town. No one knows where Taylor is.'

'So?'

'So follow me.'

She led him up the stairs. They crept through the corridors, until they reached a small wooden staircase on the eastern side of the house. The whole place smelled of damp. 'You have to be careful on the stairs,' Jenn warned him over her shoulder. 'Last time I came up here I put my foot through one of the boards.'

She led him to a small room lit only by a skylight. In some places, brittle wooden floorboards turned to dust as you trod upon them; on the walls, brown stains seeped into blue fleurs-de-lys. Jenn retrieved a stepladder and set it up under the skylight.

'I'll go first.'

Monkey held the ladder in place as Jenn pulled herself through the open skylight. The breeze inspired the room, like breath into a corpse, cobwebs jangling upon the walls, dried leaves describing vortices upon the floorboards. When Jenn disappeared, he followed. The wind whistled like a vacuum, pulling at him, and suddenly he was high above the world, the sky spreading out total and complete, an ocean interrupted only by a white geography of clouds. The wind sped quickly across the flat roof as he stood up, teasing at Monkey's clothes, wrapping around him with invisible life. Jenn waited for him by the parapet. She smiled triumphantly as he joined her at the edge.

'Beat you.'

The sun had nearly disappeared, throwing its last light up behind the hills, the sky veined with pink and blue like a cross section of cracked opal. In the final shifting glow, the shadows of the land slid gently in the light, the long fingers of hedges and conifers ticking through the slow inches of the sun's death. The time Monkey spent with Jenn always felt like a game. They compared views from every part of the roof: the pylons striding across the land to the south, the motorway to the west. They saw figures walking up the drive and hid down behind the parapet, making bets on who was returning. Soon, the sun had fallen completely and they were left with only the arc of the cold spring sky. They leant against the chimney, smoking cigarettes and talking.

'So how were things at home?'

Jenn shrugged. 'Mark still thinks that if I lived back there, everything would be perfect. Like Dad wouldn't still be running around. Like that would get Mum off her pills. He's an idiot.' She lifted her cigarette to her lips. 'Still, I managed to escape for long enough to catch up with some friends. I'd like you to meet my friends, some time. We can head over there together.'

'You've only just got back . . .'

'I know, but . . .'

'And haven't you just been telling me how much you hate it?'

Jenn scowled. 'All I'm asking is for you to meet my friends. It's not just for me. It's for you too. I'm *worried* about you. You can't spend your whole life cooped up here. So, going back there makes you feel like an addict again. It's time to move on.'

'I'm sorry,' Monkey said. 'You're right. I can't ignore it.' He was dissembling now: he'd lied when he told her why he'd come to the Mansion, and now he lied about staying. He needed to divert her. Perhaps an answer lay under the floorboards of his room.

It was an unseasonable weekend: the first freak trace of summer burning its way into spring. The sun melted a liquid sky, the thin sparse clouds like the threatened white in the centre of an ice cube. For the first time since Monkey had been at the Mansion, everyone gathered outside on the lawn. A stereo ran from a wire from the kitchen, blaring out dance music across the grass. Robert and Sadie served up a picnic on the lawn, while Taylor tried to get enough people together for a game of cricket. If the residents kept to their separate groups, at least the place had achieved a kind of calm.

Monkey left it all behind during the afternoon, waiting for Jenn at the rear of the house, eight of the pills packed up in an old film canister inside his back pocket. The night before, he'd shown Jenn the batch under his floorboards. He'd considered this move carefully. He needed to rebuild himself in her eyes; the conversation on the roof had proved that much. Subterfuge was required: he told Jenn that he'd stolen the pills from someone who'd owed him money. An old friend had become a new enemy, which had created a few hostilities, best avoided by staying away from the town. All very convoluted, and even by not saying too much ('I don't want you to get involved'), he had probably gone too far. But the conclusion was self-evident. His need to stay at the house without returning to the town: it wasn't only a weakness, it was a way to survive. Jenn had been dazzled by the sordid glamour of it all.

So they planned an expedition across the fields: to escape the Mansion, to escape a lot more besides. As Monkey had taken so long to share them, Jenn demanded that they take some of the pills. He found it difficult to refuse. Even by the time she turned up – half an hour late because she'd had to finish some work in the cellar – she was still piqued.

'I really can't believe you've only just told me.'

They walked across the garden. A pink jay fled from an overturned wheelbarrow. The Tony Blair scarecrow grinned after it, psychotic and indifferent.

'I wasn't sure how you'd react.'

'Well, I'm wounded.' She bounced her hip against his. 'There are scars upon my heart.'

The fields rolled gently upwards away from the Mansion's grounds. The purple hills took bites out of the line of the horizon. Brushed like a poem in Japanese characters, a lone Scots pine stood out against the sky. Jenn had borrowed a map from Taylor, but both of them agreed they had no idea how to read it. 'We'll just wander. Find whatever comes along.'

They crossed thin ribbon-like roads carved like ravines below the lie of the land, but mostly they kept to the fields. Passing cars, a jet plane streaming white into the sky, these were the distant signs of a life which they wanted to leave behind. In one field, they came across a stretch of dead crows crucified on wires, their wings pinned to imitate flight.

'I do find it a bit spooky being out here,' Jenn said as they crossed the field. 'Sometimes, don't you wonder what it would be like to be the last people alive? I think about it all the time. I have this recurring dream where I'm walking through a landscape at the end of the world. The grass is really bleached, the sun is hot but comes through this misty film, and the skies are black, although it's daylight. What buildings there are have been abandoned. People's things are just lying in the road, an empty pram, an open suitcase, a laptop. There's obviously been looting, violence. Cars are burned out and there are spent bullets on the ground. But I have this cat with me, a little kitten. I have it huddled down in my coat; I have to keep it alive. I need to get to the next town. I need food, water, medicine. It's so vivid, and I wish you'd stop laughing at me.'

'I'm sorry. I don't often feel like that, no.'

'The weirdest thing about it is that I'm actually happy. It's the perfect environment for me. I think that's why I'm living out here. My innate misanthropy. You're still not taking me seriously, are you?'

The church appeared out of nowhere. A squat, hefty building, it stood at the edge of a field, set back behind a wall of grey slate overgrown with moss and bracken. After years of being blasted by the wind, the soft red stone had receded from the mortar. Vines reclaimed the cluttered headstones. The bell would not ring. Jenn led Monkey through a gap into the churchyard, and they picked through the outlines of graves in the long grass, the names on the headstones blasted to sand. Monkey set his shoulder against the church door and the wood shrieked over the tiles. A lone pigeon fled to the rafters, the violence of its wings shattering the quiet.

'So when was the last time you were in church?' Jenn whispered, as though there were rules about that question, covenants.

'Me? I don't know.'

'No secret weddings you want to tell me about. No christenings.' She paused. 'OK, tell me now if you've had a painful funeral. I deserve it.'

'No, nothing. Maybe a carol service when I was a kid.'

The low sun broke through stained glass, the blues and golds and reds glowing in the arched windows. Most of the pews lay turned over on the floor. The air smelled like the pages of an old book. Mould erupted from corners; great, mouthed boles flowering out of damp plaster. A lectern stood facing the wall, a wooden eagle supporting the bookrest on its outspread wings. Beside the altar lay the effigy of a woman with a small dog curled by her feet, the stone of her face razed and featureless.

'What about you?' Monkey asked.

'Last weekend.'

'When you said you went out with your friends, I thought . . .'

'Very funny. No, it was my mum. She appears to have found God. It had to come sooner or later, I guess. Shopping worked for a while. And there was obviously golf. But our Father seems to have popped up at the eighteenth hole.'

'You don't seem very happy about it.'

Jenn shrugged. 'She's lonely. That's what it is. She spent a lot of time telling me that a church isn't just a building, it's a community. She wants to belong. I started arguing with her about it – I was overreacting I suppose, like she was joining a cult or something – but I was upset that she felt like this. Angry at Dad too. Guilty.'

'Why guilty?'

'Because I'd run away. Which is what I have, really. Anyway, she asked me to come along, to the church. To meet her friends. I said no, but, well, once my mum can sniff that guilt, she won't let go. And in the end, I thought that I should.'

'What was the place like?'

She gestured about them. 'It wasn't like here. It was

new, like a council building. Posters about Africa in the hallway. Fairtrade. Drives for recycling. Adverts for a rock band. That had me alarmed. There really is nothing so misguided as a Christian rock band. Still, my mum enjoyed herself. I looked over at her during the sermon. It was pretty boring. I mean, don't get me wrong. The man knew how to talk. He could deliver, project. But sermons only have one punchline. The look in Mum's eyes, though: it was intense. She was feeding off it all. Afterwards, as we left, she held my hand very tightly. "I'm so glad you came," she said. "Did you feel it? The energy. Sometimes it makes my hair stand on end."'

'And did you feel it?'

'No, of course not. Still . . .' She glanced over at him. 'I envy the belief, in a way. Do you know what I mean?'

The vestry lay beyond a low door with splintered hinges, a small, damp room furnished with a coat-stand, a bookcase for bibles, more foldaway chairs, and a desk pushed up against the wall. A few framed pictures hung above the desk, reproductions clipped from a book. Most were religious in subject: a few portraits of the Madonna with Child, a Last Supper, Salome with the head of John the Baptist. One showed a figure, half-man and half-goat, bent down over the body of a young girl lying in the field. In the background, the long fingers of the coastline crossed over the length of the estuary. The girl's skin was pale, the flesh tight against the curve of her skull, her forehead, the line of her jaw. A wound scored her throat, another her wrist, the blood trickling on to her bare breasts. The thin material of her dress had been torn open past her belly. It was hard to tell if the satyr had torn her clothes to find the wound, if the girl had done it herself, or if some other, darker act had been disturbed. Only a brown dog watched them, a foxglove curving to the arc of its back. On the sandy banks behind, three more dogs played in the light of the afternoon sun, brought to the shore by the sight of the birds that floated on the water. All the dogs would play until someone called for them. They would seek trails in the beach, mark out territory – and if no one called, they would play forever. Only the brown dog stayed behind, patient and sombre, obeying a word that it didn't understand.

'Come on,' Jenn said. 'We came out here for a reason. You're keeping me waiting and I don't like to wait.'

They walked away from the churchyard, leaving the dead to stare at their allotted portion of sky. But the dead were all about them, dateless and pervasive, the earth and the dust: the ancient permanence of an ancient land. Monkey divided up the pills, and they swallowed them down with mouthfuls of water. The light was slowly draining out of the day. The pills came on slowly. At first, Monkey noticed a slight drag in his retina, a way the shape of one object had of blurring into another, a tree skidding across the turf. The sunset flowed down the sky like lava, the clouds seamed with veins of molten light. Warmth spread from Monkey's stomach. His senses connected almost totally with the outside world, his skin only a thin membrane against the stimulation of the air, colours bursting upon his eyes like they were wet paint. He became obsessed with the feel of Jenn's skin underneath his fingertips.

'I want more,' she said to him. 'I don't think one is going to be enough.'

The wind stirred the feathery heads of the grass, and as Monkey trailed his hand amongst them, they almost pierced his skin. The sun was fading in the west, and the moon was as distinct as a silver disk, its shadow almost raising it from the sky. Drawing a line on the horizon, traffic flew along a distant motorway, the white beam of light resembling the flat-line of a CAT scan. At a small pond, Monkey became entranced by the movement of water. He could see it trembling to his breathing, bright and viscous as oil. It was so tactile, so fascinating, that he went to put his foot against its surface, and Jenn had to pull him back.

'What are you doing?'

'I don't know.'

'It's water.' She was laughing, almost hysterically. 'Can't you see that it's water?'

She reached out for him. He put his arms around her, kissing her mouth, her neck. They fell to he ground. His hands reached under her top, her skin smooth and cool against his hands. She groaned, pushing her jeans past the gentle rise of her hips. They wriggled against each other, the grass cold underneath them, the feel of each other's breath like fingers on the skin, so warm it made you cry. Afterwards, they looked up into the sky. It was a moment that, as you experienced it, made you ache for its passing. The sky was clearing. A wind picked up and blew the shredded clouds away. They waited for the ash of a burned out star.

On the way back to the Mansion, they became lost in the dark. The initial excitement of the pills had receded and was now replaced by a kind of hungry curiosity: the feel of grass on bare skin, the sound of their voices, shrill in the lonely fields, the way a clump of silver birches resembled disinterred bones. They took their time crossing the roads, which seemed to Monkey the width and texture of the Amazon. They had climbed a fence – the Mansion just visible across the next field, the white brick sucking the light down from the stars – when Jenn slipped. Monkey heard her shriek. When he turned around, she was lying flat on the grass.

'Are you OK?'

The dark was fuzzing over his eyes, the whorl of random fingerprints, of static raining over a thousand television screens.

'My back. I think my back's gone.'

'What?'

'I'm not joking. But I'm fairly sure that my back's gone.' She was very calm, almost resigned.

'Damn.' Why that word? he thought.

'Yes,' Jenn said. 'It's not good. You know, I'm not sure I'm going to be able to walk.'

'I don't know . . .' Monkey paused. And drifted. The moment returned. '. . . what I'm supposed to do.'

'Neither do I. Where are we?'

'We've come out near the front of the house.'

'The front of the house.' She bit her lip. 'There's a lot of steps at the front of the house. Not to mention the stairs inside.'

'Right. You're right.'

'Sssh. Monkey. Listen to me.' She reached out and tried to place her hand on his shoulder. She couldn't reach him though, and her fingertips slipped down his arm, a failed sad gesture that died on the silver grass.

'OK.'

'What about the cottage?'

'I don't think that's a good idea.' A feeling like ice began to leak into his stomach.

Jenn continued, oblivious.

'Listen, even if you could lift me, you couldn't get me up the stairs in the Mansion. People are going to start asking questions. I take it you don't want people knowing about the pills.'

'Yes.'

'Then, I don't see what option we have.'

'No.'

'Good.' Jenn folded her hands over her chest. 'I'll just wait here then. I'll wait here for you to come back.'

Monkey struggled to his feet. Jenn lay perfectly still, facing the stars. He was reminded of the picture in the church: the fallen girl and the half-animal man set against an ancient landscape. But what dog could track them down?

Alone now, Monkey wandered back to the house, easily disorientated by the dark fields, the shifting mental topography. Finally, he crossed into the Mansion's gardens, skulking around the edge of the house, the white brick like a searchlight as he headed for the cottage. The weak light of a candle glimmered in the dark panes. He reached out for the door. His hand failed and fell. He looked over at the Mansion. It seemed impossible that it couldn't hide them. He would go back. He would persuade Jenn. They could hide there until morning and then surely, her back would be recovered. The power of dawn to cure such things was very real to him. He was thinking about this when Lucas opened the door.

He didn't say anything, didn't even seem to react to the fact that Monkey was standing in front of him, open-mouthed, surprised.

'I need some help,' Monkey said, eventually.

'Yes?'

'Jenn. You know, the girl from the house. Red hair. Don't know if you've met her.'

'I've met her.'

'She's hurt her back. It's seized up. She's lying in a field just over there.'

'Right.'

'We can't go back to the house. We've . . . I'm a bit fucked to be honest. So is she. We had some pills.'

'OK.'

'I need help. Getting her inside. And we need a place to sleep. She was wondering. That is. I was wondering. Whether we could stay here.'

'Is it far?'

It was a difficult question. Monkey considered it.

'I mean,' Lucas said eventually, 'do I need my coat?'

'No,' Monkey decided. 'No. I think you'll be fine.'

Lucas shut the door behind him, and they headed out to the field, cutting down the blind side of the Mansion, away from the kitchen. They walked side by side. Once, as they climbed over a fence, their arms knocked against each other. The warmth in Monkey's veins, the ache in his groin confused him. 'We took some pills,' he said suddenly.

Lucas didn't look over. 'Yeah. You said.'

'I wanted to get out. I've been stuck in the house for so long. So we took some pills and went for a walk.'

'Right.'

'They were great pills. We fucked on them too. In a field.'

Lucas didn't look over at him. 'Right,' he said. 'Is that how she threw her back?'

'No,' Monkey said. 'She fell over. And it just went. It's a car crash that caused it.'

'Right.'

'I mean it's not like her back just fell apart or anything.'

'No.'

'It had already been injured. That's what I'm saying.'

'Yes. A car crash,' Lucas said. 'That will do it to you. That will hurt.'

It was a relief when they found Jenn. She was still lying in the same part of the field, looking up at the sky. She waved them over as they approached, her voice bright and cheerful in the quiet.

'I'm glad you came back. I was starting to get very cold. I didn't dress for this.'

They managed to lift her to her feet, taking hold underneath her arms.

'I *will* be all right, you know,' she said. 'Don't worry. This has happened before. I just need to lie down on something flat.' She looked over at Lucas. 'I suppose you can help me with that, can't you?'

'There's the floor.'

'Ah. The floor. That sounds ideal. Almost prescribed. Doctor Lucas.'

They began to walk across the field. Jenn was able to rest on their shoulders, but because of the uneven ground, the progress was slow. After his protracted journey to fetch Lucas, Monkey now concentrated on each step, as though walking a tightrope. They took a long detour around the next field, because it would have been impossible to cross the gate. 'Wouldn't it be easier,' Lucas said, after the third time they stopped, 'if we carried you flat on your back? I'd take your arms, Monkey your legs?'

'No, no,' Jenn said, brightly. 'That would be absolute agony, I'm afraid. What I need, is a chariot. Like Boudicca.'

When they finally reached the cottage, Monkey laid Jenn down on the rug by the hearth while Lucas gathered logs and coal from a small pail by the door and began building up the fire. Gradually, the flames illuminated the room.

'Do we need candles?' he asked Monkey.

'I think the fire's enough.'

Jenn glanced between them. 'Do you two know each other? I mean, should I make introductions?'

Monkey hesitated, leaving Lucas to reply. 'We met before.'

'Before the house?'

'Yes,' Monkey said. 'That's right.'

'Oh, you didn't say. Then we're all friends.'

'Yes,' Lucas said. 'All friends.'

'So is it OK if we stay here?'

'The night?'

'Please. I'm not going to be able to get up those stairs.'

'You'll be gone by morning?'

'Of course. That is, we should be. It usually takes a few hours to click back into shape.'

'Then I suppose so. If you can't get up the stairs.'

'We should be honoured,' Jenn said to Monkey. 'Lucas has really done a lot of work to this place. When he moved in here we all thought he was crazy. The place was just a wreck. But he's completely turned it around.' She looked around the room. 'So have you put in a toilet?'

Lucas shook his head. 'Have to go to the house for that. Or the woods.'

'Ah. Like a bear. Or the pope. I forget which one shits in the woods. Anyway, it doesn't matter. I think I pissed myself out there in the field.'

Lucas began to laugh, sitting with his head against the back of a chair. Monkey frowned. 'What?'

'Actually, I'm lying. I *know* I pissed myself out there in the field. But allow a girl to keep her mystery.'

When the door opened and Charley walked inside, Lucas and Jenn were still laughing. For a second everyone stared down upon the situation like it was a fallen mirror: the shattered, haphazard perspectives. Charley recovered first. She leant back against the wall, her arms folded across her chest, her posture defensive, threatened.

'So what's going on here?'

Monkey answered. 'We were just out for a walk. And Jenn fell and slipped her back.'

'He's right,' Jenn said. 'It's gone, I'm afraid.'

'And you?' Charley looked over at Lucas. 'You're involved?'

Lucas shrugged. 'I was called out to help.'

Charley had moved away from the wall, closer to the fire. As she looked down at Monkey, suddenly she erupted.

'Jesus Christ! Look at your eyes. Both of you.'

'Uh oh,' Jenn said. 'Sprung.'

'I don't believe it. I don't believe you could be so stupid.'

'It isn't what you think . . .' Monkey began before Jenn interrupted.

'I think that I ought to tell you. Charley, I have taken some illegal drugs.'

'Jenn . . . !'

'In case something happens. As the responsible adult in this situation, I feel you ought to know.'

'I really, really can't deal with this at the moment.' Charley held her head in her hands. 'I can't believe that you've been so stupid. Do you know what you've done?'

'If you'd just listen . . .'

'I don't want to hear it.' She turned before she walked outside. 'But I'll tell you something, Jenn. If you stay the night with these two, you might find yourself left out.'

The last remark was ugly and corrosive, staining the air after she'd gone. Monkey glanced at Lucas, who shrugged, non-committal and absent. He soon left the room, returning with a couple of blankets which he tossed on to the floor. 'Be careful of the fire. It spits.' With that he headed upstairs; for the rest of the night they could hear him pacing around the room. Monkey laid out the blankets in front of the hearth, and he and Jenn settled down, huddling close together. 'That was so embarrassing,' Jenn whispered. 'Did you see the look on her face when she saw we were in here?'

'I think we might be in trouble.'

'Why? Everyone knows what's going on between them. It's not as if it's a secret.' She moved against him under the blanket. 'And what do you think she meant about me being left out?'

'I don't know. I don't know what she meant.'

It took Charley two weeks to have her revenge. 'Don't forget,' she said to Monkey during what followed, 'you forced me into this. This is your fault.' He tried to explain, telling her that he'd had a few pills left over from the batch he'd taken from Lennox, but she wasn't interested. 'I warned you. I told you what would happen.'

The morning after she had found them in the cottage, she called a house meeting. All of the residents gathered around the kitchen table. Monkey sat with Jenn at the back; Lucas stood near the door, ready to escape once everything had finished. Charley and Robert outlined how they would deal with the extra work for the May festival: how they had planned for a larger stall than normal: selling the cheese, jams and preserves that Robert had prepared throughout the year, as well as fruit and vegetables and Taylor's wine and beer.

'Obviously this is going to mean more work on the garden, so some of us will have to cover a couple of extra weekly shifts.' As the residents started to complain, she began to read out a list of people. Jenn was one of them.

Immediately Jenn put up her hand. 'I won't be able to do that.'

'Why not?'

'My back.' She glanced around the table. 'I don't mind covering anything else, though. I just can't do that.'

Charley shrugged. 'Everything else is covered.'

'But I can't *do* that.'

'Fine. OK.' Charley struck her name from the rota. 'The rest will cover you.'

After the meeting it didn't take much for the residents to turn. They were so alert to inequality, so hungry for intrigue. More came: money missing from the till whenever Jenn was working. Ten, twenty pounds at a time: the figures were irrefutable. Charley added them up. When fifty pounds had vanished, it had gone on for too long.

'Tell me what I'm meant to do?' Charley confronted Jenn in the office, while Monkey tagged along. 'This is the third time that this has happened.'

'I didn't take the money.'

'OK. So you didn't take the money. So you're not a thief. It doesn't explain where the money went.'

Then Monkey blurted out, 'If you're accusing *me* –'

Charley cut Monkey off. 'Who's accusing *you*? Who even asked you to be here? I'm only saying that no one has explained to me where the money has gone. And not just this time.'

She leant back against the desk. 'First there was the incident with your brother. Now there's this. Am I meant to think they're not related?'

'But that's ridiculous!'

'Whatever it is, I'm going to put your membership to a vote. There's a few other issues as well, the distribution of work being one of them. We'll let everyone else decide. I'm sorry it's come to this, but . . .'

Jenn started packing immediately. Monkey tried to persuade her to stay, but she'd made up her mind. 'I'm not giving her the satisfaction,' she said, as she stuffed clothes into a rucksack.

'But people have to vote.'

'Oh please. That lot? Most of them would vote me out just for the fun of it.'

'You don't know that. At least leave it until the morning.'

She sighed. 'Maybe I'll come back in a couple of months when everything has calmed down. To be honest, it's probably for the best. It'll get Mark off my back.'

In the end, after Jenn called home, it was Mark who drove over to collect her. It was past ten by the time he arrived and Monkey spent all that time trying to persuade Jenn to change her mind. It was no use. They said goodbye outside the front door, while Mark waited inside the Mini, staring blankly across at them, a skinny fish illuminated inside an aquarium.

'You'll come over to visit me, yeah?' In front of Mark, Jenn seemed distant. She reached out for Monkey, but it was a tentative gesture, almost reluctant.

'When I can,' he said.

'Make it soon, OK?' It sounded like a threat. Probably Jenn realized: she leant close to him, kissed his neck. 'I'll miss you. You know that, don't you?'

He watched the car disappear down the driveway, the lights sliding into the darkness. The hallway boomed with silence as he walked back up to his room, solitary, but not completely alone. Charley was waiting for him outside his room.

'I take it you're happy now?'

She shook her head. 'No. No, I'm not. I don't take any pleasure in this.'

'Then why do it?'

'What you did was jeopardize everything we've worked for. You threatened my home, my life out here. You should have been the one to leave.' She caught her breath. 'Unfortunately, I need you. That's what it comes down to. So Jenn leaves instead.'

As he lay in his room, with only the trepanned monkey

for company, Monkey could hate Charley, and hate the residents for the easy way they had been turned. He could tell himself that he would stay until he had built up enough pills of his own; he could make this bargain. But he knew that he was as much to blame. He could have told Jenn why she had been singled out, even though it would have meant the end of his stay. By keeping quiet, he was complicit. Whether she knew it or not, Charley had given him a choice. He had chosen the Mansion, because it kept him safe.

14

Keep busy, lose yourself in the tasks, project fear and anxiety into everything around you, and yes, use your whiplash mouth against anyone that interferes: this was how Charley coped with those days. Two weeks before the May festival, she met up with Pete in a pub not far from the Welsh Bridge. He sat over in a far corner, sipping from a Guinness as he looked up at the football match on the big screen. Charley bought a rum and coke and joined him.

'Evening.'

'Evening.'

She gestured to the game. 'Are you winning?'

'My knees are shot. I'm guessing this will be my last season.'

Pete had arranged this meeting at the last market day, buying a bottle of beer from the stall when he'd seen Charley working alone. She'd been worried ever since. He appeared relaxed as they talked, but there was always a ghost of tension haunting his movements: a jig of the leg, a twitch of the mouth; he soon obliterated an empty cigarette pack, tearing it into its constituent parts. Under the low yellow lights, his skin took on the even colour of milky tea. They chatted for a while, wary of an old drinker at the table next to them, who stared at the beer foam sliding down the side of his empty glass. When he left, it was finally time to talk.

'Is everything OK?'

'I've been approached.' Pete paused, took a sip from his beer. 'I won't say much. You don't need to know.'

'OK.'

'I'd like a shipment. A large one. After that, I thought we should maybe bring things to a close.'

'Is there a problem?'

'It's nothing like that. I've had an offer. An offer I want to take.'

'When do you want them?'

'Two weeks.'

'It's short notice.'

'Can you make it?' Pete paused, cleared his throat. 'I mean, "Can they?"'

It appeared that the carefully structured architecture of lies had been designed for her comfort alone.

'I think that should be fine.' She remembered a few early conversations with the Vegan about volume and production. He'd always boasted that he'd intentionally kept everything on a small scale, although the lab was able to produce many, many times the amount.

'Good.' Pete kissed the word out. 'So. Money.'

He named a figure. Charley laughed. 'Oh no. I think we've got friendly over the last few months, Pete, but really . . .' They haggled gently, almost flirtatiously, and the eventual price they agreed upon was a little more than Charley had been hoping for. When it came to the arrangements for the shipment, Pete suggested meeting by the old football ground, during the festival. The day would be stressful enough for Charley, but she'd agreed. Business done, they had a few drinks together, as the football match finished.

'So what will you do?'

'When?'

'After this. Our deal.' She smiled. 'Are you going to be moving up the chain?'

He shook his head. 'I take this offer as being the end of my involvement.' He took a couple of mouthfuls of beer. 'I'm thinking of heading out to somewhere in the Med. Maybe I'll just disappear into the sun. Seems like the best decision you can make these days.'

He was trying to persuade her to come along with him (joking or flirting, she couldn't decide) when the pub door opened and a group of men walked in. The youngest was probably in his mid-thirties, the oldest might have been seventy. All were dressed in uniform: white collarless shirts, long socks and short brown corduroy trousers. They carried blunted cutlasses in their hands. With the festival so close, a lot of groups warmed up for the big event by performing around the town. Choreography was sharpened, routines perfected, nerves allayed. As the leader tapped time with two wooden pins, the dancers hopped into steps, and clashed their swords. Most people ignored them, but, along with a few others, Pete started clapping time.

'It's still the dance,' he grinned, as Charley glanced over at him, questioning, amazed. 'You've got to love the dance.'

As Charley walked back to the car, she thought about how her attitudes to the festival had changed. While most of the rituals had been subsumed by commerce – the great bonfire that had once burned on Beck's Hill had been replaced by fireworks – for the town it was still the most important date of the whole year. There was a flower show for local producers, a music festival for local talents, an arts and crafts fair, as well as a large market. At first Charley had hated the crowds and the drain of extra work. She had looked upon the whole weekend with a little bit of amazement. One festival was the same as another: you saw the same stalls, the same people. But over the years, something changed. She began to anticipate that time of year, work towards it, make plans. In her mind, the festival became linked with the Mansion, and she became a part of it. The build-up, the hard work, the preparation: the tradition excited her.

After the meeting with Pete, the idea of heading back to the house, finishing off chores and heading to bed didn't really appeal. The house was quiet as she pulled up ouside. She drove slowly, letting the vehicle come to rest on the wide part of the drive, near the front steps. She let herself out, locked up the van, and began walking quickly across the front lawn, towards the cottage. It was a moody eveing, monochrome, phosphorescent. She let herself in through the front door and called out Lucas's name. With no answer, she climbed the stairs. She'd seen him only a couple of times since the night he'd sheltered Jenn and Monkey. She'd tried to interrogate him, but Lucas had refused to be drawn. 'I don't see why you're so upset about it,' he'd said. 'I don't know what the problem is.'

Waiting for him now, she rolled a cigarette, and smoked it lying on the bed. A little bored, the short walk for something to occupy her attention led her to Lucas's desk. The drawer was already half open, which, as she replied to the timid voice of conscience, was no way to keep a secret. The diary was a red school exercise book, upon which Lucas had scrawled a huge pattern of interlocking circles. Charley opened it at the first page.

'Over the last few years I think I missed a lot of things. A lot of it passed me by. I don't think that's right. If I'm going to use this time for anything, it's got to be to make sense of what has happened.' There followed a short rant about the Vegan, 'Sad, pretentious, dry. Manic, desperate attention to these acquired beliefs and experiences to make up for personality deficiencies. Tossing dirt into a hole.' So far, so good. Charley felt a thrill of complicity, and started on the next page.

A memory. Not really the first thing I want to write about, but the first thing that occurs. Especially now, being out here, in this cottage in the middle of the country. Close to the land. I write that with a smile on my face, but I actually think I mean it. It has done something to me. The sound of the forest at night. This is the first time I have ever been scared of the dark and the fear is like a buzz.

Anyway.

Once, on acid, I wandered away from the group. It was at a party out in Cambridge. We had driven out into the country. I'd been invited along by a girlfriend. I was happy to be there, to be part of the crowd of beautiful people. They were so assured. There was no doubt. It didn't occur. It was like a figment, another country, something you hear other people talking about but never experience for yourself. Because of this, they were very dull. I think I admire self-doubt above anything else. It shows true bravery. It means that you are truly ready to question everything about the world.

It was a long night. One of them had scored some liquid acid. There was coke too and some black hash, runny like molasses. It was like a picnic. I don't know if it was the combination. The acid was very strong. (Strange, even to name the drugs these days seems like an act of nostalgia, acutely embarrassing. Everything is in the past. It comes at you like a shark, mouth open, eyes dead, never stopping. The person you were disappears. You are erased.) But I lost it. Nothing before or since comes close to what I experienced that night.

I wandered off by myself. They'd set up tents, built a huge campfire. Someone had even brought a stereo. I'm surprised there wasn't a fridge. I couldn't cope with it all. I needed a bit of peace. The music was too loud, the people too much. Away from them, the moonlight and stars, the light of the galaxy, reflected upon the landscape like it would on a mirror. It was incredible. I became convinced that this was a new world, one that only I had set foot in. I wandered around, seeing things clearly, as though for the first time. I think I actually hugged a tree. I became amazed by the way it connected to the sky, the way the trunk receded into branches, the branches into twigs, and the stars shattered from those twigs, part of it almost, like the structure of a lung. The landscape a kind of pure hallucination, natural forms assuming impossible shapes. It was a pure kind of life, life as total, overwhelming experience, so very, very beautiful.

I want to get it down. I want to describe what it was like. But I can't, precisely because I keep tripping over myself. Limits of vocabulary, maybe, accuracy of description. But how do you describe a moment when you as 'I' have been totally removed. 'I' was irrelevant. World a kind of pure objectivity and 'I' was only a part of it. All I can do now is string the words together and worry if they are accurate or, even worse, parodies. Because you can't even describe these things. They are ridiculous and they are lost.

I came back to that party and no one understood. My girlfriend had moved on to coke. Sniff sniff through a rolled fiver, off a copy of The End of History. *There in the middle of the country, it seemed obscene to me. I mean that literally. I told her about it. It became very important that I take her with me, out into this new world, and I tried to persuade her. She didn't want to come. I think I*

*made some kind of scene. I remember talking. I remember
everyone watching me. I think I was lecturing them. How
they were missing the point of the drugs. That they weren't
games to play with, these experiences, they were lives in
themselves.*

*The morning after we all left together. We ate breakfast
in a motorway café, lorry drivers and travelling salesmen
staring at us because we managed to waltz through the
whole meal as though everything was some comedy laid
out only for us. Place mats and menus and knives and
forks and plastic squeezy tomatoes for ketchup. All of it
was a joke that only we could see. These people . . . their
whole lives were like that for us, as though secretly filmed
with added laughter track. Irony. It is the antithesis of self-
doubt. An easy embrace of everything, and because of
this, it is the first step to total self-loathing.*

Charley smiled at her reflection in the glass, savouring the
reflexive conspiracy. She flicked a few pages before she
carried on reading.

'The other night I found a millipede on the toilet bowl,'
the section began, and continued in a similar vein, so
wilfully intellectual and despairing and *male*.

*I watched it for nearly an hour. It crawled around the rim,
coiling and uncoiling, covering the same track. Didn't know
where it was. Not understanding the land it was in. A new
territory. Bare and white and cold. Almost like a perfect
snowfall. Eventually, I decided to save it, pick it out of its
confusion. It took me a while to pin the thing down.
Finally I got it on the end of my finger. Walked through to
the front door. Opened the door. Suddenly, I realized that
it wouldn't matter, so I crushed the millipede on my thumb.
And now I write this, because I'm lonely and bored. And*

tonight, not even Charley will come scratching at my door.'

She stopped reading. Well, what did you expect? she asked herself. Don't read a diary if you don't want to know what a person thinks.

Depression. Lying around the cottage. Tried to read but the words buzzed around the paper. I paid more attention to the gaps between the words than the words themselves. These empty days: I don't know how to describe them. As though there is some kind of activity that I'm missing, one that doesn't even exist. What is it like to live in a time when your power has no channel? Do you innovate, seek out some substitute? Or do you drift, out of sync with the times?

Charley equals broken power. Her type of failure fascinates me. I only take pleasure in watching her malice whip out like a snake, whoever standing nearest taking the fangs. And the only place that she has found to thrive is out here, on the edge of things. Nowhere. The blank white stone of an abandoned house. You'll find it between a couple of villages even the inhabitants have forgotten. A place that is nothing but a figment, a delusion.

Last night she came around again. She seems to want me more and more. I say this without arrogance. You can smell it on her, it comes off in waves. It's intriguing watching a woman grow old like this. To be the last bit of vitality that she rubs against. She is so conscious of fading, so vocal about it. But it's an act of denial. It's like a magic spell. She talks about getting old and turns it into words. The words are out there, outside of her, but they don't connect with her. They are abstract. Alien. They don't mean anything.

191

She tells me that she feels she is intensely attractive to other men. She says that when she walks into a room she knows that most of them, all of them, would sleep with her. She says it gives her a feeling of power. She misses the point. Men will sleep with anything. I wonder if she does it on purpose. Even intelligent people succumb to the comfort lie. Sometimes, when I put my face to her cunt I only feel disgust . . .

Charley didn't hear the back door open, or the footsteps in the room underneath. The boards of the stairs brought her around, the dreadful shrieking of tired, ancient wood. A few things went through her mind, and one of them, strangely, was fear. Even so, she remained seated at the desk with the book open on her lap, and it was with, she hoped, defiance, that she stared at Lucas as he walked into the bedroom.

'Evening. How are you?'

He was shocked to see her, shocked and angry that she was sitting at his desk. She saw it in a burst of blackness in his eyes: a black circular mouth of a seabed hugging fish.

'Fine. I'm fine.'

'Been out for a walk?'

'That's right. I've been having trouble sleeping.'

'Perhaps it's guilt.'

'Or paranoia.' His jaw was set, his mouth thin. 'But then, apparently not.'

He moved towards the desk by the window: the doorway was open to her. 'The other night,' he said. 'I was out there and I found a rabbit, a baby rabbit in the grass. A fox must have got it. Maybe one of the dogs. There was a tooth hole near its neck. But it was still alive. Did I tell you this already?'

'No, you didn't.'

'That's right. I thought that it would upset you. Anyway, I'd heard that animals like that died as soon as they were taken. The heart beats so fast that the shock kills them. But this little thing had lived through the trauma. A survivor.'

'Is this going somewhere, because really, Lucas, if you're going to play the same games as you do with Taylor . . .'

'Who knows, maybe I could have saved it. Fed it with milk, shared my body warmth. But it was late and I was tired. What could I do? The fire had gone out. There were no logs left. To get more, I would have had to come over to the Mansion. I just wanted to go to bed. I didn't plan on lifesaving.'

'Now I see. I'm the rabbit. This is a threat.'

'Not a threat. But yes, I broke its neck. It didn't take much. Gripped it with two hands. Crack. The flicker of current in the nerves and it was gone. It's crazy, don't you think? That a life can be that meaningless. Something you dispense with because you won't walk across a field to fetch a log. But these things have to be done. I wonder . . . do you understand that? They have to be done.'

Charley didn't glance or look or spy. She watched him, openly, silently, as she would a film: the violence of subtle movement, the trick of the light.

'Will you write it down?' She pressed her palm against the diary, the easiest weapon. 'Try to make sense of it? Like your night with your friends?'

'I wasn't going to write it down. But I will, if you want. We can turn our relationship into that. You can come to the empty house and read the diary. I'll put messages in it, just for you.'

'That doesn't appeal to me.'

'I suppose not.' Lucas's face betrayed no thought or emotion but it was a mask of sinister vapidity, a cruel emptiness. 'I always wanted to ask you,' he started, but paused and cleared his throat, and it was a little bit theatrical. 'I wanted to ask you because you're a woman of lots of men. When the way you feel about a particular man changes: has that happened when the man has actually been inside you?

'It occurred to me the last time we spent the night together,' Lucas went on. 'Halfway through, you were on top of me, I remember. You were very good. You performed. But suddenly, I realized that I felt nothing. It was very odd. To lose the taste for sex with someone. But that's what it is like for men. For women, I'm not sure.' They stared at each other. 'Violence, is what I mean. I imagine it must feel more like violence.'

'They are never really inside you,' Charley replied. 'You were never really inside me.'

She threw the book on to the bed and hurried downstairs. Outside, the night came to meet her with smells of wet earth and leaves. She hurried into it, panting in the cold, the damp grass whipping at her jeans. When she reached the kitchen, she found Taylor passed out on the floor, a small cut on his forehead, an empty bottle of white rum discarded upon the table. The yellow greyhound kept watch. Because she needed someone to be close to, she tried to wake him, calling his name and slapping at his face. Eventually, she'd shoved a bucket underneath the taps, letting the cold water hammer out full blast. As the water level rose, she glanced up into the black glass of the kitchen window: the lonely and scared woman who stared back only accused. She looked away. With the bucket full, she hefted it out of the sink, staggered a couple of paces to stand directly over Taylor's head. The yellow greyhound had moved to the edge of the kitchen, whimpering softly. She tipped the bucket, preparing to shock Taylor from his dream. 'This is it,' she told herself, as the water fell. 'This is it, for ever.'

15

Three months, three weeks, four days. With Jenn gone, evenings were long and lonely so one night, Monkey headed down to the living room to spend an hour or so on the edge of the Mansion. A fire crackled in the hearth. Smoke from cigarettes and green marijuana hung in the air. The final scenes of an old colour Western played on the TV: Joan Crawford fleeing from the flaming torches of an angry mob. Disputes over territory, sexual longing and bad blood had finally led to this flashpoint, this climax. The white hotel, the first building in what would soon become a prosperous new town, burned to the ground.

'The hunger of the pack,' Andrew said from his perch of the chaise longue. 'That's the message. McCarthy witch-hunts and mob rule. Let loose, it will turn civilization to ash.'

Monkey left for the kitchen, and stole one of Taylor's beers. He sat drinking it at the kitchen table, while leafing through a calendar advertising a brand of chicken feed. Three months, three weeks, four days: Monkey worked out how long he had been insulated from Herointown. Days of chemistry and Jenn, of power struggles and recovery. And soon, those days would be gone.

The day before, Charley had visited the lab. The three of them faced each other under the electric light: the

Vegan by the shelves, Monkey slumped against the metal table, Charley leaning back against the locked door. Her voice was clear and piercing in the confines of the narrow room.

'There's been a change of plan.'

The Vegan cleared his throat. 'What change of plan?'

'I had a meeting with our dealer, earlier in the week. He's asked for a larger shipment. Significantly larger.'

She named the amount involved, adding that they would need to produce the pills within two weeks. The Vegan scowled. 'That's absurd. There's no way –'

Charley cut in like a blade. 'Of course you can make it. You've told me yourself that this place can produce far more than we're doing at the moment. So, we produce more.'

Caught out by his own mouth, the Vegan began to babble. Charley cut him off again.

'Anyway, it's not up for discussion. It's a significant amount of money, which I can't afford to turn down. If we don't make this shipment, then I really don't see the point of continuing. We may as well stop the whole thing right here.'

'And after this deal,' the Vegan asked. 'What then?'

'We'll see where we stand. But I guess we'll go back to the smaller quantities.'

He nodded. Monkey almost thought he looked relieved. 'Then I guess I can't say no.'

'So.' Charley turned to Monkey. 'The upshot is that, after this, we won't be needing you any more.'

He didn't say anything. He didn't even look at her, only stayed slumped against the table, picking at the sleeve of his tracksuit top. He'd been partly expecting this. With Jenn removed, his presence in the Mansion had become unstable, the sand shifting under his feet.

The Vegan spoke up. 'Do you think that's wise?'

Monkey could almost have cheered at the recurrence of *this* particular irony. Faced with admitting that he had no control over the lab, the Vegan had been forced to defend Monkey's version of how he'd come by the pills. While he was more attentive around the lab, he hadn't asked Monkey to return the duplicate key.

'Of *course*, it's wise. The way he's behaved over the past months . . .'

'He already explained about that.'

'I don't *care* what he's explained. I don't really care that it'll slow down production. He's not staying.'

It was final. Butch Vegan had failed to save the Monkey kid.

'One thing . . .' the Vegan continued as Charley moved towards the door. 'I want to come with you on the day. When you sell the pills, I want to be there.'

'Why?'

'I just think it's wise, that's all.'

'Worried that I won't be able to cope?'

'Yes, actually. I'm guessing that there's a lot of money changing hands. Don't forget that some of it is mine.'

Grudgingly, Charley agreed. After she left, the Vegan spent the whole morning complaining: about her shortsightedness, her hunger for power, the pressures that he had to work under, the total ingratitude that came his way. They worked until eight. Monkey spent the rest of the day in his room, avoiding the rota, wondering if Charley would send someone to hunt him down. He was left alone, however, and that evening, he called Jenn to give her the news. Rather than breaking off contact, as he'd feared, she'd called three or four times a week. 'Charley's started on you too?' she said when he told her that he would be leaving soon.

'I guess so.'

'Oh the irony.' She laughed drily. 'Looks like you'll be heading back to town sooner than you thought. You know I always wanted it. I just didn't expect it to be so permanent.'

'It's nothing to do with you. I'll tell you about it later.'

'Well, I'm sorry if it was. Are you worried?'

'I'm OK.'

'Things will be different this time. We'll make them different, I swear.'

For the next two weeks the other residents ignored Monkey, and he, in turn, stopped pretending to ingratiate himself. He worked with the Vegan, he took meals alone, he enjoyed bad novels and cigarettes on his camp bed, appreciating the last spell in his room. Bored with that, he would take long walks in the woods, simulating his escape. Spring bloomed. Above him, green flames trickled along the branches of the trees. Summer was waiting to explode.

On the last morning before the festival, there were no flags or ceremonies, no fireworks or rewards. He woke up and walked out to the outhouse. The Vegan arrived an hour later and spent most of the morning picking through magazines, while Monkey put the finishing touches to the batch. They finished early, and parted in front of the outhouse, with barely a goodbye. Monkey headed around the back of the house, past the gardens which had been harvested in preparation for the festival, past the Tony Blair scarecrow standing over a section of empty beds. He performed a full, lazy circuit. The Vegan's car had disappeared along the drive. Monkey walked back to the outhouse and let himself in. Working quickly, he opened up the freezer and pulled out the plastic bag containing the latest batch of pills, and counted out fifty. These he sealed into a small bag, which he slipped into his back pocket;

resealing the main batch of pills, he put them back in the freezer. After checking the lab one more time, he turned off the lights and walked outside.

As Monkey had turned to lock the door, he didn't see Lucas approach. Suddenly, his voice cut across the morning quiet.

'You're up early.'

Monkey turned to see him standing by the corner of the outhouse. Lucas was leaning against the wall, dressed in the green parka, his blue jeans drenched from the grass. A finger scratched idly at lichen on red brick.

'That's right,' Monkey said.

'I heard about your friend.' His smile was thin and humourless, as though he knew that a joke had been played upon the world, but that it was a bad joke, predictable and misjudged. 'Bit of an overreaction. Seeing as all she did was hurt her back.'

'There were other things going on.'

'I'll bet. All that time you spend over here, for example. Doing what you do.'

As Lucas stood in front of him, looking to gain power the way he always had, it occurred to Monkey that he wouldn't have cared about that night if he hadn't associated it with heroin. Whether this was true or not, he couldn't say. It was an easy release. Perhaps this was the reason he had allowed such a vacuum into his life: to eat up mistakes and digressions, to consume regret, memory and pain, to swallow a whole life. Never to have to face up to the things he had done: perhaps that had always been the need.

'I'm leaving tomorrow,' he said. 'None of this really matters to me.'

'You've been removed too? So what *were* you doing?'

Monkey hesitated. 'You can find that out for yourself.

But I'd be careful. I don't think things are going to work for this place.'

'Why should that bother me?'

'With me gone, I think they're going to be looking for someone else to blame.'

He let the sentiment hang, turned his back and walked away. Upstairs in his room, he retrieved his collection of pills from under the floorboards, and packed it up in his rucksack. He spent the day as he would any other, even deciding to return to the rule of a rota that would soon mean nothing to him. He fed the goats, and washed up after the evening meal. Rather than heading for the living room, he walked up to the deepest corner of the third floor, where Jenn had led him that time. Monkey let himself out on to the roof, and, underneath the cloud-covered stars, he smoked cigarettes looking down upon the landscape. As the wind whistled across the parapet, he built the streets of Herointown in his mind.

The next morning everything was bright and hot and it was suddenly 6 a.m. Charley woke the house, knocking on doors, charging along the corridors with the dogs. Monkey could hear them down on the second floor: yapping, whining, barking, excited by the rebellion, as normally they would not be allowed beyond the stairs. After he'd dressed and packed – he sat on his camp bed. Despite the damp, the lack of furniture, his monkey partner on the wall, it felt as if he was leaving something important behind. He concentrated upon the stillness, that singular sound which all rooms have: the vibration of air between four unique walls. This quiet had always felt eloquent and fleeting to him, like music written for his recovery.

Eventually, he shouldered his rucksack and walked out. Downstairs, he found the kitchen already busy. Robert had woken at five, and started cooking a preparatory break-fast, a huge Spanish omelette and fried field mushrooms, served with lots and lots of coffee. The morning was a small festival in itself, everyone tired, red-eyed, a little edgy, but still excited about the day. After breakfast, Charley and Taylor organized groups, and everyone set about load-ing the van. It took nearly an hour, packing the boxes of fruit and vegetables, roping the trestle tables to the roof rack. Charley ticked off an inventory until everything was accounted for.

Monkey rode in the back of the van, crushed by a card-board pallet of vegetables. Every metre of road that trailed behind the back window, every second they travelled brought him closer and closer to Herointown. A few familiar land-marks appeared: the red plastic and blue glass of the ten-screen cinema, a dilapidated warehouse. And then came the first heroin landmark, a road he had walked once through a slush-filled December, on his way to sell a bag filled with stolen meat, the acquisition of which he no longer remembered. Later, the van brought him past a disused service station where he'd once smoked heroin. He remembered the way the sunlight had woken him in the morning, coming in through the cracked wooden boards over the window. The first moment of wakefulness returned to him, that groggy innocence when you couldn't really recall where you were, or what you were doing. And then it came to you: you were a space for the need, a hole to be filled, an absence in the shape of a drug-skinny man, and the course of the next twenty-four hours would be the pro-cess by which you would make yourself whole. As Mon-key watched the town grow around him, these thoughts lingered. Marked out by his hunger and loss, those streets charted the network of his heart.

16

Calling themselves Woman and the Chieftain, later they would decorate any number of the town centre pubs. 'Woman fetch drink,' the Chieftain would say, from whatever corner he had chosen to occupy. 'Chieftain much drunk.' Now, they sat placidly on a bench in the market square. Taylor watched the attentive, intimate preening they performed upon one another: straightening tassels on the fake straw skirts, smoothing the feathers of head-dresses, touching up the horrid comedy of their mouths. The Chieftain had done without the pair of coconut shells which barely covered Woman's low-slinging bosom. As she bent forward, applying the bright white and red grease-paint to the Chieftain's lips, Taylor was treated to a sight which broke taboo. The Chieftain glared over, his eyes displaying a stark, blue cruelty amidst the black face paint. Taylor looked away as the woman began to reattach the fake bone to the Chieftain's nose.

By eleven o'clock, the stall still hadn't seen many customers. Mostly, people stopped to browse before heading towards the gardens by the river, where the funfair had been set up. The majority of the residents had been given the day off as a reward for the labour over the previous weeks; of those working the stall, most passed the quiet time with a game of cards while one person looked after the till. Only Monkey carried on working for the whole morning, always looking for work even when there was very little to be done. Taylor had expected him to leave as soon as they pulled up into the town; Monkey had brought his rucksack, and Charley had made it clear that he had spent his last night in the house. When he'd asked if he could work for some cash in hand, Taylor had agreed. He felt a little sorry for the way Monkey had been treated, so he wanted this last generosity to be the act upon which they parted.

Once Woman and the Chieftain moved away, Taylor was deprived of a way of passing the time. More than anything in the world, he would have liked a beer, but he'd promised Charley that he'd stay sober at least until all the work had been done. To satisfy some kind of fix, he sneaked across the square to a stall selling pork roasts. He ordered two rolls with apple sauce and returned to the stall, where Monkey was moving beer crates. 'Going-away present,' Taylor said, offering the white paper bag. 'My treat.'

They pulled up a couple of beer crates and ate sitting side by side. More people had drifted into the market square, families with children, teenagers in groups, as well as a few more people in costume: a couple of clowns, a Marcel Marceau, two women who made up the bisected parts of a pantomime horse. 'Listen,' Taylor said, breaking off to finish the last remains of a mouthful. 'I wanted to say . . . I know it hasn't been easy. But, well, Charley and I . . . That is . . .'

Monkey almost choked on his roll. 'Are you trying to thank me?'

'Whatever else happened, you put a lot of work in.'

'Not sure anyone else feels the same.'

'I believe in gratitude,' Taylor said. In front of him, an old man ambled past, aimless and forlorn, the bells of his jester costume chiming with every step. 'I'm the last of a dying breed.'

The Vegan headed over to the Mansion during early afternoon. A tailback at one of the main roundabouts slowed him down, but he was too preoccupied to notice the delay. He spent the whole journey brooding upon the day ahead, driving almost on autopilot. From the moment that he'd learned about this pill deal, he'd been suspicious of Charley's motives. He felt marginalized, and this disturbed him: his plans for the Mansion had been clouded. Soon the view of the town's outskirts – the bowling alley, ice rink, cinema, the retail parks – were replaced by fields. The uncertainty continued to gnaw at him. It may be time to reveal a few things.

Charley had warned him to be discreet when he came to the house, as the place wasn't completely empty: Lucas had stayed behind. The Vegan almost delighted in driving slowly up the drive, letting the car roll gently over the grass towards the outhouse. He left the door open as he walked inside, and set about packing the shipment of pills into a large, shapeless canvas holdall. When he heard footsteps behind him, he wasn't surprised to see Lucas standing at the door.

'So this is it, then? The big secret.' Lucas stepped through the door, approaching around the metal table.

'I thought you must have had an idea that something was happening.'

'What is it?' He took in the equipment on the table, the chemicals in jars. 'A lab?'

'That's right.'

'For what?'

'Well, let's just say we've been securing a future for this place.'

'A future?'

'It's all part of the plan. The lab. You being here. It's all connected.'

Lucas scowled. 'What do you want from me?' he said, finally.

'What do you mean?'

'You keep on coming around. Always hinting at something, but never really saying what you want.'

The hostility confused the Vegan. He tried to retain his poise. 'You impressed me. I liked your mind.'

'"Liked my mind."' Lucas drummed his fingers on the metal table. 'You see, I don't even think you know what you want. From me or anyone.'

A group of performers had set up a stage near the market hall. Four men, with wooden swords, tasselled masks and a sadly made papier-mâché dragon – their speeches soon echoed over the crowd.

> I am St George the bravest man
> With blazing sword I stalk the land
> Dragons I've killed and gryphons slain
> I made away with the Queen of Spain.

By now, the stall was doing good trade. They'd almost sold out of the sandwiches and beer, Robert's preserves had been popular and even the supplies of fresh fruit and vegetables were dwindling. But it all made for a stressful day: Taylor had hardly any help in managing the workers on the stall as Charley was distracted, irritable, brooding on the meeting with the dealer. Monkey had proved to be the most reliable worker, always moving, always busy. Taylor needed a break, and when a pregnant woman bought a box of mixed fruit, he saw an opportunity to get away. As he followed the woman through the square – she wanted to store the box in her car before heading down to the funfair – they passed the stage. By now, a large crowd had gathered. The fight between St George and the dragon ended quickly, the dragon despatched by a meaty thrash of a sword. Another performer pushed to the front of the stage: dressed in crude chain mail, with an old woman's hat topped by a cone of silver foil.

Here am I, the Turkish knight
In desert wars I learned to fight
I'll send St George to meet his God
I'll pierce his body, spill his blood

The Vegan had been explaining why he'd arranged for Lucas to move to the Mansion, when Lucas interrupted him.

'You did me a favour. And I appreciate it.'

'It was part of a plan.' He cleared his throat. 'I put you here for a reason.'

He started to explain that Lucas would only be the first of a number of people – students and activists – who would come to the Mansion. The speech should have felt like a release, but even as the Vegan spoke, the impetus fell from his words, as though his imagination had suddenly been exhausted, and the words failed him.

'To learn what?' Lucas was almost deliberately obstructive. 'What do you expect them to learn?'

In reply, the Vegan told Lucas how he saw people coming to the Mansion to experiment with drugs and art, and how these experiments would go on to forge a new kind of politics. Automatic writing, experimental film and 'happenings': he described to Lucas a terrorism based upon aesthetics, exploring hidden areas of the human mind. The people who came to the Mansion would be sent out into the world, part of a global force seeking to undermine, to persuade and to disturb. Hidden, largely forgotten, *clandestine*: the Mansion would become central precisely because it had been left behind. A time of remission, the Vegan said, was as instructive as time spent travelling: think of Gramsci or Bunyan in their prison cells, or even (why not?) Bin Laden in his Torah Borah cave. Some people thought that the perspective of the world had shifted: not London, not even Europe, old or new, was important any more. 'I do not believe this,' the Vegan said. 'Our dreams can effect the changes. And the Mansion will help us.'

Lucas stared at him. It was a clear look of total, uncomprehending, amazement. 'I don't know what to say.'

'I thought you'd approve.'

He shook his head. 'I don't approve. I think it's crazy.'

'Crazy?'

'What else do you expect me to say?' He took a step back towards the table. 'I mean, what were you thinking?'

'But . . . Wait a minute.' The Vegan felt confused, anxious.

'Jesus Christ, I came here to recover. It wasn't part of some scheme.'

The Vegan scratched at the skin of his neck. 'I think you're ignoring how much time I've spent with you over the year,' he said. 'How much I've taught you . . .'

'How much you've *taught* me?' Lucas scowled. 'What the hell are you talking about?'

People of this noble town
Now you'll see me mourn.
I have hacked down the brave Turk
Like the harvest corn.

For a Doctor I beseech you
A Doctor must be found

To heal a brave knight
Of a dolorous wound.

The Turk lay stretched out at the very front of the stage.
The crowd bayed in approval. But St George only begged
for a doctor to help revive his enemy. On the way back
from the car park, Taylor had stopped to watch the play.
He stood behind two men at the very edge of the crowd.
Cashing in the silver of his years, one of them provided a
commentary.

'Of course, if you really want to know, this lot have
taken it completely out of context.' Like all experts, he
sounded bored. 'These plays were the remains of winter
rituals. Struggle, death and resurrection: it's all there. When
people thought that everything was dying, the rituals were
a way of bringing on new life. Originally, that meant human sacrifice – the failing king offered in return for bounty
– but no community could survive with that kind of system. The king was substituted for a fool, but eventually,
over time, it was considered too much to kill even a fool.
Play was introduced. The rituals became drama.' He gestured towards the Turkish knight, who hinted at his coming resurrection by scratching his nose. 'He's a sacrifice. A
symbolic sacrifice by a community to bring about the
spring.'

By the time Taylor headed back to the stall, Magalene
was nowhere to be seen. 'She said she had to meet a friend,'
Monkey explained. 'She said to say she'll see you tomorrow.'
A long line of customers was waiting. Wearily, Taylor
moved behind the till. On the other side of the square, a
man in a white cape took to the stage, his face obscured by
a fringe of tassels attached to a stovepipe hat.

Here am I, a Doctor of Physick
Friend to the fallen, aid to the sick

I have a little tincture, a reviver of men
A mixture of honey, curled dock, bitumen.
To his hurt I'll apply it, to his lips, to his eyes
I'll say, 'Come awake knight, return to us, rise.'

Lucas spent a long time explaining where everything had gone wrong. He was animated now, more animated than the Vegan had seen him in a long time. He paced the floor, once he even kicked out at the metal table. The Vegan had bored him, he said. All the talk, the frustration: it had all been tedious. Lucas had only ever come to him for drugs. He'd always been mystified by the talks, the offers, the endless recommendations. And as for his plans for the Mansion: couldn't he see it was ludicrous, divorced from reality. 'You're completely deluded,' he said. 'If you think that's why I came here, you're completely insane.'

As the Vegan listened, his thoughts were unclear. For a second there was a white spot of violence within the blur. The chest freezer, the lonely house, the outhouse with a lock for which he had a key: an intricate plan burst into his mind like a firework, but faded just as quickly. In the end, he turned his back and stared at the wall until Lucas left. He waited before heading back to the car, hefting the bag to his shoulder to test its weight.

The air felt clear and pure as he walked outside. By now, Lucas was level with the house. The Vegan breathed deeply, filling his lungs with the air, hoping to be calmed. When he reached the car, he stowed the canvas bag in the boot, and let himself into the front seat. Before starting off, he rolled himself a spliff and sparked it, looking out at the sedate landscape out of the windscreen, the swollen belly of the land. He needed music, and, after rooting around the floor of the car, he found a tape of Gaya trance, and placed it in the stereo. The music intensified as he passed Lucas walking across the grass towards the cottage. Lucas didn't look over at the sound of the car. The Vegan smoked his spliff, probing at the situation in his mind. In that shapeless canvas bag, he carried the future of the Mansion; he imagined himself absconding with the pills, and destroying the whole commune with this magnificent act. This plan distracted him as he reached the road, offering a pleasant diversion.

But the dream soon failed. A few minutes later, trawling gently through one of the narrow roads that snaked behind the Mansion, the trance accelerated over the stereo and he'd almost finished the spliff. He'd started feeling a little more at peace when he looked up and saw a police car in the rear-view mirror. It came from nowhere and was suddenly and irrefutably *there*. The Vegan stubbed the spliff out, unwound the window and threw the butt on to the road. Paranoia exploded: he imagined the police stopping to check on what he'd thrown away. 'Stupid, stupid,' he hissed at his reflection in the rear-view mirror. 'I really must stay calm.'

Stan Laurel. Charles II. A Routemaster painted bright green. Las Vegas Elvis. Bugs Bunny. Scooby Doo. *'Everywhere we go, everywhere we go . . .'* A float bearing the local scout group. The Grim Reaper. Eric Cantona. Henry VIII. Groucho Marx. Humphrey Bogart. A float for the football team. *'People always ask us, people always ask us . . .'* A float for the fire service. Flash Gordon and a female Emperor Ming. Another Las Vegas Elvis. A gang of at least twenty Freddie Flintoffs all with the same beaten cardboard mask. *'Who we are, who we are . . .'* Daffy Duck. Shaggy. Osama bin Laden. The Lone Ranger. Freddy Krueger. Abba, all of them. A float for a major high street supermarket. *'And where we come from, and where we*

come from. . .' Jordan and Peter. Posh and Becks. Rod
Hull and Emu. Darth Vader. James Dean. Pamela Ander-
son (male) and David Hasselhoff (female). *'And we tell
them, and we tell them . . .'* Jesus Christ. God. Merlin.
King Arthur. Bill Clinton. Prince Charles. Tony Blair and
Gordon Brown dressed as cavemen. Captain Caveman.
Captain America. Captain Kidd. Captain Kirk. Mr Spock.
Dr Watson. Sherlock Holmes. *'We're from Amwythig,
we're from Amwythig . . .'* A float for the local hospital. A
float for a major high street building society. Free pens.
Free cardboard hats. Free card wallets. Free goodie bags.
'Mighty, mighty Amwythig, mighty mighty Amwythig . . .'
Jimmy Saville smoking a big fat cigar.

'How much is your apple juice?'

An old man stood opposite Taylor, his lips pursed into
fine vertical wrinkles like notches of every year he had
been disappointed.

'It's £1.50 a glass.'

'Ridiculous.' What little remained of his lips contracted
even further. 'I won't pay.'

Taylor took a deep breath. 'There's a shop open . . .' he
began, but the old man cut him off.

'It's all organic, these days. Seems like a very convenient
way of bumping up the price.'

Their eyes met over the rows of bottled beer. Taylor
didn't know whether to break one open to drain its contents, or crack one over the old man's skull. The old man
pointed along the stall.

'And how much do you think you're charging for a jar
of that jam?'

'Oggy oggy oggy . . .' Michael Jackson. Dracula. Oliver
Cromwell. A group of children dressed as fire sprites. *'Oi,
oi, oi . . .'* A samba band. The real live, actual Alvin Star-
dust, invited to judge a talent contest. Luke Skywalker.

Cardinal Wolsey. Another Las Vegas Elvis. William Shakespeare. Groucho Marx. Marilyn Monroe. The Krankies. George Bush. '*Oggy* . . .' Snow White and the Seven Dwarfs. Men and women in white yoghurt pot costumes. '*Oi* . . .' A float emblazoned with the logo of the local dairy plant. Frankenstein's monster. '*Oggy* . . .' An American footballer. The Pink Panther. Mickey Mouse. '*Oi* . . .' The Beatles. A man dressed as a fox. A woman dressed as an owl. A man dressed in green, head to foot in green, with leaves in his hair. '*Oggy oggy oggy* . . .' Superman, Wonder Woman and Spiderman at different corners of the market square, like superheroic security. '*Oi oi oi* . . .' C3PO consoling Oliver Hardy: both of them drunk and hopelessly alone.

The Vegan controlled his fear. He couldn't hear sirens, the car hadn't moved towards him: these were all good things. The main road was still a couple of miles away, but only a couple of miles. He took deep breaths. The police weren't following him: he was sure of it. He was in control. Five minutes later, he'd hit the main road and, within the acceptable limits imposed by the state, he began to put a little distance between himself and the police car.

He was doing forty when the tyre burst. The pop sounded to his right, and the car suddenly lurched underneath his hand. For a second, he looked out over the hedgerow into the field beyond, and with an insane clarity he decided that this was where he was heading. He only just managed to wrench the steering wheel away, and pulled over at the next lay-by. His hands were shaking as he left the car. Except for a blue boarded-up caravan, 'Café' scrawled upon it with yellow paint, the lay-by was deserted. The tyre lay shredded around the wheel, the metal of the hub scraped by the tarmac. Just as the Vegan popped the boot to retrieve the spare tyre and the jack, he saw the police car approaching.

'Go on,' he said through his teeth, bending down to push the canvas bag to the back of the boot. 'I'm OK. I'm alive. You can pass. Don't worry.'

The police car slowed down. An indicator winked. The Vegan slammed the boot shut. The police car pulled into the lay-by and came to a stop a few metres away. The Vegan squatted down over the ruined tyre and began to fit the jack under the axle. His stomach felt sour. When he glanced up, the policeman had left his car. He was a tall, thin man, his neat slick black hair combed back from his bloodless, pointed face.

'Everything all right, sir?'

The Vegan stood up to meet him. 'Everything's fine.'

The world smelled, suddenly, of marijuana. Cowslip and dock leaf blooming in the verge behind him, the purple flowers bobbing in the breeze, the white barbs of pollen that chased themselves forever across the tarmac, the fumes of petrol, the minute evaporation of breath: it all reeked of sweet skunk grass. The Vegan tried to ignore it. The law and I can meet each other as equals, he told himself. We are citizen and public servant. We represent the benign workings of pleasant democracy. The policeman bent his head to look past the Vegan at the state of the tyre, whistled, and shook his head.

'What happened here?'

'Tyre blew out,' the Vegan replied. 'I was lucky. I wasn't going fast.'

The policeman glanced over at the car. 'The limit is forty around here.'

'I know.'

'It's OK, I didn't mean anything. Only stating facts.'

The Vegan turned back to the tyre. He pumped the jack, ratcheting the wheel up from the ground.

'You know what,' the officer said, 'I think you could do with a hand.'

'That's OK.'

'I insist. I'm off duty now, anyway, so it's not as though you're keeping me from work.' The Vegan tried to protest but the officer held up his hand. 'Really. It's OK. I've stopped now.'

The Vegan glared at the bolts on the hub, the grey indifferent eyes. 'Thank you, officer.'

'Call me Dave.'

'I'm worried.'

'What about?'

'He should have called by now.'

Taylor and Charley stood away from the stall with their backs against the window of a building society. A gang of teenagers gathered in a small car park opposite. Three of them pissed against a ruined brick wall, while the rest threw chips at each other. Charley watched them, holding a cigarette close to her mouth. She hadn't stopped smoking all day, and, with no time to roll her own, had soon disappeared from the stall into a nearby pub to buy a packet of Superkings from a machine. Almost half the pack had already gone.

'What time are you meant to meet him?'

'Six.'

'But it's only four. There's no need to worry.'

'But he was going to call on his way over.'

Taylor took hold of her arm. 'Everything is going to be fine. Try and enjoy it.' This was the wrong thing to say.

'Enjoy what? That in about three hours' time, I'm going to be taking part in a fair-sized drug deal. How can I enjoy anything?'

'I meant the festival.'

'I know what you meant. But you didn't think it through.' She turned away and looked over as one of the teenagers began to retch against the wall, while his friends pelted him with chips. 'I've got a bad feeling, that's all.' She reached for her pack of Superkings. 'Do you think I should call?'

'Is that your phone?'

'Don't worry about it. It's nothing. I'll call them back.'

'How do you know it's nothing?' Dave continued. 'A friend could be in trouble. Imagine, if your friend had broken down in *their* car.' He shook his head, amazed at the possibility of such a coincidence.

'Yes. Imagine.'

The phone stopped ringing. They returned their attention to the wheel. They worked together, quickly and neatly, taking turns to unscrew the bolts from the hub. To his utter horror, the Vegan found himself deferring to the police-man's directions. 'Hold on to the jack now. That's right. Good. Well done.' Soon the wheel had been replaced. The two of them stood side by side, staring down at their work. The policeman gestured to the ruined tyre. 'Do you want me to throw the old wheel in the boot?'

'No.' The adrenalin pumped into the Vegan's stomach. 'I'll take care of that.'

'But you will, won't you? Terrible thing fly-tipping like that.'

'Of course.'

'Have you got a bit of old rag?' Dave offered his hands, streaked with black oil.

'Of course.'

Dave tidied away the tools as the Vegan walked to the back of the car. Hurriedly, he opened the boot, threw the old tyre and jack inside, retrieved a piece of old T-shirt, and slammed the boot shut behind him.

'You forgot the tools.'

'Oh don't worry. I keep them in the car.' The Vegan passed over the rag. 'They belong to a friend. Anyway,' he nodded his head in the direction of the road, 'thanks, for your help, officer.'

'Dave.' He passed the rag back over.

'Thanks. Dave.'

Dave pulled on his jacket. 'So where have you been?'

The Vegan wiped some axle grease from his fingers. 'Oh, seeing some friends.'

'What, in the village?'

'That's right.'

'I thought you joined the road near the old house.'

'Yes . . . That's right.' The Vegan paused. 'I mean . . .'

Dave's gaze was empty, his smile vacuous. 'It's fine,' he said. 'It's all right.' He walked to his car. He rested his cap on the bonnet, and then leant down beside it, resting against the car. 'So you've had a good day, then?'

'That's right.'

'Catching up with old friends?'

'Yeah. You know.'

'Nice out here isn't it, for things like that. Old friends. Talks and walks. Out for miles across the countryside. A bit of lunch.'

'Yes.'

'It's what England is. Good day for it too. Lots of your kind around here. I don't know what the word is now. But you are certainly a type.'

'Not everyone . . .'

'Likes the way society works?' Dave enjoyed finishing the sentence for him.

'Well, you know . . .'

'It's OK. I understand. The capitalist machine. It gets too much. Money, money, but you can't eat money.'

'It's true.'

'There are other things. Love, say. Children.' He began to recite as though from memory. 'Good air. Friendly people. The walk to work. Work itself. The land.' He glanced around them. 'Yes, the land. It's a great answer to modern life.'

'I think so.'

'Dropouts. That used to be a word for your type. Hippie as well. But that's so dated now.' Dave looked him up and down. 'Are you an anarchist?'

'I didn't vote.'

'Good answer.' Dave stared at him, a cold look of approval in his light blue eyes. 'Because, you know, I didn't vote either. Does that make me an anarchist? Probably not.' He nodded. 'Yes, very good answer.' It was hard to separate the colour of his skin from the colour of his teeth. 'We're probably not so very different. Me in my uniform, you in . . . well . . . But there I go. Point proved.' He pointed at the Vegan's clothes. 'Khakis. There we go.'

'Yes.'

'A uniform.' He glanced over at the car, at a 'Bliar' window sticker. 'My brother just got back from the Gulf, you know.' He clicked his tongue against his teeth. 'A haunted man.'

'Really?'

'Terrible story. Lost a friend in friendly fire. A targeting system malfunctions and a missile takes you out. Those bloody Yanks. They shoot first and ask questions later. Except they don't ask questions. Sign of an enquiring mind, you see.'

'I don't . . . I don't really know what to say.'

'Hey. No problem.' Dave pushed himself up from the bonnet of the car, retrieved his cap. 'Just making conversation. Community policing and all that. You can drop out, do whatever it is that you want to do to exclude yourself, but we will still care. You are never divided from the community. We will always take you back.' He looked back at the tyre. 'Well, you can get going.'

'Think I'll wait for a while. Bit shaky.'

Dave frowned. 'You're all right, aren't you? It sometimes has delayed effects. Shock. They teach us this in training. If you want I can give you a lift back to the town. It might be safer.'

'No. Really. I'll be fine. Need a breather.'

'Well this is the place to get it. I'm right, eh?' He inhaled deeply. 'Smell that air. Good country air. It's why I'll never leave this place. The land. It's in your soul, isn't it? Once you're born to it. You never want to leave.'

'You're right.'

'Well. Have a good day, sir. Drive carefully.'

Dave pipped his horn as he pulled away. The Vegan sat down on the thin bank of grass by the side of the road and rolled a cigarette. He looked out across the countryside. Behind him, towering above the land on the vast wire pylon, cables hummed with power, a drone that he could feel reverberating in his skull. Finally he reached for his phone.

'He's called,' Charley said. 'Got held up.'

'I told you. There was nothing to worry about.'

'We haven't sold them yet. There's plenty that can still go wrong.'

'But he's on his way?'

'He's coming. I'd better go and meet him soon.'

Charley left as things began to wind down, leaving Taylor to pack up the stall. By now only Monkey remained: all of the others had drifted away, to meet friends or follow the procession. The crowd had dwindled too, leaving only a few performers entertaining passers-by. A stilt-walker dressed as a great blue fly stalked the square flanked by two jugglers with flaming torches. Fireworks popped in the backstreets. Monkey and Taylor finished loading up the trestles into the van, and finally, for the first time in a long while, they stopped. Taylor sat back on the inside of the boot, while Monkey squatted on the ground. He looked tired, drained. As he lit a cigarette, a firework burst in a nearby street. Monkey flinched, as though the lighter had exploded in his hand.

'Hard day, eh?' Taylor said.

'Yeah.'

'Oh yeah, I nearly forgot.' He reached into his pocket and withdrew a roll of cash, the last of the takings from the day. He counted out thirty in tens, and, at the last minute, added another, passing the notes down to Monkey.

'Cheers.' He folded the money into his tracksuit top and reached for his rucksack. 'Well . . .'

'So what are you doing now?'

Monkey shrugged. 'Heading for the music festival.'

'I'll give you a lift.'

Inside the van, they opened up bottles of beer and Taylor set the van moving towards the music festival, on the northern outskirts of the town. Within the cordoned area around the centre, there was a reckless, almost chaotic atmosphere. The crowds ruled the streets, and the few cars and vans caught behind the cordon moved slowly. As Monkey and Taylor waited, a group of men dressed in ponchos and sombreros serenaded with 'La Bamba' in bad Spanish accents. Nearby, a Las Vegas Elvis threw up on his shoes. Soon, Taylor moved them out of the cordoned area, and the traffic flexed like a concertina through a region which, despite a few George crosses, had been more or less untouched by the celebrations of the day.

'So what next?'

They were waiting at a set of traffic lights beside the old brewery recently renovated into a fitness centre. Even today, a woman and a man stood side by side, running on treadmills. The look in their eyes – strangely frantic as they tried to achieve the limits of an imaginary distance – reminded Taylor of rats in a laboratory maze.

'Now that you're out of here,' he continued, 'what's the plan?'

Monkey shrugged. 'Not really sure. I'm going to talk it over with Jenn.'

'So you're still seeing her? That's good.'

'I'm meeting her tonight.'

The first trace of alcohol in Taylor's blood had given him a feeling of glorious rightness. It pleased him that these two young people had met while staying in the Mansion. Somehow, however indirectly, he had been a part of this coming together. He took another sip of beer.

'We're probably going travelling,' Monkey said. 'Eventually.'

'That's good. I always wished that I'd travelled,' Taylor added, although really he had never wished any such thing. He gestured towards the beer bottle he had clamped between his thighs. 'Always spent too much time drunk, that's my problem.'

Monkey nodded, but didn't speak.

'Travel.' Taylor shook his head, bemused even by the sound of the word. 'Any idea where you're going to go?'

They had stopped by the old Rolls Royce factory. In the fading light, the imprint of the old sign was still visible along the side of the building: an old, corrupting failure branded on to the corrugated walls.

Monkey lifted his beer to his mouth. 'I think we'll go anywhere away from here.'

17

The stage – a covered platform bearing the logo of a local radio station – had been set up on a large field out past the railway line. After Taylor dropped him off, Monkey hung about the entrance, trying to pick Jenn out of the moving crowds. A row of food stalls stood on the other side of the entrance gate; the air reeked of meat fumes and sodden grass, chip fat and sugar, beer and cigarettes. The rain fell lazily, gentle and persistent. Taylor passed by fifteen minutes later. 'Still here?' he remarked, as he walked by without stopping, presumably on his way to find a drink.

When Monkey finally saw Jenn, she was walking arm in arm with a woman wearing a long white dress, straight and sheer as a wedding gown. After a whole day of the carnival, the sight of the costume hardly registered as a curiosity, not even the crown of green leaves pressed down upon her straight black hair seemed out of place. Both of them were drinking from bottles of beer.

'Oh hey!' When Jenn caught sight of him, she jagged from the direction in which she had been walking, dragging the woman across the grass. 'He's here. He's *here*.'

She threw her arms around Monkey. 'I wondered where you were!' Her eyes were like crushed green glass and the alcohol was sweet upon her breath. 'I've been back here three or four times and you were . . . Yeah. I was *looking* for you.'

Jenn wrapped his arm around her own, and all together the three of them walked across the field towards the stage. 'Monkey. I want you to meet Tess. Tess this is Monkey.'

'It's my fault,' Tess said. 'Us being late. In fact all of it. It's my fault.' With her mid-length sleek black hair, and eyes the colour of dry slate, Tess was strikingly attractive. She took a sip of beer, but as she removed the bottle from her lips a surge of foam spat all over her dress. 'God, Jenn how did you let me get in this state! How can I even trust you any more?' Wiping beer from her chin, she turned to Monkey, and curtsied slyly. 'Jenn has told me *so* much about you.'

'I like your dress.'

'Tess is the queen,' Jenn said. 'Queen Tess.'

'This? Blame my father. Every year since the day I was born. He and his friends . . .' She broke off, to look at Jenn. 'You know, it's cruel when you think about it. It's almost sinister. Him and his friends, pimping out their daughters. And of course, in the old days, I would have ended up dead. That's the joke. Thank you, Father. It's no wonder I'm screwed up. Really, I'm crazy. You don't want anything to do with me.'

Jenn smiled over at her, her eyes liquid and smashed. 'Queen Tess. Isn't she beautiful?'

The football ground had once been the site of an old cotton mill, an apparently magnificent example of industrial architecture razed to the ground in a mysterious fire during the first few years of the twentieth century. Arson or accident, it was never established, but when the club accepted investment from a local entrepreneur some wondered if the site had been cursed from the start. Soon it became obvious that the new owner's blood didn't run blue-and-old-gold. The third round tie with Newcastle meant nothing to him; neither could he name the nifty winger kept out of the Fulham first team by a wasted George Best. He only wanted the land. Investment in facilities and the team dwindled. Debts soared. Managers were fired and players sold. Eventually, the club dissolved in bankruptcy and, under a new name, moved to a ground-share in a neighbouring town. Only the colours remained.

Charley had arrived half an hour early, the festival traffic less problematic than she'd imagined. Waiting became immediately more painful when she discovered that she had only one cigarette remaining. She smoked it, cursing darkly to herself, and after it was gone – still well over an hour to go – she left the car. The rain smashed into the potholes of the ruined tarmac. She picked her way around the edge of the abandoned ground, where even the padlocks had rusted shut. Regular proposals for development included a theatre, a block of exclusive flats, a casino, but these were only questionable theories applied to an insoluble problem. Pieces of corrugated iron were missing from the roof of the West stand, and dripped rusty rain on to the concrete of the terrace. The turf of the pitch had been stripped away, but the frame of one goal remained, with one post staggering away from the other, as though caught trying to run off.

Charley returned to the car. She had taken a position by the fence, kicking idly at a back tyre, when the Vegan approached. His car rolled down the bank to meet her, describing a half loop and reversing so the boot faced the back of the fence. The Vegan stared out, a neutral look on his bland, spoon-shaped face.

'Everything all right?'

It took the Vegan a while to respond. His gaze was absent and distracted, as though he were listening for some glitch in the engine, or a familiar voice on the radio. His eyes flicked over towards her. Charley realized how unpleasant she found him, how desperate she was never to be in his company again.

'Yes,' he said, after a pause. 'Everything's fine.'

The crowd had grown around them. A burglar with swag bag, a Grim Reaper with damp cardboard scythe, a group of ex-prime ministers in grey suits and garish pink papier-mâché masks. On the stage, a lone man tested the monitors and speakers. 'One two. One, two, three. Three, four. Three, four.' Tess had wandered off in the direction of the open-air bar. After hitching up the grimy hem of her dress to reveal a money belt above a set of ribbed thermal underwear, she had grinned wickedly at Monkey. 'You have no idea how cold it gets in this dress.'

'Her dad takes the festival very seriously,' Jenn explained as they watched Tess cross the field. 'They re-enact a ritual up on Beck's Hill. She usually has to play some part in it.'

'What do they do?'

'I don't know. I don't get invited. Very exclusive group. Very secretive. Very weird. She's probably right, in the old days she'd have been sacrificed.'

She rested her head upon his shoulder. 'I'm very drunk, I'm afraid. You have some catching up to do.'

'It's good to see you,' he said.

'It's good to see *you*. How was the stall?'

'Hard work. Kept my mind off coming back here, I guess.'

'Everyone miss me? I've seen a couple of people around.'

'Taylor's here somewhere.'

'I hope Charley turns up. Get me drunk enough and I might punch her in the face. Really, I'll do it. You can drag me off her if you like. "She's not worth it, Jenn!" It would be good to make a scene.'

He laughed, but he felt awkward seeing her again. Nothing was how he'd imagined it. And he regretted mentioning his return to the town: it had only made him look weak. Jenn put her arm around his waist and they kissed while the roadie continued his serenade. 'Four, five. Five, five. Five, six. Five, six.' Soon Tess returned, clutching three bottles of beer by the necks, a mobile phone pressed to her ear. The rain had beaded upon the leaves of her garland like clear exquisite fruit.

'I got a call from the boys,' she said. 'They're on their way.'

'The boys?' He glanced over at Jenn.

'Some friends,' she explained. 'We're meeting them.'

The bald roadie had left the stage, leaving an idle microphone, a drum kit and guitars. Music played over the PA: the rehearsal of a ghost band.

'So.' Tess took a sip from her bottle, a look of mischief in her slate-grey eyes. 'Did you ask him?'

'I hadn't got around to it, actually.' Jenn's cheeks were already blushing as she glared over at Tess. 'But I was going to.'

Monkey glanced between them. 'Ask me what?'

Tess stared up at the empty stage. 'She was going to talk to you about the pills.'

Pete was already ten minutes late. Charley sat in the passenger seat of the Vegan's car. Rain licked against the bleak kidney-coloured brick of a haulage company over the road. The waiting was all so tedious and anxious, the day so dour, that Charley had to ask the Vegan for a cigarette, although it irritated her to reveal this weakness. She rolled the tobacco inside one of her own liquorice papers, and when the smoke filled her lungs, it went some way to calm the scratching in her blood.

'So, any problems on the way over?'

'Had a bit of a glitch with the car. It's all sorted now.'

Charley bunched her hand inside her cardigan and wiped the condensation from the inside of the windscreen. The Vegan opened the window a crack, but closed it again when the rain began to spray upon the side of his face. He flicked on the radio but turned it off soon after. He drummed his fingers against the lower half of the steering wheel. He was obviously brooding upon something, and finally, he spoke.

'This dealer of yours. Do you trust him?'

'Yes. Of course. I've had no reason not to.'

'So you think everything's going to be fine?'

Charley sighed. 'Like I said, I have no reason to think otherwise. What about you?' She turned to face him. 'What do you think?'

'I've never met him. But I want to be prepared.'

'What do you mean, prepared?'

'In case something goes wrong. We've been too fucking blasé about all of this.' His eyes flicked over her again. 'I shouldn't have let you lull me into a false sense of security.'

'Please don't make this any more difficult than it has to be.'

'But how difficult *is* it going to be? That's what I want to know. We have to be prepared,' he continued, glaring at the car floor, 'for betrayal.'

'Betrayal?'

'It has to be considered.' His expression was almost comically solemn and severe. 'It has to be kept in mind.'

Charley put her face in her hands, her breath warm on

the cold skin. 'Oh God. I am so glad that I don't have to do this any more.'

The Vegan frowned. 'What?'

She had intended to tell him after the deal had been completed. It was meant to be the final act of her celebration of the day, but instead, it had slipped from her, and she saw no reason to delay it.

'Taylor and I have decided. We're not going to continue with the pills. This deal, and then the end.'

The Vegan opened his mouth to protest but she cut him off.

'Don't worry, you'll get paid. We can divide the money tonight, and that will be it. We're very grateful.' She aimed this last, spurious courtesy at the side of the Vegan's head, as he had turned away to stare through the windscreen. 'But we think that it's the best idea.'

'So, what?' The Vegan spoke to the road. 'What am I meant to do?'

'Come and collect the lab stuff if you want. But it's probably best if you don't come around after that. In fact, it's probably best if we break off contact. You never know, after all.'

If the Vegan wanted to argue, Charley would take time to explain exactly why she wanted shot of him, how the greatest hazard all of them had faced throughout this very hazardous business was his disturbed, isolated personality. But the Vegan didn't have time to argue: Pete's car turned off the road and pulled up next to Charley's side of the car. She unwound the window, as Pete did the same. The air between them fizzed with rain.

'Everything all right?'

'Everything's fine.' When Pete glanced across at the Vegan, she explained, 'This is a friend of mine. He's here to keep me company.'

Pete nodded thoughtfully. 'I guessed. You're all right aren't you, mate?' he called to the Vegan. 'Knock once for yes.'

The Vegan shifted in his seat and looked over at Pete.

'I'm OK.'

'Then, I suppose we should do business.'

Bardo Nightwatch had taken to the stage. All four were proficient, experienced performers: a Hammond organist, a drummer who'd been nominated for Young Musician of the Year and suffered a nervous breakdown from the pressure, an ex-choirgirl vocalist, a guitarist who'd auditioned for The Fall. They mixed the roots folkiness of Sandy Denny with the sinister fairground music of *Carnival of Souls*, had released an EP on a small label in Birmingham, were due to tour Sweden, and would split up by the end of the night.

'We'll give you money,' Tess said. 'Don't worry, that's not an issue.'

The fading light danced in her slate-grey eyes. Monkey wanted to escape. He wanted Jenn to come with him, for both of them to run far, far away. But there was Tess, there would *always* be Tess, seducing them both with her regal, voluptuous power. Although the rain had abated slightly, the wet grass reminded him of the smell of the river, how it had permeated his clothing and even now followed him. Herointown, he thought. Always Herointown. Tess smiled at him. Jenn stared across at the band, her cheeks flushing slightly. They stood together, a triangle of people pressed in by the crowd, and each one of them was fixed in place.

'OK,' Monkey said. 'How many do you want?'

The Vegan walked around to the back of his car and popped the boot, while Pete retrieved a jiffy bag from underneath the driver's seat. Charley waited on the patch of concrete between them. A few cars passed on the road in front of the haulage company, but these were only flashes of colour tearing up the rain-soaked air. The Vegan came to stand by Charley's side, bringing along with him a shapeless canvas bag. Pete handed the envelope over to Charley.

'Count it,' the Vegan said.

She almost cracked at this, almost snapped back at him that she was about to do that, of *course*, but she held her breath, feeling that it was best they kept a united front. She walked to the Vegan's car, and sat down in the passenger seat, keeping her feet on the ground outside. She tore open the envelope. The money had been packed inside in slim, equal bunches. As she counted through it, Pete and the Vegan stood facing each other: Pete with his hands in his back pockets, the Vegan with the bag down by his ankles, like a traveller waiting for a train.

Charley looked up from the money. 'It's fine.'

Pete began to reach across for the handles of the canvas bag, but the Vegan stopped his hand.

'Wait a minute. Is the money real?'

'Is the *what*?'

'Have you checked that the money's real?'

'I don't believe I'm hearing this.' Pete nudged Charley's arm. 'Can you talk to him, please?'

Staring steadily into his eyes, Charley tried to hold the Vegan's attention. 'The money is *fine*. Everything is OK.'

'But have you checked? It's not padded out with newspaper, anything like that.'

'Please . . .'

Pete finally snapped. 'Jesus Christ! Can we just finish this?' He reached out to take the bag, but anticipating this, the Vegan pushed out with both his hands. Pete lost his balance on the uneven concrete and fell sprawling on to the wet ground.

'What the fuck are you doing!'

He was already getting to his feet as Charley started up from the car.

Tess took three of the pills, necking them with a gulp of her beer. 'These things are like aspirin for me, I swear,' she said. 'Three will only give me a little buzz.' He didn't argue; he didn't care. Covered by Jenn and Tess, Monkey had sorted out a handful of pills from the main bag in his rucksack. Tess had pushed a twenty-pound note into his hands, while Jenn looked the other way. 'I insist.' Monkey had passed a couple of the pills over to Jenn. She swallowed them down with her drink, risking a glance at him.

'Come on. You too. You're a part of this.'

He didn't have time to answer, because suddenly the boys arrived. Tess called them over and they came pushing through the crowd. Monkey didn't even catch half of their names. It didn't take long for Tess to tell them about the pills. One by one, they came to him. They fed from his palm like birds. As he took their money, Monkey kept his eyes upon some distant space in the general direction of the stage. This drug-deal look, feigning innocence and projecting himself into a world without blame, sometimes, he felt that he'd been using it all of his life. Jenn waited beside him. She sipped from her drink, accepted a cigarette from one of her friends, looked over at the stage and shared a joke with the group. After the last deal had been made, she moved closer towards Monkey, brushing cold fingers against his cold hand.

'Everything OK?'

'Everything's fine.'

'Have you taken one?'

'Not yet.'

'But you will.'

'It's been a long day.'

'Don't be like that.' She spoke softly. 'I'm sorry about all of this. Tess kind of gets carried away. You've seen what she's like.'

While he might have felt betrayed, disappointed or even jealous, instead, he felt only numb. That was Herointown: it killed the pain. Jenn reached out her hand, her eyes already swollen with an ecstasy that was not for him.

Charley moved around the fight as though she were practising a baffling dance step: one arm outstretched, a pace in, a pace out, two steps to the right, one to the left. Pete and the Vegan ignored her, even as she screamed at them.

'What the hell are you two trying to prove?'

In the end, Pete punched the Vegan on the jaw and Charley gave him an extra shove to send him sprawling on to the ground.

'OK. *Now* can we try and talk?'

The Vegan sat up slowly, apparently winded by his fall. Pete was breathing heavily beside her. She could see signs of calculation moving across his face. He looked from her, to the Vegan, to the bag and the envelope of money. A blankness welled in the dark green-rimmed pools of his eyes, a twitch pulled upwards at the corners of his mouth. She knew what would happen, perhaps even before he did.

'Oh Pete, no.'

He punched Charley in the face before she had finished speaking. As she flinched, he hit her twice more; and as she slipped to the floor, he kicked her in the chest. She went down into the dirt, all the air pushed out of her body, and she felt the envelope getting whipped from her hand.

Pete moved to the Vegan and kicked him two, three times, in the side, in the face. Charley watched her life being wrenched from the fingers of a man she despised. She wanted to comment on this, she wanted to scream, shout and in this way arrest the utter ruin. But the air would not move from her lungs, and the silence stayed heavy and rigid in her throat. It remained as Pete succeeded in prising the handles of the bag from the Vegan's fingers, as he wrenched it away and began to run back to his car, his footsteps large and flat and solid against the wet surface of the tarmac. Only as the car squealed away, as she rose up on her hands to watch it streak into the road, was Charley able to cough. 'No,' she said, her eyes burning as the breath finally dislodged the silence. 'No, no, no.'

A stall by the entrance to the field sold cheap toys: cap guns, light sabres, and bubble machines that inflated the froth of soapy water to the size of illuminated globes. The bubbles floated above the heads of the crowd, promising, but always failing, to disappear into the limits of the quickly fading sky. In some places, the arc of their surface caught the reflection of the surrounding lights, creating an optical trick which made them seem as flat and feature-less as two interlocking metal rings. Jenn and her friends pointed them out as they slipped by, marvelling at these trembling, precious miracles. Perhaps the pills were already beginning to work, but Monkey couldn't have known. He had left them and pushed his way through the crowd, heading towards the bar. One of the bubbles fell from the sky and popped against the side of his face. For a moment it had been whole, huge and beautiful and strange; the next, it had vanished in a slightly sticky residue that he wiped from his skin with the sleeve of his tracksuit top.

He lit a cigarette and bought a bottle of beer. The music

brayed in the speakers. The crowd massed in front of him. He felt awkward, unable to hide in the stark surroundings of the field. Further along the bar, Taylor was standing alone. Monkey bought him a drink, and they stood for the entire set of a band, cheering, calling out requests. And when the three cello players failed to break into 'Ace of Spades' they began to jeer. When the lead singer of the next band became distracted by a disturbance in the crowd, Monkey didn't pay any attention. He thought that someone had started heckling a song which was very earnest, very slow, and very bad. Only when a gap formed in the crowd did Monkey realize. He tried to ignore it – Taylor said something, which Monkey decided was the funniest thing that he had ever heard. But the hollow in the crowd had grown. When the band stopped playing, the bassist bending down to talk to one of the roadies, Monkey left Taylor's side, and picked his way back through the crowd. He walked unhurriedly, trying not to appear concerned, trying not to appear involved. But he was concerned, and he was involved, even more so when the crowd thickened around the place where he had been standing. Monkey pushed through the thick wall of the crowd, where Satan was waiting for him.

Satan was a tall man, long-limbed, skinny, and his red leotard and red tights only exaggerated the meanness of his body. The dye from his bright-red goatee beard had streaked slightly in the rain, leaving small capillaries seeping into his jaw. The red pointed tail which poked out above his fleshless backside was muddy from the wet ground, and his sparkling red pronged fork flashed sadly on the grass. He crouched over Tess, slapping at her face. The panic brayed in his voice as he shouted out to the surrounding crowd. 'Can someone call an ambulance! Can somebody please call an ambulance now!'

Other people attended to the four boys, who sat looking yellow and dazed, guarding their own private pools of vomit. Monkey's attention moved to the far side of the clearing, where Jenn lay stretched out on the grass. A teenage boy sat beside her, a smudge of a beard on his chin, his black hair bedraggled from the rain, matted into locks above his neck. He sat with his hand resting upon her shoulder, while beside him a rangy brown dog surveyed everything with patience and calm.

Charley pulled herself to her feet, wincing from the pain in her chest. The rain cooled the heat of her inflamed lip. The Vegan lay on his back, blinking up at the sky. His bottom lip had burst like fruit, and his nose was trickling blood. Charley squatted down beside him, the pain in her chest overwhelming. She coughed and checked her hand for traces of blood. Slowly, clumsily, the Vegan sat upright, the grey dust from the beaten tarmac smeared over his back. His face remained fixed in an expression caught between pain and confusion. Charley leant close to him.

'I never want to see you again.'

She almost headed home. She had been driving for the bypass, returning, returning, returning, when she pulled over outside a newsagents for a pack of cigarettes. The first touch of smoke on her lungs made her cough, and the coughing brought tears. She cried briefly, until fury overtook her, the fury at the situation and the fury of the tears. She slapped at the steering wheel with the flat of her hand, slapped it so hard that the pain brought more tears. She collapsed over the steering wheel, the wasted effort seemingly commensurate with the exhaustion that swamped her. Finally, she picked herself up and wiped the tears away, swearing at herself for being so fucking pathetic. She wouldn't head home, not yet. She couldn't face it alone. She started up the car and headed for the festival.

Most of the band had left the stage once the ambulance crew arrived. One guitarist remained, strumming along to his guitar while the monitors started piping out a compilation of anodyne pop songs that everyone knew and everyone loved. Monkey went to find Taylor. If he'd tried to run away, everything would have become a little too real for him. Taylor was arguing with a barman. Monkey was able to intercede, divert, and, when they were at a safe distance, explain. It took Taylor a while to appreciate the situation. 'They *collapsed*?' he said, when finally he realized. 'They collapsed?'

The first of the ambulances pulled away, the blue lights leaking into the moist darkness of the night. Taylor and Monkey walked side by side, drawn together by their conspiracy. Because of this, it seemed only natural to find Charley waiting. She stood leaning against the van, scanning the faces of anyone who walked past. The high white halogen lights illuminated the bruises on her face, the cut above one eye.

'I found the van, so I thought I'd wait.'

Taylor didn't notice her injuries. He was too drunk, too scared. His voice was shrill and impatient as he tried to describe everything he'd left behind in the field. Charley interrupted him.

'Taylor. We really need to talk.'

'Then you've heard? The pills?'

This made her falter. Monkey saw it in her eyes. She had been sure that this was her story to tell, but now Taylor had intruded upon it unexpectedly. 'Heard? What do you mean? Heard what?'

Around them, more people were heading for their cars.

The white halogen burned above them. To give space and time and privacy, they retreated to the front of the van, to share everything that had happened.

Charley watched the road. It came towards her, the colour of gunmetal under the headlights. Catseyes sparkled in the centre. Taylor sat beside her, Monkey on the edge, all of them cramped into the cab of the van. They had left her car behind in the field. Charley had felt too exhausted to drive, but one look at Taylor – sweating, drunk and reeling from what had happened – told her that she would have to make the effort. It was up to her, it would always be up to her to hold everything together.

'What are we going to do?'

Monkey had spent most of the journey staring out at the blur beyond the passenger window, but now he'd decided to involve himself in the situation. Charley wondered if the question was supposed to be an offer of culpability. As the road gulped them down, she brooded upon her blame: imagining Monkey, out there in front of the van, pulled towards it by the inevitable acceleration, ridden over, destroyed. Monkey thief, Monkey dealer, Monkey wrecker of ordinary dreams. When she ignored him, he repeated the question.

'Charley. What are we going to do?'

Her mouth was so dry she could hardly talk. 'Tomorrow. We'll think about it. But right now, I want to get home.'

She set the van weaving through roads and corners and along the driveway, until they got to the house. Later, when she thought back to that night, she would remember the way the atmosphere had been charged as they let themselves in through the front door. It had almost hissed, like something pressurized. All three had headed for the kitchen, although they should have fled from each other, their company was so poisonous, so ridiculous and doomed. However, the air in that cold grey chamber of the front hallway had felt so full of menace, full of old sorrow and doubt, that, as they approached the kitchen, she would later think, they had clung together because it had affected them. When they opened the door, they could only guess what had happened. What looked like a rat had crawled up from the cellar, a huge, juicy brown country rat. It had somehow got itself trapped and the dogs had gone crazy, tearing it to pieces on the kitchen floor. After that, it looked as if they had fought amongst themselves: the collie had a cut in its ear, the retriever a nasty scratch above its eye. Only the yellow greyhound was unmarked. It sat away from the rest of the dogs, looking a little terrified, shaking slightly, staring at them with upturned black eyes. Blood dripped from its mouth, leaving marks all over the tiles: smashed crimson circles, the shape of dwarf stars.

18

Whispers and theories in cold stone rooms. Monkey could almost feel all the talk going on around him during those days after the festival. It rose like smoke through the boards of the house into the empty chambers of the third floor, poisoning, suffocating. Monkey spent hours on the camp bed, his chest thick with cigarettes, staring at the picture of the monkey on his wall. *I let us down*, he explained. *I am the enemy now*. The monkey probed its skull for a solution.

When Taylor knocked on the door and asked him to come down to the office, it was almost a relief. Charley was sitting on the office chair, with her knees pulled up to her chest. When she wasn't speaking, she touched the inflamed flesh of her lower lip against her jeans: testing her pain. Taylor leant against the desk, while Monkey rested himself against the radiator, his hands held behind his back in a firing squad pose.

'So,' Charley said. 'Take us through it again.'

Monkey sighed. 'I'd been skimming off pills here and there for the past few months. Enough that so when I left here, I'd have a bit of an income. No one had made any promises to me, so I had to look after myself.'

'You only had to ask,' Taylor said.

'What were you going to do? Offer me a room for life?'

Charley started laughing, a hard, dry, mean sound in the cramped confines of the room.

'Exactly. It wasn't likely to happen. Besides, I wanted to get out of here. I wanted to save some money. I didn't think you'd miss a few pills here and there.'

He told them how he'd taken pills from the new batch, how he'd put most of them aside, and taken the rest to the festival. 'Jenn and I had already tried some of the other ones,' he said, 'and they were fine. No problems at all. So . . .'

Charley finished it for him. 'It must have been the new batch. What could have gone wrong?'

Monkey had wondered about this himself. 'I'm not sure. You're talking to the wrong person, really.'

'We've tried speaking to the right person. He's not exactly been forthcoming.'

'I went round to his house,' Taylor said. 'There was no answer. We don't know where he is.'

Monkey tried to recap what he knew about chemistry. 'Maybe we made some mistakes increasing the amounts for the big shipment. He didn't exactly have his mind on what he was doing towards the end. I don't know. I suppose it doesn't take much for these things to go wrong. It would make sense.'

Taylor shook his head, and caught Charley's eye. 'One burn will spoil it all.'

She glared at him. 'What are you *talking* about? Why can't you keep your mind on what has happened?' Stung, Taylor stared down at the floor. Charley turned to Monkey. 'What I want to know is, why didn't *you* take any of the pills that night? Why aren't you lying in a hospital bed?'

'I didn't really like Jenn's friends. I wasn't comfortable.'

'Well, you certainly put them in their place.' She smiled, finding a little weary comedy in a terminal situation.

'So. What happens next?'

'What do you mean?'

'I mean, what do you want me to do now?'

'You stay around here. For the time being at least. The last thing I want is you running around town.'

They had taken only a few steps into the hallway when Magalene ran up from the living room.

'You've got to come and see this.'

The TV flickered in the corner, an almost liquid brightness in the dull light of the day. The newsreader sat at a silver desk, talking about the poisoning of the carnival queen, about epidemics and these malign seeds we plant, and who will save us from their fruit? Photographs flashed up on the screen: Tess in jodhpurs astride a white horse, seated on the steps of a beach hut. Finally, Jenn appeared. She stood in front of a green garage door, hardly smiling. Far far too young: awkward, altered, removed. The picture changed. No one spoke. Monkey left the room.

He took a short walk around the grounds. The same longing which he'd experienced in the clinic overcame him: the possible world restricted by his weakness. When he reached the wall, he realized that there was nowhere else to go. The route across those fields led only to Jenn, to the spring day they had spent together, sharing an experience which would eventually bring about the end. Trapped again, between the past and his own inability to confront the future, he froze, lighting a cigarette, watching the sky. A scattering of residents still tended the garden. He wanted to tell them all to move on, to find a better way to spend their lives. But if he told them that the Mansion was doomed, if he managed even to drive them away, he guessed that they'd return. A solution of sorts, this land distracted them from everything that was happening.

He returned to the house. He'd become like the rest of

them, reliant upon it to protect and offer diversion. He had spent too long in his room, so he walked into the kitchen, where Robert was bent over the stove.

'Do you need a hand?'

Robert smiled. 'Oh, we always need help around here.'

Monkey dissolved into the steam of the kitchen. He peeled and chopped the contents of a basket of vegetables; he made bread, losing his fists inside the pale, flaccid belly of the dough. Beside him, Robert was only a blur of activity, of purpose. Robert knew what he was doing and Monkey could only follow him. Later, they sat outside the back door, smoking, talking, Robert squatting on the door-step, Monkey perched on a green plastic garden chair. When the yellow greyhound joined them, wriggling out through the kitchen door, Robert bent up close to it. With his cigarette clamped between his teeth, he took hold of the dog's jaw and stared into its eyes, blinking against rising smoke.

'Dog, I don't trust you,' he said. 'What do you think of that?'

The dog whined, but didn't pull away until Robert removed his hand. Freed, it trotted away to the far end of the patio, staring back accusingly at them both. Robert tossed his cigarette away, a thin orange arc that burst in the night.

'When I was fifteen,' he said. 'I was still at home. Me and my dad never got on. He was old-school working class. Didn't like it that I wanted to cook. Anyway, I was sixteen and he got cancer. He went in with a pain in his chest, and the doctor broke it to him. He smoked forty a day, so it shouldn't have been too much of a surprise.' A car passed on the road down beyond the cottage, the headlights rising like a ghost amongst the hedges. 'He went into hospital and they opened him up and he was all rotten inside. More cancer than man, that's what he kept saying. They gave him three months to live and the old bastard, rather than dying in hospital, where they could look after him, where they could make it easy, he demanded to be sent home. Those three months, I'll never forget them. Him screaming through the night, swearing at the top of his voice. And the smell of him. It came through the whole house, so that none of us could eat. I mean, we'd sit down at the table together, food on the plates, and all that we could smell, the only thing in front of us, was *him*.

'And when he went, the night he died, all the dogs went crazy. Not just next door, or along the street; you could hear them barking, two, three streets away. I went out right after he died. I left my mum up by his bedside, let her say goodbye. I had to get some air. I've never forgotten the way those streets felt that night. They were hungry for him. They could smell that he had gone.'

They walked back inside. They tidied up the kitchen, and went their separate ways, Robert to the living room to catch the last hour of the evening film, Monkey to his room. To entertain himself, he retrieved the bag of pills from underneath the floorboards. Two days ago, they had represented an escape, now they were as worthless as sand. He threw the bag into the corner of the room, and set about packing his rucksack with clothes. He left the picture of the trepanned monkey on the wall. 'We are on the outside now,' he told it, by way of goodbye. 'Things have slipped.' The monkey could only grimace in reply.

Outside, Lucas's cottage smoked in the early morning. Birds called, scattering from one tree to the next like a handful of gravel. Monkey left the drive and walked the narrow road that bordered the forest; soon, he had reached the A road. HGVs passed him by, sleepy travellers trying to beat the rush hour. No one stopped on those roads. No one stopped anywhere. He walked along the green verge separated from the road by a grey plastic barrier, dawn a sickly yellow that spread over the horizon. It took a while for the landscape to change. He watched white water towers, a rural church, a barn and farm machinery, the hills. Gradually, the outskirts of the town rose up to dominate all around him. Gradually, the town became distinct. Monkey walked the road to Herointown.

19

On the outside, you see things more clearly. People come, people leave: you witness their passing. Mostly it happens by accident. Voices drift from the roadside or the edge of the forest: the walls of your home are very thin. Cars disturb the gravel of the drive, legs sweep through wet grass. You try not to be involved, but this stasis becomes like anticipation. People come to you, in confusion, in need. You let them. Escape might not have been the reason you set yourself on the outside – escape brings with it the idea of fear, and you don't believe you are afraid – but you needed a distance. Later, you will realize that by the accident of your attention, you have become involved. On the outside, you see things more clearly, and if you see things, you have caused them to be.

That day, Lucas had been free to work entirely on the cottage; more than ever, this was the epicentre of his days. He touched up the paintwork in the ground-floor room, tried to fix a catch on the window, filed the edge off the front door to stop it sticking on the floorboards. Tools, off-cuts of wood, tins of paint and paint stripper lay scattered around the floor, the living room forced into a state of ruin before it could be improved. Afterwards, he had sat back in his chair, reaching for a book on a whim. 'But if man surrendered unreservedly to immanence he would fall short of humanity; he would achieve it only to lose it and eventually life would return to the unconscious intimacy of animals.' This sentence, the first he'd read after cracking the spine, had many places in which to fall; Lucas lost himself in the gaps between the words. He returned the book to the shelf and decided to head over to the Mansion. Apart from a bag of porridge and the packet of porcini mushrooms, his supply cupboard was empty. He was hungry.

Although the day had been dull, moist and overcast, there was a pleasant stillness in the air. It was just over a week since the festival. Lucas remembered how, the morning after the festival, he had walked over to the kitchen to check the rota, but there had been no rota, and the house had been almost deserted. As he dawdled, a little uncertain whether this meant a day of freedom, Magalene had accosted him. Not since his first week in the Mansion had she spoken to him directly, avoiding him because she hadn't liked the way he'd responded to some idiotic question she'd once asked him. All that had been forgotten. 'Did you hear?' Magalene's eyes had brimmed with excitement and conspiracy. 'Did you hear what happened last night?'

And so, Lucas had found out about Jenn.

This evening again the house was quiet. A pot of kidney beans was bubbling unattended on the Aga, like something from a ghost ship. The purple froth bubbled over the water, while, stoked by the draft from the open door, the bitter-smelling steam filled the room. A lot of people had stayed away from the house after the festival; Monkey had vanished early one morning. Only a few of the older residents remained. As Lucas approached the Aga, the border collie picked itself up from its warm spot and padded to another part of the room. Lucas boiled pasta in an old red pan and heated up some left-over stew. He glanced through a copy of *Jane Eyre* which had been left behind on the counter, but he quickly discarded it. When the pasta was boiled he poured in the remains of the stew and mixed everything together in the pan. As he moved to the table, the collie sniffed at the steam. 'It's good,' Lucas said, but it was a strange thing to speak your first words to a dog, and did not try again.

Charley didn't notice him as she walked into the room. The doorway through from the hallway created a blind spot of the kitchen table, and Lucas was able to watch her for a few moments as she moved to the area by the cooker. She stopped by the sink and poured a glass of water from the tap. When she turned and saw him, she hardly registered any surprise at all. She leant back against the sink and drained her glass. The bruises on her face had already yellowed: an ugly nicotine colour on the left side of her jaw, the patch above her eye topped by a black graze. She had told everyone that she had been mugged at the concert by two teenage boys. Magalene had passed on that conversation too. 'And you'll never guess what else happened . . .' Lucas had listened. And thought.

Charley turned to wash her glass under the tap. She glanced over her shoulder. 'I expected to find Robert.'

'He left a pan boiling,' Lucas said.

'Right. Well, if you see him . . .' She turned as though to leave, but patting the pocket of her cardigan absent-mindedly, she remained where she was standing.

'Bad news. About Jenn.'

He didn't know what made him say it. Ever since the confrontation over his diary they'd avoided one another. It had even occurred to him that he was lonely without her, but this had made him feel foolish and exposed. He stared down at the plate and speared a mushroom with his fork.

The sound of the pan seemed to grow louder, a thick sucking and popping, building in fury.

'Yes,' Charley said. 'Bad news.'

'Place isn't the same.' He ate the mushroom and chewed it slowly. 'Obviously, she left a while ago now. But it's certainly not the same.'

'A lot of people have left. But they'll come back.'

'Why do you think they've gone?'

'It's always like this a few days after the festival. Always. They stay in town. A lot of parties. It's always like this.'

Lucas speared a piece of pasta. 'Still. It's very quiet.'

He wanted to hint at the failure of her plan with the Vegan, because it had failed, Lucas was sure of that. As he glanced over at her he noticed how pale she looked under the bare electric light bulb. She fiddled in her pockets, pulled out a pile of tissues and papers and sorted through them until she separated a cigarette lighter. She returned the paper mass to her pocket, and kept the lighter in her palm. She flicked at it a couple of times, the white spark flashing like a star.

'Don't you think it's time you left here?'

Lucas had been expecting this conversation for a while. 'No,' he said, remaining impassive. 'I don't think so.'

'Not even if I asked you to go?' She paused, and flicked the lighter again. The gas caught the spark, showing as a small round pebble of flame above the silver casing. 'Even if I *told* you to go?'

'I don't want to leave. I'm happy here.'

The flame faded, and Charley replaced the lighter in her pocket. 'I suppose you're right,' she said. 'I suppose there's nothing else. Where else can you go? Head back home? Run back to some old friends? Take up some of your old nasty habits?'

Lucas pierced onions and mushrooms on the tines of his

fork. 'Old friends.' He glanced over. 'Do you mean the old friends who have been helping you?'

'I don't understand.' Her eyelids fluttered as she spoke, a flaw in the mask of her complacency.

'The old friends,' Lucas went on, through a mouthful of food, 'who have been helping you in that outhouse.' He swallowed, and even while he spoke, he hated the way the conversation had run away from him. 'Or should I call it a lab?'

At that, Charley hurried out of the kitchen. Lucas finished his meal. The emptiness poured in on him, the sound of the bubbling pot torturing the silence. He moved to the sink to wash up the dishes. A radio lay discarded on the windowsill, a small grey portable flecked with old splashes of paint. Lucas switched it on. It was tuned to a late-night dance station. The beats trembled in the stillness of the house, chasing away Charley's departure, drowning, or at least allaying, the sound of the boiling pot on the stove. As he worked along to it, his movements matching the patterns almost unconsciously, Lucas felt that it was the first time he had *heard* music in a long time. It accompanied him, providing rhythm and order to his tasks. When he had finished, he reached out and flicked the switch on the radio, and the sudden loss of that music – a guillotine slice – affected him so much that he took the radio with him when he left, hurrying quickly over the wet grass to his home.

Back in the cottage, he picked his way through the litter of his earlier work, navigating paint tins and tools and off-cuts of wood. He built up a fire in the hearth, prodding at the flames with the old poker. Soon he turned on the radio, and the order he had felt back in the house returned. He was staring into the flames when two cars slowed down at the junction and took the turning – one, then the other –

grinding past the cottage walls. Lucas turned up the volume to shut them out, and, screwing the poker into the fire, he gave himself over to the oblivion of the radio.

20

Rats run from sinking ships, so when monkeys run from mansions it should be time to evaluate the situation, but Taylor and Charley hardly spoke after the festival. Taylor spent most of that time losing himself in jobs around the house: fine-tuning the generator, mending the fence of the chicken run, or working on the third floor. But eventually, Charley tracked him down. It was past seven, and he had headed upstairs after the evening meal to strip the rotten floorboards from one of the damp rooms. Stiff Little Fingers, a bottle of beer and organized destruction: it felt like the best way to spend his time. He lost himself entirely in the work. When Charley crept up on him, he almost jumped out of his skin.

'Sorry,' she said. 'I did say hello.'

'It's OK, it's OK. Just gave me a fright.' He smiled and patted his palm on his heart. 'Getting too old for things like that.'

The joke hung in the dusty silence of the room. Charley lowered herself down on to an old chair, wincing with a hand clutched to her ribs.

'Still sore?'

'Getting better. But yes, still very sore.' She glanced down at his afternoon's work, the rotten splintered boards, the denuded floor. 'Listen. We need to talk. I know we've been putting things off. Both of us. But we really need to decide what we're going to do.'

'Right.' More than ever, he wanted to be left alone. Charley sensed this: her eyes were hard and piercing, forcing him into the situation.

'Last night, the police released a description of the pills. That circle-cross thing. I've been thinking through what links us to them. Monkey is on his own. In some ways, it's the best thing that happened that he's run off. And, assuming that he's heard about what happened, I'm fairly sure that Pete will just dump the pills he took. He was talking about getting away, anyway. We don't need to worry about him.' She paused. 'But there's another problem.'

'What?'

'Lucas knows about the lab.'

Taylor winced. 'How did he find out?'

'God knows. But I've just left him in the kitchen, boasting to me about it. So we can't just leave all the equipment out there.'

'The door is locked.'

'I *know* the door's locked. But we're too close to this. Surely you can see that?' The strain sounded in her voice. 'Sooner or later – if they aren't already – someone is going to start asking questions about Jenn, and those questions are going to lead them over here. Do you trust Lucas to keep his mouth shut?'

'So what do you want to do?'

'Head down there tonight, while everyone's asleep. We'll load up the van with the equipment.'

'And then what?'

'Drive it over to the Vegan. He can take care of it.'

'Who knows,' Taylor said, to fill the gap, 'he might be able to make a bit of money out of it all.'

He intended the remark as a joke, but in that place of

rot and damage, it didn't seem funny. After Charley left, he gave up any pretence of work and drank the rest of his beer, sitting with his feet dangling through the ruined boards. In this space between the floors a person could hide, he told himself. They could live there forever, never to be found.

The gossip of the residents, the reports on TV, the fears she kept pushing to the back of her mind: none of these had been able to move Charley. But Lucas had managed it. After talking to Taylor, she killed time in the office, clicking through game after game of patience on the computer. This was a terrible way to spend her time, but she remained in her seat, smoking and sorting, until an impression of the cards burned under her eyelids whenever she blinked.

'For God's sake,' she muttered to herself. 'What am I doing?'

The collie was waiting for her outside in the hall, and the look of bored longing it shot Charley was enough for her to decide to take it for a walk. As she headed for the kitchen, Magalene appeared from the other direction, cradling a pile of logs in her arms. She wore a jumper, brand new, expensive cashmere. Charley noticed it because of the way it clashed with the hairclip clamping Magalene's topknot, and her bright yellow sunflower leggings.

'Nice jumper.'

'Oh this.' Magalene blushed slightly. 'I've had it ages.'

Charley gestured to the logs. 'Building a fire?'

'That's right. It's freezing in the living room.'

'Make sure someone watches it.'

'Don't I always?'

'No. You don't. You never do.' But Magalene had already walked away.

Lucas, thankfully, had left the kitchen by now. She collected a torch from under the sink and headed out of the back door. With the dog at her side, she walked around the side of the house on to the drive. As she continued down to the road, she ignored the cottage, blanking the light in the window like she would the eyes of an enemy. Once she had crossed into the field, the dog soon disappeared beyond the range of the torch. Charley walked quickly, her breath steaming in the light. Eventually, she reached the oak tree. Elegant and graceful, the shape had always seemed human to her, but tonight the narrow crown reminded her of arms raised aghast, in surrender or despair. She felt almost threatened. While the dog roamed in and out of the torch beam, Charley settled herself against the bark, rolling a cigarette, and shivering slightly in the breeze as she tried to find a little peace.

She had no idea of the time as she headed back. Calling the dog towards her, she held it by its collar as they crossed the dark road, and trudged up the gravel of the drive. She had walked halfway towards the house, when she heard the cars pulling on to the driveway behind her. Because she didn't recognize either car, she stood her ground. Just when she thought she would have to leap out of the way, the lead car pulled up, grinding stones. She was close enough as to be able to see through the windscreen, but even so it took a while for Charley to recognize the driver as Jenn's brother. When he stepped out, she hated him immediately, hated him and the six friends who followed him from the cars. All of them shared a nasty intent.

'Remember me?' There was a brightness in his eyes and a sharpness to his teeth that made him as sinister and attractive as a knife.

'Of course.' She cleared her throat. 'I'm sorry about what happened.'

Mark stared at her with open contempt. 'I'm touched.'

'What can we do for you, anyway?' Charley kept her voice as soothing as she could manage.

'What do you think? Since the police seem to be doing fuck all, I thought I'd come out here and find out what happened.'

'But she wasn't even living here any more.'

'What about that boyfriend?'

'He's not here, either.'

'Don't give me that.' Mark's voice became shrill, uncontrolled.

'It's true.'

'You're protecting him.'

'He left not long after it happened. I don't know where he is.' She took a deep breath. 'Listen, I can see you're upset. I don't want to have to call the police . . .'

Mark laughed. '"Call the police." Don't make me laugh. My Dad's been on to the police every day to see what they're up to. I'd be glad to see them.'

'Maybe not, Marky,' someone in the group cackled loudly.

'Yeah, well. Maybe not.'

It was clear to Charley that if she let these men near the house, it would be the ruin of everything. She had tried diplomacy, but diplomacy had failed. Now, there was only diversion.

'Anyway, you better get out of the way,' Mark said. 'Because one way or another we're going in there to find him.'

'You're going the wrong way,' she said, as Mark walked back to the car.

He turned to face her. 'What?'

'Over there.' She pointed over at the cottage. 'I think *he* might know what happened. I think *he* might have had something to do with it.'

'You're fucking lying. There's no one there.'

But all the same he had turned, and the light showing in the window of the cottage had caught his eye. 'We were going to wait,' Charley went on, trying to keep his attention, 'until things blew over. To get rid of him. We don't want him here. It was him and a friend of his. Jenn's boyfriend. That one you met.'

'He's over there?'

'That's right. I'm pretty sure he sold the pills.'

'Why didn't you call the police, then?'

'We didn't want the hassle.'

The friends now stared over at the cottage, passing a bottle of vodka between them. Mark turned towards the car.

'If no one's there, we'll be back.'

He left this last threat over his shoulder. Charley began walking back towards the house as the cars moved gently across the grass. Her mind streamed with panic, but as she moved through the possible outcomes of this situation, Lucas was only an absence for her, a hole into which the problem could be pushed. But he *would* tell them about the outhouse. It was inevitable. As she hurried along the drive she could feel that she was magnifying the danger out of all proportion, but this realization only increased her sense of desperation. If someone called the police, if the police realized that this was where Jenn had stayed, if they started asking questions, then nothing would be safe.

Walking through the front door, she met Taylor coming down the stairs. Quickly, she told him about Mark and his friends. 'I sent them over to Lucas,' she explained. 'They headed over to the cottage.'

'Why?'

'I told them that he gave Jenn the pills.'

'But why?'

'Because, obviously, I didn't want them coming over here.'

Taylor had moved halfway up the stairs by now, to glance out through the hallway window. 'I heard the shouting . . .'

Charley insisted that she wanted to move the lab equipment that night. Where didn't matter: they had to remove it from the house. She soon persuaded Taylor too. Perhaps this was the reason that she remained so close to him: he could be so easily persuaded, he lived so close to a state of fear. They headed to the kitchen to pick up keys and a torch; Charley brought the mobile phone. 'At least this way no one can call the police,' she explained. 'It buys us a bit of time.'

As Taylor unlocked the van, he could still make out the two cars parked outside the cottage. The shouting had now subsided. He fired the ignition, and moved the van towards the grass at the side of the house, turning off the engine once the wheels began to roll with the gradient. He glanced over at the house; the few lit windows stared back at him stupidly.

Inside the outhouse, Charley had started packing up the lab equipment, a tangle of tubing and glass sticking out from a cardboard box at her feet. She had rested the torch upright on the floor, and the dramatic up-lighting accentuated her expression of exhausted concern. She had wanted to drive the equipment out to the town. Where they would leave it, why they would expect an easy sanctuary, what danger, anyway, actually threatened: these things didn't matter, only that Charley acted rather than remained powerless. Instead, Taylor had persuaded her to store the equipment in the old shed he'd found while walking the dogs.

'Everything OK?'

'Fine.' She gestured towards a pile of discarded card-board boxes. 'These must have been left over from when the Vegan set up the place. There should be enough to hold everything.'

Taylor began helping her with the equipment. 'The cars are still outside. I don't know what they're doing, but they don't seem to be making too much noise.'

Charley didn't look over. 'They'll just frighten him. That's all. A gang of kids who got talking and thought this was a good idea.'

With the chemicals and equipment packed up in boxes, they were even able to fit the shelving and tables inside the van. Only the chest freezer was left behind. Taylor started the van, and once Charley had climbed up beside him, they headed back to the drive, the van rocking awkwardly with the uneven ground. At first he drove slowly, steadily, until they passed the house; with relief, he pressed his foot down on the accelerator. A warm yellow light glowed behind the windows of the cottage. The chimney stoked the night with white smoke. The two cars had disappeared: tyre marks in the grass led back to the road.

'They've gone,' Taylor said.

'So?'

'So do you think we should stop? There might be no need to carry on.'

Charley kept her gaze fixed ahead. 'We have to get rid of it.'

'You don't think we should at least stop off?'

'He'll be fine. I'll bet he's headed back to the house.'

'What are you going to say to him?'

'About what?'

'About sending them around there?'

'I'll tell him that they asked for him, that I thought they were old friends. He's been into all sorts of nasty stuff in the past. If it comes back to haunt him, it isn't my problem.'

The cottage slipped past the car window. Soon they turned off the driveway on to the road. The headlights burrowed through the darkness as they traced the edge of the forest. At the turning, there was no road, only a wide path carved by previous vehicles. The suspension of the van shrieked as the wheels rolled over the uneven ground. Taylor moved them through into the clearing. He'd wanted to park the van as close as possible to the edge of the forest, but at the edge of the trees, and too late, he saw that the clearing gave way to a ditch. The left wheel suddenly pitched downwards, the view through the windscreen toppling as they were shaken like coins in a tin. Taylor stayed upright by gripping the steering wheel, but Charley cracked her head against the door.

The van jerked around them like it had been stunned. Taylor killed the engine.

'Are you all right?'

Charley held a hand to the side of her head, for a second too enraged to speak. 'Jesus Christ! Can things get any worse?'

Firing up the engine again, Taylor tried to reverse out of the ditch, but the van had stuck fast. They climbed out through the driver's door. Outside, Taylor shone the torch upon the stricken wheel while Charley stood silently beside him, huddled inside her jumper.

'Don't worry,' Taylor said. 'It'll take us five minutes to get it out. It's still early. We'll just let out the tyres a little, jam the boards underneath. It'll come up easily.'

'It's just . . .'

As Charley's voice faded, Taylor reached out and laid his hand on her shoulder, but gently, almost politely, she eased herself from under the pressure of his fingers.

Together, they set to work. Charley crouched inside the van, while Taylor laid the boxes on to the clearing; this done, they began transferring everything to the shed. The walk through the forest was awkward, dangerous. There was hardly enough light to see, and with his hands full, Taylor couldn't get sufficient grip on the torch. Once, Charley stumbled over a root, and only just regained her balance. It took them five trips – fraught, awkward, tiring trips – until they were done. The shed, smaller than Taylor remembered, had soon been crammed full. Charley worked in silence. If she noticed the interior of the shed – the discarded underwear, the porn mags – she didn't mention it. Her boot squeezed the grey carcass of an ancient condom, as if it was only cartilaginous sea-matter, exhausted upon a beach. Finally, Taylor pushed his shoulder to the door, while Charley wove the chain around the handle.

'There.' He slapped his palm on the door. 'It should be fine for a couple of nights.'

'We'll call the Vegan tomorrow.' Her voice was tired, but almost on instinct, she'd corrected him. She couldn't let it go, Taylor thought; she had to have the final word.

'At least tell me you feel better now,' he said, trying to provoke a little gratitude.

'I won't feel better until all of this is behind us.' She turned away from him. 'Come on. Let's get those boards and pull out the van.'

The route they took through the forest should have been a short cut, but in the dark, not really knowing where they were heading, Taylor led them too far. Soon he was reduced to flashing the torch through a dense part of the woods, hoping to make out the field beyond the trees. When they finally emerged, they were at the back of the garden, beyond even the outhouse. Taylor could smell the smoke in the air.

Charley stood beside him. 'Do you smell that too?'

'It's the house.'

She scowled. 'What time is it now?'

'Must be gone two.'

She pushed past him along the path. 'If they've left that fire burning again, I'll kill them.'

Approaching the house, they heard the fire before they saw it, heard it spitting and cracking through wood. Charley started running. 'I told them,' she shouted as Taylor followed her. 'I've *always* told them.' She was faster than Taylor. He had never felt so heavy. She ran parallel to the garden, aiming, he guessed, for the kitchen door, but as soon as she passed the wall she stopped in her tracks. It took Taylor a few more seconds to reach her, and then he was almost tripped by the sight: the cottage streaming with orange fire.

Again they began to run, but this time Charley jogged by Taylor's side. The flames were pouring from the windows and doorway, leaking upwards in ragged, shuddering fangs. The group of residents huddled together to one side, defining the limit of the radiated heat. Robert was bent over double, coughing drily, his face streaked and grey with smoke, while Magalene stood with her arms around him.

'He tried,' she said as Charley and Taylor approached. 'He really tried.' She looked away from them, and bent down towards Robert, hugging him close. The fire filled the silence, hissing and spitting with accelerating fury, exploding into a sudden dull pop of a pane of glass. 'There was nothing he could do,' Magalene said, and only when Taylor saw the look upon her face, did he understand. He looked beyond her, shielding his face with his hand. The wind had caught the smoke, casting it back from the frontage, like white hair from a skull. One of the residents tossed a bucket of water into the fire, defiant in the sheer face of what everybody knew.

Charley dialled 999. Taylor had offered, grabbing hold of her arm as she started from the flames, a bizarre gesture, which she assumed he saw as a kind of chivalry. She had shrugged him off and now ran back to the house. 'I couldn't find the phone,' Magalene shouted after her. 'I looked everywhere.' Maintaining the façade, Charley waited until she was out of sight before she retrieved the phone from her pocket. She was very calm. The operator came on the line, and Charley explained that there had been an accident in the grounds of their house, a fire. Someone may have died. Before she knew it, she had started trying to piece together the story, as though, right there, approaching the steps of the house, she was being asked to defend her actions. 'I don't even know if he was in there. I saw him earlier in the evening and we . . . The point is that I was the last one to see him and I . . .' She stopped herself as the story broke apart, and she hung up the phone, a thumb pressed quickly on the button.

Walking up the steps into the cold of the hallway she headed through to the kitchen, because, she told herself, in here she might be able to find something to help. She was looking out of the window, filling a washing bowl with water, when the chimney collapsed. All of a sudden it shifted downwards, into a dense shower of sparks, and when everything had settled, a large portion of the roof had been replaced by flames.

Charley looked down at the water brimming in the bowl and turned off the taps. She sat down at the kitchen table, the muscles of her legs and back palpitating with the beat of her heart. The dogs moved around the kitchen, agitated and unable to settle. Only the yellow greyhound remained in its bed, trembling slightly, a look almost like despair in its dark eyes. Charley smoked a cigarette, and stayed where she was sitting, even when, across the length of the field, slight streamers of blue light began to decorate the window pane.

When Taylor tracked her down, she hadn't moved. He didn't speak at first, only walked through into the alcove to retrieve a beer from the fridge. After popping the cap with his back to the window, he drained half of the contents. Everything that had happened had been sewn into his flushed, exhausted face.

'Are you OK?'

Charley nodded. 'I'll be fine. You?'

The smell of smoke was thick upon his clothes, the carbon residue stank of singed flesh.

'What about . . . Outside?'

'Nothing. There's nothing they can do.'

'But he was . . .?'

'Yeah.'

She continued nodding her head, as though she had been expecting it, as though she were prepared. 'And where are the others?'

'Still out there. No one seems to want to come back inside . . .' He let his voice trail away, thinking, she guessed, that this sounded like an accusation.

'And the police?'

'Not yet. Probably be here soon, though.'

'Send them over to me when they come.'

'What do you want me to say?'

'I don't know. Say the two of us went for a walk. It was late, we had argued, we went out to talk about things. Say I saw him last, if you want.'

'Do you think they meant to do it?'

Charley shook her head. 'I don't know. I don't think so.

He had the fire in there. He lit the place with candles. It would only take something to get spilled.'

'So quick.' Taylor shook his head. 'How long do you think we were gone. An hour? Two?'

She looked away from him, at the window. The kitchen light felt suddenly severe.

When Taylor placed a hand on her shoulder the gesture felt so tense and premeditated that Charley stiffened and, although she wanted him to stay near, she shrugged him off. Her fear suddenly became very transparent. She stood up from the table and walked to the nearest wall, where a litter of scraps had been pinned. A calendar given away free with a brand of chicken feed. A photo of one of the residents, long since gone, wearing the Tony Blair mask which now decorated the scarecrow. A postcard from Llandudno. A note from Sadie. 'Whoever cleans out the fire,' it read, 'can you PLEASE make sure you move the washing? Unless you want to clean my pants, which I doubt you do. Love Sadie xxx.' The note was written in blue felt tip, with a rounded, fluid script, and Charley could easily imagine a time when all the O's had little faces and the I's were dotted with hearts. Apparently, Sadie had used the nearest piece of paper that had come to hand, in this case a weekly rota, on which Charley could still read Lucas's name.

She turned around to Taylor. 'Can you just leave me alone? I'd like some time by myself.'

'Of course.' Taylor turned to go, but stopped before the door. 'But if you're feeling guilty . . .'

She turned to face him. 'What? If I'm feeling *guilty*?'

'I don't know. I just . . . It was him. Or it was us.'

'But this wasn't anything to do with me. This was them.'

'I know, I know. But if you were. I meant. You didn't need to.'

'OK. That's good to know. But I don't feel guilty. Now please leave me alone.'

Charley sat at the kitchen table, listening to Taylor's footsteps echo down the hall. She picked at the skin on her fingers, and once more she tried to piece together the shattered events that had led to this moment. In a kind of tribute to what lay beyond the glass, she rolled one of her liquorice paper cigarettes. The smoke burned in her lungs, but it was a good feeling, it felt pure. Her thoughts were calm now, static and huge, and in their inevitability she saw the extent of her failure. The house lay quiet around her, large and empty and dead; she felt that room by room, space upon space, it had been constructed like an intricate Russian doll with herself at the heart. When she heard the knock on the door, she felt no fear. She stubbed out her cigarette and walked over, ready, once again, to defend her home.

The Vegan heard about it all a few days later. He had spent this time almost entirely at home: sleeping most of the day, drinking tea, reading through a few books, even rationing his marijuana intake so he didn't provoke too many bad ideas. One night, when someone had knocked on his door, he'd frozen in his chair, fearing that any moment he would finally be called to account. But the door stayed shut and no one knocked again.

To check up on the events which might still overtake him, he'd watched the news. The slow poisoning of the festival queen: the national news had revelled in the story. Reporters gathered outside the hospital, witnesses from the festival talked directly to camera. The parents even sanctioned some pictures for the tabloids: ugly tubes and wires intruding upon the grey, sad skin of a young woman. But she didn't live and she didn't die: she persisted, and because comas make for bad news, eventually she disappeared.

After spending nearly a week inside his house, he ran low on supplies, so a trip to the town became necessary. The day was overcast and bleak, rain threatening all around him, a mushroom sliminess coating the streets. He moved furtively, wearing the hood up on his parka. It wasn't quite enough to protect him. On his way through one of the cramped passageways behind the market, he bumped into Jed, whom the Vegan hadn't seen since the time he'd been looking for Monkey. Jed was heading back to his record shop with his lunch, a white bag of sandwiches and a coffee in his hand. When he called out the Vegan only stopped because it would have been worse to carry on walking. Once again, Jed brought significant news. 'Sorry to break it to you, like this . . .' He told the Vegan about Lucas and the fire at the Mansion. 'I know you two were close.'

After that, the Vegan headed over to The Swan and sat in the corner near the fire. He drank a beer, saying goodbye to old friends and protégés, and the plans that were made. Later, it would seem synchronous. Someone at the bar caught his eye. Only when he moved across the pub towards him did the Vegan place him: it was Andrew from the Mansion.

'Do you mind if I sit down?'

The Vegan gestured to the stool in front of him. 'Not at all.'

It had begun to rain. The window beside them glowed with a bland grey milkiness from the overcast sky. Andrew removed his suede jacket and let it fall upon the stool next to him. A book filled the inside pocket.

'Bad news,' the Vegan said. 'About everything . . .'

Andrew shook his head. 'Terrible. I mean, I hardly knew Lucas, he kept mostly to himself . . .'

'It was a terrible thing.' The Vegan paused, and wet his mouth with beer. 'So what's going on there?'

'It's been crawling with police. Lucas's parents have been demanding an inquest. All of the hassle means that a lot of people have left. I'm not going back there until everything has settled down, but I wonder if it will.' He sipped from his pint glass. 'It'll probably be the death of the place.'

'Do they know what happened?'

'No. No one saw anything, or they say they didn't. But still . . .'

The Vegan took the news calmly. An inquest meant pressure, and pressure meant that inevitably something would give. He thought of Charley and Taylor, even Monkey, and how glad they'd be to drag him into this great white hole that the Mansion had become. It might be time to leave for a while, perhaps for good.

'It's strange . . .' Andrew said. 'I'd been thinking of moving on but I never imagined . . .'

'Why did you want to leave?'

Andrew scratched at his jaw. 'The place had been failing for a while. I just got bored, you know?' He swilled the remains of his drink around the bottom of his glass. 'These past few days, I've been wondering why it did fail. I mean, it could have worked out, that place really *should* have worked out. The location, that house. Do you know what I mean?'

The Vegan was intrigued. The fear of capture, the need for flight, it suddenly all felt a long way away. 'So what do you think?'

Andrew cleared his throat.

'Maybe it was because the time had passed. That they were people holding on to something that had died a long time ago. Or . . .' He paused and sipped from his beer. 'But perhaps I shouldn't say this? They're friends of yours, aren't they?'

'Go on.'

'Or it wasn't meant for them.'

He glanced over at the Vegan for encouragement, but finding nothing, he reached for the book from his jacket pocket. He placed it very definitely on the table, one palm pressed down upon it as though it was a totem. 'I've just felt that the house . . . It was something more than just a farm. Or a home, or a business. There was just something *about* that place. It was unique and it always seemed a waste to me, the way they were using it. It could have been something important. Do you know what I mean?'

'I know what you mean.'

'Do you?'

Beside them, the rain ticked against the glass, insistent, demanding. They stared at one another. No matter what happened, the Vegan told himself, a few months, perhaps a year, and everything will have settled down. It will all be about timing. I may have to go away into hiding, but if I have someone around here, the old plans can be reborn. This is not the end of things. Andrew had looked away, and was glancing back at the book now. The Vegan picked it up and flicked through the pages.

'It's good,' he said. 'It's very good.'

When Andrew looked up at him, the light from the window reflected in his eyes, illuminating their ready questioning openness. The Vegan stared at this for a moment, his lips pursed over the rim of his glass.

'Have you read it?' Andrew asked.

'Yes,' the Vegan replied. 'I first read it in India, I think.'

21

People who eat, don't want to know. This was the first lesson Monkey learned when he started work. The owner of the restaurant had made a point of establishing the rules. Monkey was the disposer of rancid meat and green potato peelings, the rinser of curdled cream. If flying ants gathered at the back of the kitchen, it would be Monkey who doused them with boiling water. If the fat had caked on to the metal of the grill, Monkey would clean it. Because of this, he must never appear at the front of house. An ugly mechanics was part of all pleasure, but the customers need not be reminded of it. To eat meant not to know.

Monkey didn't mind. It was all a logical progression. He remembered the evenings he'd spent washing dishes in the Mansion, the long days spent with the Vegan amidst the fumes in the laboratory. It occurred to him that the past months had been training for this new life. He enjoyed those busy hours, the air thick with the smells of charred meat and warm cream, the steam of vegetables, the bitter smoke of garlic and herbs burning in a forgotten pan. He moved between the chefs as they cooked over the flames, collecting discarded pots and pans, the black metal hissing in viscous water. He loaded the dishwasher with crockery and cutlery. He wiped down surfaces and washed walls. He kept moving all of the time, and all the time he moved, it felt like he escaped.

At first, he'd returned to the wrecked house along the river. The water had receded for the summer, so the house was at least dry, but the floor was hard, and rats often crawled up from the river. He avoided getting in touch with Rose. Even if she was back from Dubai, he would be too much like the old Monkey for her; nothing would have changed. Instead, he found a room in a hostel. He went to the social services and explained his situation: that he had left the clinic late last year and that he had since found himself homeless. They asked him where he had been during all that time.

'I had friends I could stay with,' he said. 'I've managed by myself.'

'And heroin?' the interviewer asked. 'You've kept off heroin?'

'I've been clean ever since I got out.'

They congratulated him. He was their polished little apple, their performing chimp. They found him a room in a halfway house out by the station. A single bed and a bare wall, with a window that looked out on to the rail tracks. He thought about tracking down one of the Vegan's magazines, for a picture of a monkey to provide a little decoration. Those days were gone, however, so he kept the wall blank. It said more than his old monkey picture ever had.

It might have been a life. He only had to ignore the threat of capture, but mostly, he managed this. He made no moves, but he avoided all traces of the story. There was a TV in the communal room of the hostel but Monkey never watched it. He stayed in his room, reading through paperbacks which he bought from a bookshop near the restaurant. He lost himself in doomed planets and fragile beings forever lost in time. Despite these diversions, he couldn't escape all of the story. From snatches of news, he discovered that Tess remained in a coma, but Jenn and her other friends had been released from hospital. Monkey allowed himself to feel grateful about Jenn: this was the extent of his contact. He wanted a quiet life, serene, uninvolved. But then one day he met up with Lennox, and he was suddenly released.

It had been a dull morning at work. Most of the kitchen staff spent the time hanging around the back of the kitchen, smoking cigarettes and talking, but Monkey didn't like to be idle. He invented work for himself: mopping down the floor and making more French toast than the restaurant would ever need. Towards the end of his shift, Monkey carried the stockpot outside the back door. It had been bubbling for hours on a back ring of the hob. The patio was quiet. Caged in creepers, in the summer it would be the romantic setting for alfresco meals under candlelight, while piped Dean Martin CDs drowned out the traffic crawling on the road. Now it was empty. Monkey lit a cigarette and stretched out the cramp in his back. The smoke blended with the wisps of steam from the stockpot. He pulled out the larger bones, and strained the liquid through a colander; splashes of stock congealed like white wax upon the concrete. He returned the stock inside, where it would be boiled further, intensified and reduced. Afterwards, he bagged up the steamy remains, the yellow bones and destroyed meat, and walked around to the bins. A door slammed in the car park. Subtle murmurs approached him and a family of four appeared, well dressed, laughing together in the warm afternoon. Monkey dropped his gaze, shielding the rubbish bag until they had walked inside. People who eat don't want to know.

After the morning shift, he was free for the afternoon, until six in the evening. Most days, he would head for the town park and sit watching the river, or hide out in a small café not far from the restaurant, where he could drink tea and smoke cigarettes, and where the radio played only music. He'd been paid that day, however, so to celebrate he went for a drink in a pub not far from the hospital, a vast place which filled its hopeless silence with widescreen TVs. Monkey was in the process of creating a new town for himself, no longer Herointown. He would wait for a new need before he decided upon the name.

He sat alone, reading science fiction between watching repeats of an old detective programme. All of a sudden, he looked up from his book to see Lennox walking towards him. He must have been sitting in the pub for a while, as he was carrying a half-empty pint glass. 'I thought you'd left,' he said. Right away, Monkey knew that this conversation would mark the end of something. Lennox checked his shoulder as soon as he sat down. 'I thought you'd got out of here.'

'No, I stayed with some friends . . .' Lennox didn't give him time for the lie.

'When you stole those pills, I was pissed off at first. Now, it looks like you've done me a favour.'

Lennox told him how the police had released a description of the dealer who had sold the pills at the festival, a description which Lennox had been able to identify easily. 'Don't worry. I haven't said anything to anyone. I mean, it's only because I knew you had the pills . . .' He cleared his throat, and reached over for Monkey's arm, the gesture almost alarmingly intimate. 'You won't bring me into this, will you?'

They sat together side by side, Lennox tracing his finger in the residue of his beer while the detective programme boomed across the chatter of the pub. It was an awkward, uncomfortable situation, and by changing tack and discussing his other news, Lennox was only reacting to this. He had thought that everybody knew about Lucas. At first, Monkey had laughed but the look in Lennox's eyes meant it was all true, it had happened. Lennox didn't stay much longer. He told his tale, and left. In the absence that remained, Monkey ordered another drink, chasing vodka with beer, his mind running, running, running. He should have been starting work in an hour, but he wouldn't be going back to the job. He thought about hitting a few pubs, doing a tour of the whole town until he'd drunk enough to erase himself. But he could never drink that much. He only knew of one way to get what he needed.

As he walked over to the estate on the edge of town, he thought about how inevitable it had all been. The roads of Herointown would always fall under his feet. He would always fail. This was my story, he said to himself. It had to end like this. The need lay inside him, heavier than an emptiness should be, a great, draining weight that grounded him. When he reached Teal's house, however, he could tell that something had changed. The curtains weren't drawn. There was a child's bike outside. When he rang the doorbell, a woman answered. She told him that the previous tenants had been forced out by the council. She and her family had lived there for six months.

'If you knew them, well . . .'

'What?'

'Then you know what they were like. Too much trouble. It's best that they've gone.'

As Monkey walked back to the main road, the woman stood watching him from her front door. He caught a bus back to the town centre. He had a new plan. It took him most of the evening but in the end he found what he was looking for. An old friend of Teal's gave it to him, in exchange for a couple of drinks in The Fox, down by the weir.

The old friend gave it up quite willingly. He offered Monkey much more. He offered the promise of a long night and an early morning. He even offered heroin. Monkey refused it all. Instead, he took Teal's address and returned to his hostel room.

He set out the next day. The town stood over the Welsh border. Monkey struggled to pronounce its name. An old mining town, it lay pooled around the base of a hill of black rock, tall, thin and crooked, like a figure gesturing lazily at the sky. A long road, wrapped in a helix around the hill's edge, led up to the abandoned colliery. A few houses were scattered along the way. Although the sky had glowered with low clouds earlier in the morning, gradually the sun had burned through; the air drowned in wet heat. Monkey had waited an hour for the only bus; no trains ever stopped here. He walked slowly up the hill, stopping occasionally by the side of the road. Down in the valley, the town lay like something whole that had been shattered over the rocks: a rubble town. Monkey's legs hurt, as did his back and his shoulders. But this did not matter. Quite soon, all pain would be gone.

The bungalow stood on an isolated patch of ground, the stones of the pebble-dash as silver as bullets in the white sun. A wooden sign on the front gate read, 'Paradise'. In the overgrown garden – a mess of grass bleached by the sun – a faded, orange plastic doll lay on its back, grinning up as though its fate was perfectly acceptable. Monkey rang the doorbell. A shadow oozed behind frosted glass. Teal opened the door. A short, scrawny man, with olive skin and a slanting chip in his front tooth; his eyes were the yellow-green of fading grass. He had shaved his head close to the skull and his pale yellow T-shirt, illustrated with the fading silver print of a baseball player, clung damply to his skinny frame.

'Monkey,' he said.

'It took me a while to find you.'

'I thought you went away.'

'I went away. But now I'm back.'

He followed Teal into the hall. The house smelled of damp and gas fires. A great bay window looked out over the town. 'Have you got money?'

'Don't worry. Everything is fine.'

A woman in her late forties was smoking from a square of foil. Her hair, once black, had greyed in fine dry threads, which crinkled up like the burned out wires of a short circuit. Her skin was pale and bright and translucent, like some kind of wax. She shivered in a green woollen cardigan. On the other side of the room, a man with a thin beard stared at the TV. His T-shirt said 'Vacant'. He didn't say a word. Neither of them looked over as Monkey came into the room. On the floor, sat Teal's daughter, drawing on a piece of paper, a wallet of brightly coloured felt pens by her side.

Teal sat down in an armchair. Monkey sat down on the settee. Out of the sun, the material of the cushion was cool on his arms. The TV talked. The man with the thin beard walked over to the woman and took the pipe and foil. He returned to his seat. No one spoke. Eventually, after thrashing the blue pen over the top of the paper, the girl stood up and walked over to Monkey, chattering as she approached. She handed him her piece of paper. She had drawn a large green man with wide fan legs. A yellow-cross sun boiled in the corner of the thrashed blue sky. The girl described the picture, but Monkey didn't understand. Her words were new words, a little soft-edged. He could have fallen in love with the world they created.

Teal stood up and retrieved the pipe and foil. The smell of the smoke was fierce and acrid in the room. Teal said,

'She's bored. She wants someone to play with her.' He brought the pipe to his mouth, burned the foil, gulped the smoke.

'It's story time,' the man with the beard said. He spoke slowly. 'She wants someone to tell her a story.' He looked over at Monkey. He stared at him, almost in shock, as though someone had suddenly whipped away a sheet to reveal him. 'Yeah,' continued the man. 'Yeah. Well, why don't you tell her a story? Why don't you do that?' The TV screamed about soft drinks and fast meals and a car you can drive away to a house of which you have always dreamed. The man answered its call.

'Tell us *all* a story,' the woman corrected. 'We all want to hear one.'

At some stage, Teal interrupted, and passed over the lighter and foil. It was Monkey's turn, apparently. It came and went. He was involved, of course. It happened. Afterwards, he bent down and put his arms around the girl. She pointed out details of her picture. He began to tell a story. He stumbled at first. The girl continued chattering to him, occasionally interrupting his story. It all felt a little too complicated. Everyone else ignored him. They stared at the TV. Monkey told them anyway. It was important. He told them about stars that fall like rain, and rain that falls all the time. He told them about a town that was nothing but a memory of need, about the stories of our lives, how they lie in wait for us, pure and predetermined, impossible to escape. And he told them about people who eat and people who know, about all the dogs and cancer, and how he could boil the meat from the bones.

About the Author

DANIEL BENNETT was born in a small village in the Shropshire countryside in 1974. He has worked in bookshops, offices, libraries, wine merchants and factories around the country. His short stories have appeared in literary and crime anthologies and magazines. He lives in Hampshire with his wife and daughter.

Acknowledgements

Like the house it describes, *All the Dogs* seems to have seen many people pass by over the years. I would like to thank them all. In particular: Ron and Linda Bennett for their love and support, as well as their time living the good life; Tom Bolton and Richard Bancroft for their friendship; Luke Brown, Alan Mahar and Emma Hargrave at Tindal Street Press. Finally, I'd like to dedicate this book to Violet, for helping me concentrate, and Catty, for whose love, tolerance and belief I'll always be grateful.